About the Author

Jill Yielder, PhD, is a Jungian analyst and psychotherapist working in private practice in Auckland, New Zealand, also writing part-time. Previously she worked as an academic in the medical programme at the University of Auckland. This is her third novel in the Anam Cara Trilogy.

The Rising of the South

Jill Yielder

The Rising of the South

Olympia Publishers
London

www.olympiapublishers.com
OLYMPIA PAPERBACK EDITION

A CIP catalogue record for this title is
available from the British Library.

ISBN: 978-1-80439-690-2

First Published in 2024

Olympia Publishers
Tallis House
2 Tallis Street
London
EC4Y 0AB

Printed in Great Britain

Acknowledgements

Special thanks to Andrew, Rachael, Christine and Glenda for their support, advice and editing. I'm also very grateful to Juliet Sharman-Burke and Liz Greene for their generous support in giving me permission to quote and reference the book that accompanies their wonderful Tarot deck, The Mythic Tarot.

Preface

Stories bring people together. Through stories we can connect to experiences or feelings and explore them as if they were our own, finding a sense of connection from a 'safe' distance, allowing them to percolate in our psyche. We don't have to do anything other than read or listen, just absorb the story and grow our understanding through the effect the story has on us.

This is the third book about two teenagers, Tom and Sarah, who have found their way into a parallel world called North Feasgar. It picks up the threads about six months after the conclusion of 'Return to Greyvyn'. This book too, can be read in two ways: either as an adventure story; or for older readers, as an allegory to illustrate the tasks that a person, male or female, may need to undertake psychologically in order to find a sense of wholeness. Because of this, a section called 'A Jungian perspective for the older reader' can be found at the end of the book.

The story so far…

In 'Through the Labyrinth', Sarah and Tom, both thirteen, struggling with their home lives, found themselves in a parallel world after slipping through a rift. The land they arrived in is called North Feasgar. They were initially helped by a healer called Morwyn, but it quickly became apparent that Morwyn had ulterior motives and kept Tom captive while sending Sarah on a quest to find an elixir that would prevent her from aging. During her travels Sarah rescued Mary and Arthur Birch from where they'd been kept captive by a man called Willard, and they became friends to both Tom and Sarah. They also met Hermione, a magical cat, and a hawk called Ryder, both of whom can communicate with them. In the climax of the story, Morwyn dies and Sarah and Tom's new friends helped them to choose whether or not to return to their own world through a labyrinth at the resolution of their adventure. Sarah chose to go; Tom chose to stay with the Birches.

'Return to Greyvyn' began with Sarah in England, two and a half years later, at fifteen, trying to find a way to return to Tom and the Birches in North Feasgar. Eliciting the help of her grandfather, she managed to find her way back through the rift and the story unfolded with the four of them finding their way inside a volcano, Mt Greyvyn, to try to prevent dark magic from invading the land. The shady character, Willard, reappeared, teaming up with brother and sister, Jonnie and Kayla, who also arrived in North Feasgar through a rift. They followed Tom and Sarah and the Birches into the volcano, where Willard got into a fight with Arthur, resulting in Willard and Jonnie falling into the river that flows under the mountain. Having to accept that Jonnie was gone, Kayla decided to stay in the mountain with Galawand, an elderly woman who uses her magic to control the dark elements seeking to threaten the land. Sarah chose once again to return to England, but was devastated on arrival to find her grandfather had had a heart attack.

'The Rising of the South' is set six months later, when Tom and Sarah are almost sixteen. It begins with Sarah still struggling to cope with her grandfather's death…

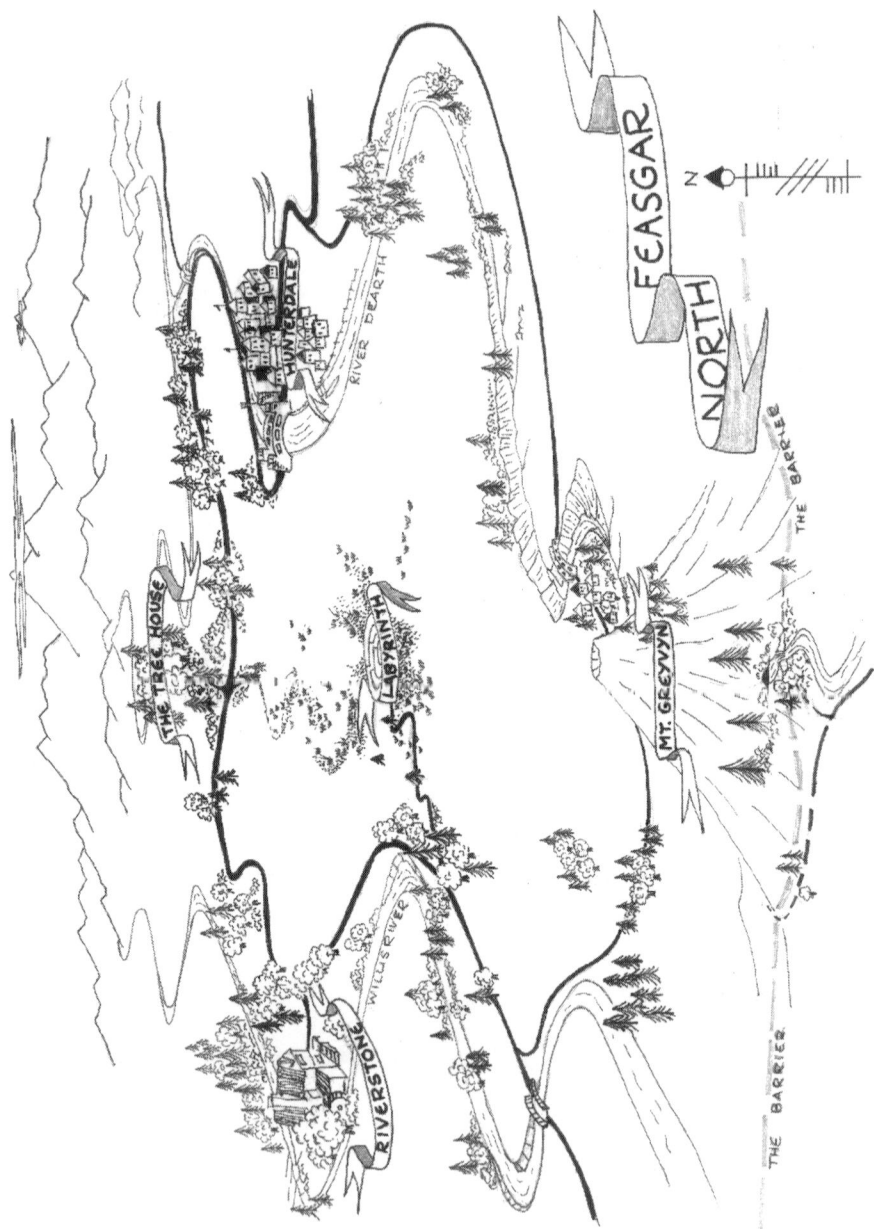

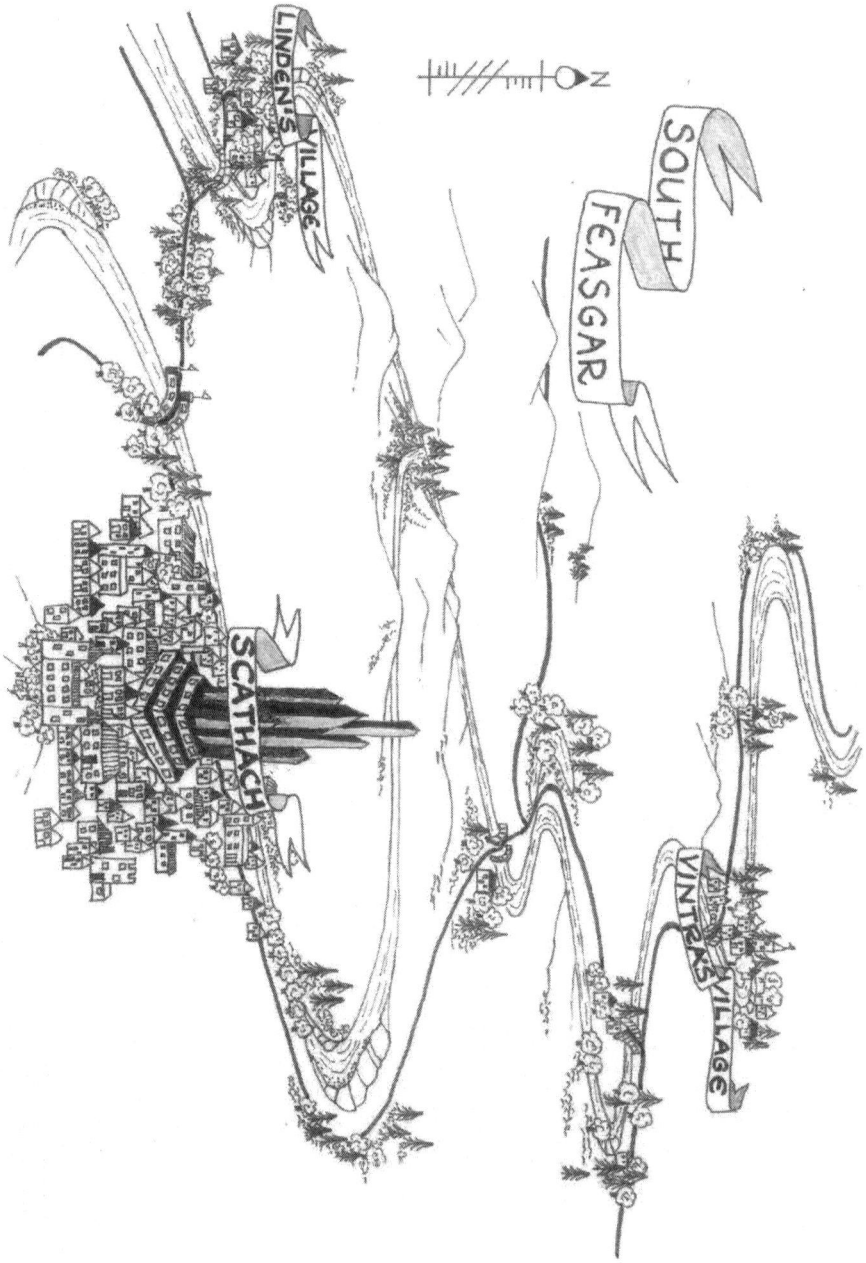

Chapter I

Searching for a Rift

Sarah reluctantly pushed unconsciousness away from her sleep-hungry body. Her mouth felt dry and gross. Sleep crashed in on her every night at the moment – she couldn't get enough of it. It tore her away from the life she was so happy to escape and then spat her out the next day, offering no relief from her deep sorrow.

Six months had passed since her grandfather had died and Sarah couldn't shake her grief. It was such a complicated mix of sadness and fury that it left her not knowing how to deal with it, so instead she'd withdrawn, keeping very much to herself back at school, not even having the energy to interact much with her friends. They were concerned about her, but didn't know what to do and they'd gradually drifted away during the lead up to the Christmas break. She supposed she was a bit of a wet blanket. When they were cheerfully planning getting away from school to be with their families, her mood just poured a cup of cold water over their excitement.

Sarah's parents had arranged for her to have a week with them in Singapore for Christmas, where they'd lived for the past few years. While it had been great to leave the depressing cold of England, it had hardly felt like Christmas. Her dad had scarcely stopped working to spend time with her and it was too hot to do the usual Christmasy things she'd loved as a kid, even though the decorations on the outside of shops on Orchard Road were seriously amazing! There was also the matter of all the unsaid things from when she'd last seen her mum in the hospital and her grandad had died. They spent her time in Singapore pretending, as usual, that nothing had happened, and she was just too tired and worn out to try to bring it up again. Her mum and dad didn't feel real to her somehow when they wouldn't talk about the important things, and she was left thinking they were far too busy to be interested in how she was. Nothing new then. Or maybe they just didn't know how to talk about the difficult stuff.

When she returned to England just before the New Year, her mum had tried to make her stay with her gran until school began again, but she couldn't do it. She still felt so angry with her. It made her mad thinking about how her gran hadn't trusted her grandad. He'd told her Sarah wasn't really in a coma, had tried to explain about how she'd travelled through a rift into another parallel land and that her vital signs showed that she was okay. But she just couldn't get past herself to believe him and insisted on calling her mum and shifting Sarah to hospital. Sarah was convinced that what her gran had done had stressed her grandad so much that he'd had a heart attack, especially by destroying Sarah's wallplate, the only means she had to return to North Feasgar in the future. She hadn't been able to face her gran since her grandad's funeral. Even the thought of that day, somehow now reduced to a blur of sadness, made her eyes tear up and her throat constrict into a lump. So instead of staying with her, Sarah had gone back to board at school, along with a few other kids who had nowhere else to go, and had been wallowing in feeling miserable ever since.

It was so hard to motivate herself to even leave her room, but today she made herself go outside. Walking alone through the school grounds, Sarah pulled her woollen coat more closely around her body, her gloved hands plunged as deeply as possible into the pockets. It wasn't as icy as it had been last week, but a creeping, damp chill sneaked its cold fingers right down deep into her bones. The grounds wore their winter bareness; no colour, just trees stretching their branches above her, dark and naked, exposing themselves to the endless, dull grey sky. They looked like they were desperate to find just a little bit of sun to caress their arms. They must be so disappointed!

Tears were leaking out of the corners of her eyes as she walked. She felt so alone in this dull dull world. Longing for someone to give her a hug, someone to laugh with, someone who cared, brought her suddenly to her knees. She slumped to sit awkwardly on the path. Huddling on the cold ground, Sarah wrapped her arms around her legs and hugged them tight, giving in to her grief. She felt consumed by sadness for her grandad – she missed him so much that her heart ached. She grieved for Tom, and Arthur and Mary, and Hermione of course, who seemed so very far away from the miserable world she now lived in. She grieved for her parents, not as they were now busy living their own lives in Singapore, but for the parents she'd wanted them to be and was beginning to accept they never would be. First her shoulders, then her whole body was shaking, partly with sadness, partly from the bone-numbing cold. She needed to move or she'd become an iceblock, though that somehow seemed fitting to her mood.

Pulling herself slowly to her feet, Sarah made her way back towards the school buildings. What was she going to do over the next week before her friends came back? There was only a handful of girls who had nowhere else to be over the Christmas/New Year break. She'd been avoiding them – her heart felt so overwrought and kind of numb that everything happening outside of her seemed superficial and pointless. Imagine if this barren life stretched out forever in front of her. She knew that she could probably make a life for herself once she left school with new friends and maybe even a boyfriend, but she'd already had all that, and so much more, in North Feasgar. There she'd had a sense of purpose! *So why am I still here?* The thought just dropped, unbidden into her mind. She'd thought so many times about going back over the past six months, but each time she'd become overwhelmed with the impossibility of finding a random rift somewhere in the world. She didn't even know where to start, and tears came to her eyes again at the misplaced anger or fear her gran must have felt in order to smash the plate, her only known portal to North Feasgar.

Each time she'd thought about a rift she'd been left feeling so defeated and depressed that she'd tried to keep it out of her mind. This time she let it hover over her as she made her way inside and back to her room. What had Hermione said? If she was open to an experience, help would come to her? Where was it now then? Maybe she'd been so full of feeling sorry for herself that she hadn't been open? Hermione had also told her to follow her heart, and she knew that her heart was in North Feasgar with Tom and Mary and Arthur... Mary and Arthur! They'd told her about the rift they'd passed through, they'd even drawn her a map – why had she forgotten that? It was as if she'd been so overwhelmed that she'd gone blank. Even now, remembering how they'd described the village they'd been brought up in, and how they'd found the cleft in the bank that they'd gone through, she could feel overwhelm stealing up on her, trying to take her over, making her memory fuzzy, like waking after a dream and having it drift away even as she tried to remember it. Even with what she could remember, it would be like looking for a needle in a haystack. But better a needle than a big nothing stretching out into the future!

After closing the large front door behind her, Sarah made her way to the staircase that swept majestically up two flights as if the house was still the Victorian mansion it once was. The worn, thready green carpet gave away its fall from grandeur, trampled by hundreds of young girls and teachers over the past fifty years. She forced her heavy legs and heart to pull her up to the top, where she stepped into a long, empty corridor lined with oak doors on either side. Her room was half way down, number 202. As soon as Sarah got into her room, she pulled out some paper and wrote down everything she could remember about her conversation with Mary and Arthur. Scrolling through the images on her phone she found the map she'd taken a photo of, along with the ones of Riverstone she'd taken for her grandad. She hadn't wanted to look at them because they were so upsetting, but there they were now waiting for her, and the name of the town was written in Mary's hand at the top of the map. Getting out her computer, she searched for it and found that it wasn't all that far from where her grandparents had lived before they'd gone to the retirement village.

Her decision dropped into her, sudden and fully formed, with a clear sense of 'rightness', before she was even really aware of it. She was going to find a way back – right now! Lying back on the bed to think it through, Sarah knew she had a week before anyone would notice she'd gone, so now was her chance. She was so miserable that she had nothing to lose. Even if she couldn't find the rift – she drew in a sharp, anxious breath even thinking about the possibility – at least she'd be doing something instead of sitting in her room feeling sorry for herself.

But what about her parents? It was possible she'd never see

them again. Her eyes misted over, but she swallowed and blinked, taking a deep breath. She couldn't let her wish for things to be different stop her, but at the same time she'd need to let them know somehow that she was okay, even though they didn't believe in the possibility of the existence of North Feasgar. She suddenly had an idea and got out her phone again. Taking screenshots of two photos – one with Tom and the Birches at Riverstone and the other of her and Tom, she made sure they preserved the date above the photos, clearly taken during the time she was supposedly in a coma. Sarah then emailed them to her computer and after sending them to print, she went downstairs to the small room that housed the printer and retrieved them, scrawling *Hi Mum and Dad, I'm okay, don't worry about me, love S xx* on the lower edge of the one Mary had taken of Tom and her, and slipped them into an envelope. She'd post them at the corner shop in the village when she left, thinking that they would arrive in Singapore after she could no longer be traced and stopped.

Not wasting any time that might change her mind, she packed what she wanted to take with her, mostly just essentials like clothes, plus a few personal things including her tarot book and cards, and some photos of her parents and grandparents. Doing a last check around her room she looked under her bed and spotted something a purplish-blue colour lying on the carpet. Getting down on her hands and knees she looked more closely and stretched out her arm until she touched it, pulling back a tarot card. *How weird.* She hadn't looked at them for a while but she was always really careful with them, wrapping them in their black cloth when she was finished with them, and couldn't imagine how the card had escaped from the pack. She turned it over and saw that it was The Star.

It wasn't a card she knew, so she pulled the book out of her pack. Opening it at the correct page she found an image of a young woman with long, fair hair, kneeling in front of a chest that something (the book said a swarm of flying creatures) was flying out of. The girl wasn't looking at that though, she was looking at a star above her. Sarah read the card, which was about the myth of Pandora, a story she'd read when she was younger, but she hadn't come across the specific bit about the star before. After the myth there was a section that talked about what it might mean to her: "On an inner level, the image of Pandora and the Star of Hope is a symbol of that part of us which, despite disappointment, depression and loss can still cling to a sense of meaning and a future which might grow out of the unhappiness of the past... it portends the experience of hope, meaning and faith in the midst of difficulties... an augury of promise."[1] pp.69-71 Like the last time when she'd happened upon her first tarot card, it blew her away. It felt like it was affirming her – her loss and depression and her decision to go back to North Feasgar. She'd learned each time she'd gone there to trust her intuition, but she still seemed to need something to confirm that she was on the right track when she was back in her ordinary world. It was like here she was so unhappy that she couldn't trust herself the same way – she found it hard to experience hope. Right now, it felt like she was doing totally the right thing when she slung her pack on her back and walked right out of the school – no one even saw her – and headed for the village. Posting the envelope to her parents, she caught a train heading in the right direction with only a twenty-minute wait.

On the trip south to the village Mary and Arthur came from, Sarah had plenty of time to reconsider her decision, but she remained strangely certain. Changing trains to a more rural line near her grandparents' old place brought up lots of memories that were disturbing, reminding her of how much she'd loved them, and had loved feeling secure in their house. But they weren't there any more. She would never see her grandad again. She remembered so clearly one time she'd stayed with them when she was about ten and she'd woken from a bad dream.

"Sarah, sweetie, are you okay?" her grandad was leaning over her on the bed, and when she moved towards him he'd sat on its edge and put his arm around her.

"Just a horrible dream," she'd replied, "I was so afraid because I was lost in the woods and couldn't find my way home."

He'd stroked her hair and told her that he'd always be there for her. He'd really meant it too, but now he wasn't. She was alone.

Sarah pressed her forehead to the glass of the window, staring with unfocused, tear-blurred eyes at the countryside whizzing by, until a large woman manoeuvred herself and two large shopping bags into the space opposite her, sitting heavily, the cushioned chair beneath her giving up a whoosh of air as her bottom plonked down.

"Ooph, that was the chair, not me," she exclaimed with a laugh, but on seeing Sarah's face said, "Oh, are you okay, love?"

Sarah just nodded mutely and gave her a wan smile, turning back again to the window. A little later she heard paper rustling, followed by the woman's voice asking her if she'd like a crisp.

"I'm okay thanks," she said, looking briefly at her. She instantly regretted her decision, as her stomach rumbled – it had been an automatic reply designed to keep herself feeling remote and sorry for herself, but in reality, she was starving. "Actually, that would be lovely, thanks," she managed to say. The woman smiled and pushed the open packet over to her.

"Here you go, love, you can have them all. I've got plenty more in my bag," she said with a smile.

Crunching on their crisp saltiness helped Sarah to pull herself out of her sadness. She started taking more notice of her surroundings, watching the wintry landscape, the small towns, woods and fields as they passed. The woman tried to talk to her a couple of times, and although she didn't want to be rude, she didn't say much – it was just all too hard. As the train drew up to a station, she was relieved to see on her phone that the next stop was hers, and gathered up her belongings, smiling and thanking the woman, walking down the swaying corridor to wait by the luggage rack near the door. She held onto a bar on the rack, noticing as they drew near to the village, that it wasn't so much a village as a town – it was much more built-up than she'd expected and it took a while to reach the station from the outskirts. Eventually the train drew to a stop and she opened the door, stepping down onto the platform.

With her backpack slung over her shoulder, Sarah made her way through the turnstile and towards the exit. A board near the door displayed a map of the town with a 'you are here' sign marked in red. Getting out Mary's map on her phone, there was little resemblance between the one on the board and the hand-drawn version, other than the very centre of the town she was about to exit into. Where Mary's map petered out, the current day one had a lattice of streets stretching away from the centre in all directions, including the place where the rift was marked. Her heart sinking, Sarah walked out onto the street and looked around her. This part was quite quaint – a cobble-stone road and stone-fronted shops with painted signs hanging from their lintels. Looking further to her left and right, she could see where newer buildings had sprung up to extend what was the old village into a more modern town. Office buildings jostled for space behind the shops, with the narrow walkways leading to them from the main road still decorated with Christmas lights.

Turning to the right, Sarah set off down the road, past cafés, a bookshop, a post office and several places selling takeaway food. As the older village gave way to more modern buildings it became more focused on services, like a laundromat and real estate agents. Further out these were replaced by a petrol station, mechanics' workshops, a hardware shop and even a large Sainsbury's. By now she'd been walking for about twenty minutes and her bag was getting heavy. According to Mary's map, she shouldn't be too far from where she and Arthur had found the hill with the rift in it. Not only was there no countryside as far as her eye could see, but there was no hill! She'd now come to a housing development – rows of neat, semi-detached, tile-roofed houses with brightly painted doors. Overshadowing them from where the hill should have been, were two tall apartment blocks that looked like a newish council estate.

Feeling totally defeated, Sarah turned around and headed back towards the station, lugging her bag on her back, disappointed feet plodding heavily, tears streaming down her face. All she wanted to do was sit down and sob, but she couldn't find a seat until she got to Sainsbury's, where a bench was placed near the front doors – one end of it already occupied by an old man. Sniffing, she wiped her face on the back of the sleeve of her jacket and sat down as far from him as she could. He turned to look at her and grunted.

"You all right?"

"Yes, thank you," she replied stiffly.

"What've you got there?" he asked, seeing her looking at the map on her phone.

She suddenly realised that he was a lot older than Mary and Arthur and might have known the village back when they were there. She moved over more closely to him and held out her hand to show him Mary's map.

"Well, it's a long time since it looked like that!" he exclaimed. "They call it progress, all those new houses and all, but all the green has gone and the place is full of people. Can't move for them. Where did you get that map from? Look, here is about where we are now." He pointed to the map, confirming that Sarah had worked out correctly the direction of the rift.

"Friends of mine used to live here, years ago," Sarah replied.

"What're their names? Chances are I'd know them."

"Mary and Arthur Birch."

The man screwed up his face, thinking back, then an expression of possibility came to his face. "Arthur Birch? Not that young nipper from over yon," nodding in the direction a bit north of the village. "I knew his dad, a good man, a farmer, hard worker. That Arthur, he up and ran away with a girl, broke his mother's heart, even though they had lots of other children – he'd been the clever one and they thought he'd do well by them."

"Oh… well he's a wonderful man and I think maybe he thought they didn't like Mary. She's wonderful too. They're very happy."

"Well, his mum died a while back, and his dad lives with his eldest son. You could tell Arthur to visit him sometime… he'd like that."

Sarah suddenly panicked – she didn't want to have to answer any more questions about Arthur and Mary, like where they lived and why they hadn't been back, so she quickly got to her feet.

"Thanks so much for your time – it was fantastic to find out a bit more about the village. I've got to go and catch my train now." With a smile, she picked up her backpack and quickly walked off up the road.

"Say hello to Arthur from Jack Houghton," he called after her. Sarah turned and waved before continuing back to the station.

Having found out that a train to her grandparents' old village wouldn't be passing through the station for another forty-five minutes, Sarah sat down in a café nearby, ordering a sandwich and a glass of juice. She'd been distracting herself by thinking about what Jack had said about Arthur, wondering what he'd been like as a young man and how he and Mary had got to know each other. As she stared out the latticed glass window, she suddenly realised that she'd started worrying about what Jack had said about Arthur breaking his mother's heart. Would she break her parents' hearts if she went back to North Feasgar? That would be awful, and it would be horrible to feel guilty and responsible forever. But then again, she wouldn't know, would she? Could she find a way of not worrying about it now that Jack had put it into her mind? Well, it looked like she wouldn't be finding her way back now anyway!

Disappointment that was more like despair overtook her and she rested her head in her hands, elbows on the table in front of her. Feeling sad, it occurred to her that going back to her grandparents' old place was going to be like rubbing salt into her wounds. She might as well give up now – she hadn't bought her ticket yet – she could get on a train heading north and be back home before dinner. Except it wasn't home, was it? It was school. She didn't have a home and the nearest thing that felt like it was in North Feasgar. Sarah had the strangest feeling that it was today or never. She owed it to herself to follow through with the impulse that had taken her away from school by going to her

26

grandparents' old property. She would ask the owners if she could have a look around – hopefully they'd understand her need to reconnect to her grandad as a way of dealing with her sadness, and she'd try to stay open to what she might find. She made a pact with herself. She'd keep herself open with anything that happened today, and if she didn't find a rift she'd let it go and never let herself think about it again.

The train trip was short. Sarah got off at her destination after only fifteen minutes and made her way along the familiar country lanes until she got to where her grandparents used to live. The lanes were as she remembered – little had changed since she was last there. Her breath came out in little huffs of white as she walked, warm and snug in her woollen jacket, hat and gloves. The weather was cold, crisp and clear, the lanes narrow, bordered with neat hedgerows. Houses snuggled into copses of trees, smoke trailing from chimneys into the wan, faintly blue sky, inviting the idea of the warmth and acceptance she'd experienced when she'd stayed with her grandparents. Sarah felt almost overwhelmed by her memories of them, which jostled alongside an inconsolable sadness. And she felt her memories had been betrayed by her gran… Not wanting to feel angry, she pushed that thought away and concentrated on finding the right driveway. Their old place was set back a little from the lane, down a long tree-lined driveway that led past a road-fronted cottage to their property beyond. It was just as she remembered – the same slightly crooked mailbox in front of a cluster of silver birches bared to the winter. Sarah shivered a little as she headed up the driveway, her body acknowledging that this was no longer her place to be.

As the house came into view, there were small signs of change – a few different plants, unfamiliar objects in the garden and near the front door there were brightly printed Wellington boots that her gran would never have worn! But essentially the new owners seemed to have kept it much the same. There was no car in front of the house, although that didn't really mean anything, as it could be parked in the closed garage. Her grandparents usually left theirs out, after years of being the local doctors on call and the frequent need to leave quickly to see a patient. There was no smoke coming from the chimney either though, and Sarah had the impression that the house was empty. Knocking on the front door brought no response, so after waiting for a short while, she decided it wouldn't do any harm if she had a look around the property – such a waste to have gone all that way and not have the chance to say goodbye to it properly.

Walking around behind the house, Sarah took the path leading from the woodpile stacked at one side, into the woods. Under the cover of the trees it was suddenly quiet, with the sound of her footsteps dampened by leaf mould lying on the path. The slight smell of decay, the light breaking up as it danced off branches above her, and the sound of birds sitting up high, chattering about her as she passed beneath them, were sensations so familiar to her that she caught her breath. She passed the clearing where her grandad had built a small shed to house extra firewood and to keep the tools he used to keep the paths through the woods clear. The paths weren't as well cared for now – she had to step carefully to avoid muddy patches and rucked up mounds of gravel. She remembered how much pleasure he'd got from spending time quietly raking the leaves to the sides and pulling the gravel into indents in the ground before they became potholes. Walking deeper into the trees, she started to cry again, and eventually slid to the ground, her back leaning against a tree trunk, feeling its solidity behind her like her grandad, as she let go of her sadness and disappointment. With no knowledge of how long she'd been sitting there, eventually her tears stopped. She felt like someone had wrung her out, every last drop, leaving her in a strangely light, but vulnerable place that she guessed she'd have to get used to.

Getting to her feet, she made her way back, but as she neared the shed, she heard in the distance the sound of a car drawing up on the pebbles in front of the house. A door slammed and she heard a dog bark. A man's voice shouted "Brutus, where are you going? Come back here!" More barking – it sounded like a big dog, throaty and deep. "Brutus, Brutus, where do you think you're going?" She realised with a start that the barking was moving towards her. She hated big dogs – she found them really scary and knew they could smell her fear. She decided the best thing to do was to shut herself inside the shed – if the man found her there she'd think of something to say, but at least he'd stop the dog from savaging her. The door was stiff and creaked as it opened, as if it hadn't been used for a while. Sarah imagined that the new owners may not have got around to clearing it out, and sure enough, inside was just as she'd remembered it. It was like her grandad had just walked out and left everything behind: a bench along one wall with small tools on top and sacks and sprayers piled under it, wood stacked along the other walls, with various larger implements placed wherever they would fit.

It was only a small shed and was quite dark, lit only by one narrow window above the bench. The only place she could hide was under the bench behind the bags. As she crouched down to push them to the side, Sarah glimpsed something blue on the ground and recognised with a start an old toy her grandad had given her that was sticking out from under the bench. It was a carved wooden rabbit that he'd made, with a blue jacket; Peter

Rabbit from her favourite childhood stories. She wondered how long it had been there – it was so familiar, but she couldn't remember the last time she'd seen it. She got down on her hands and knees to pull it out. It was stuck on something, so she yanked it and it came out into her hands. She could see something else too, further back, with a hint of colour. But pushing more of the bags out of the way and extending her arm back as far as she could, she wasn't quite able to touch whatever it was. Frustrated, but determined to check it out, her fears disappeared and Sarah inched her body into the gap, pushing the things under the bench out of her way, crawling right under the bench and towards the back of the shed. Somewhere in the distance she could hear the dog scrabbling at the closed door, but that faded into the background as she crawled, because whatever it was seemed to always be just out of reach. It was weirdly expansive and she kept going further and further into a space different to what it should be, a bit like the way she imagined going into Doctor Who's Tardis. She kept crawling and slowly realised that there were earth and twigs under her hands and knees. Foliage caught at her, pulling at her hair and snagging her backpack and clothes. Her hat was stolen from her head by a branch, but she kept going and eventually she pushed her way through a patch of dense growth towards the light.

Sarah pulled herself to her feet – she was in dense, scrubby undergrowth in the middle of the woods. She was still clutching a slightly grubby Peter Rabbit, which she stuffed into her pack, and then clapped her hands together, dusting the worst of the dirt off the palms of her gloves, then rubbing them down the legs of her jeans. Pulling one glove off, she put her hand to her hair and pulled out bits of twig and leaves. The light was dim, but she could see rays of sun streaking down through a break in the tree canopy above. What had just happened? Where was she? She didn't seem to still be in the same woods that surrounded the shed… Everything around her had changed. Could she have gone through a rift? Could she be in North Feasgar? Pushing aside the foliage, she made her way to a clearer patch of ground and turned around, trying to work out which direction to take to get clear of the trees. That didn't help – she had no idea where she was or which way to go and there were no obvious paths, so she started walking in the direction she was facing immediately ahead of her, thinking that would be as good a decision as any.

A few feet into the bushes though, the foliage became very dense again, and it was almost impossible to push her way through. A branch at waist height was immediately ahead of her and she pushed hard on it, trying to get it to move so she could inch around it, but it wouldn't budge. Getting down on her hands and knees, she decided to clamber underneath it. Crawling forward, hampered by her backpack, she was about to get back to her feet when suddenly she found herself hit by something so powerful that it pushed her backwards, making her land on the ground on her back with such a thump that she was completely winded. She lay there for a while feeling so shocked that she couldn't think straight. Her body felt pummelled, her back hurt and the branch had collected with the back of her head and it was throbbing. She felt dizzy and disoriented. *What on earth just happened?* she wondered. It kind of reminded her of once when she was about ten when she'd put her hand out and grabbed hold of an electric fence. It gave her a real jolt, but strangely it was like she'd been hit, and she'd looked around her to see who had done it, even though she'd known she was alone.

When she recovered enough to be able to pull herself into a sitting position, she looked more carefully ahead of her. She couldn't see anything other than bushes. But as a branch from a tree above shifted a little, letting through a shaft of light, she thought she saw something rippling a few feet in front of her. Getting back onto her hands and knees, now without her backpack, she carefully crawled again towards the disturbance she'd glimpsed. Sure enough, up close there was a faint purple-toned shimmer. A forcefield, just like the one Tom had described around Morwyn's tree house. Did that mean she really had come through a rift into the woods surrounding the tree house? Had the rift been there all the time right beneath her nose, waiting for the right time and place? Manoeuvring herself away from the shimmer, she managed to get back onto her feet. If it formed a dome around the tree house, as Tom and Arthur had described, that meant she could make her way around it, keeping it on one side of her, and eventually she'd have to come to the road that led from Morwyn's place to the main road.

It wasn't that easy. Sarah started off walking to her right, keeping the dome to her left, but trees and foliage kept blocking her way and she was continuously having to clamber over fallen tree trunks, through patches of undergrowth, or veer off her path and then try to re-find the forcefield. Eventually, tired and fed up she emerged through some vegetation onto the grass at the side of a narrow, unkempt road. It just had to be that she was back in North Feasgar, and that she was near the treehouse! Excitement overtook her, realising that something so unlikely had actually happened. Here she was, just where she'd hoped to be! She wanted desperately to sit down and catch her breath, but instead dusted herself off and walked down the pot-holey road to the main road, knowing that she'd hear any approaching vehicle with enough time to be able to hide. Getting back to Riverstone was so near now and she didn't want to waste any more time. She still couldn't quite believe that she'd made it!

Arriving at the main road, she tried to remember what Tom had said way back the first time she'd been there, about how far it was to Riverstone. Something like it was fifteen minutes by car, and she was pretty sure he'd then said that meant it was about fifteen kilometres. How far was fifteen kilometres? She didn't know much about metric distances, but she knew it was less than that in miles. Maybe something like about two thirds? Well that was walkable, and she had no choice. Sarah set off in the direction of Riverstone.

Chapter II

A Second Chance

Water enveloped him, frenzied and insistent, forcing itself up his nose and into his lungs. He felt like a great sponge soaking it up through every pore of his body. It tossed him upwards – momentarily his head was above water, gasping, before it immersed him again into its fury. His body scraped against rock walls, pummelling and punishing, all his bones and skin screaming. Now above the water again, another gasping breath, this time a sensation of red-hot needles in his lungs, but even that was suddenly eclipsed by a searing pain in his leg as it hit a rock. It was total agony, and his involuntary cry swamped him with water that rushed in to replace the small amount of air remaining in his lungs… He felt as if he was dissolving, becoming one with the water. *What have I done? I'm so sorry Kayla, I'm so sorry. I'm not going to survive this.* Jonnie gave up his fight and gradually lost consciousness, drifting into a state of oblivion that he vaguely registered wasn't as unpleasant as he'd always thought dying would be. This strange peace belied the continued buffeting of his body as it passed down the narrow chasm through the mountain.

His inert form was spat out of the rock face, where it was propelled down a small waterfall, dropping into a rock pool below. From there it continued on down the river, which was at first turbulent and fast moving, but then changed into a steady flow, finding its way south through countryside that became steadily less barren and increasingly dotted with signs of cultivation and habitation the further it travelled from the mountain. Eventually his body was dumped, face down, on a small silt embankment that protruded from a bend in the river. There was no sign of life as the water eddied around him, pulling at his clothes and nibbling at his many cuts and abrasions, sending trickles of reddish brown to swirl in the water around him.

***

Jonnie emerged from somewhere deep and heavy and sticky, like pushing himself up from beneath boggy marshland. He coughed and passed out with pain. A little later his battered and aching body forced itself into his awareness again. Every inch of him was on fire! He slowly came back to consciousness, emerging to the feeling of a rough hand on his forehead.

"He's waking up again," a gravelly voice said.

Jonnie forced his eyelids open to narrow slits, through which he could blearily see the shape of a man leaning over him, mopping his brow.

"I thought you were a goner, boy. There was very little life force left in you. If I hadn't gone to the river when I did..." He left his words hanging.

Another voice emerged from further behind him, deep and silky smooth, with something in it that sent prickles down Jonnie's spine. "Wake him up properly. I want to ask him some questions," the voice commanded.

"Here lad, have a sip of water," the first man said, lifting his head slightly, supporting his neck with his arm, holding a cup to his mouth with his other hand. Jonnie took a sip, then another, choking a little. The other figure, dressed in black from head to toe, came over towards them. As the man came into view, he could see that he had a strange burqa-like head covering with a heavy veil enclosing his face, mesh over his eyes, and a black tunic reaching right to the ground. Well, he assumed he was a male – his physical presence was large and he had a male's voice.

"Give him some of this," he commanded, handing the man a vial of liquid. Jonnie felt apprehensive, but acquiesced and swallowed a mouthful. A good feeling immediately spread through his body, like blue light through his veins, cleansing, purifying, and his pain started to disappear. As it left him, he had more capacity to be curious about his surroundings. Looking around he could see he was in a small dwelling, with just one living area. It had a kitchen on one side, a table, the couch he was lying on, white-washed walls and one internal door opening into a room that looked like a separate bedroom. He felt remarkably peaceful and idly wondered why he'd been anxious just minutes before.

"Boy, what's your name?" Burqa-man asked.

"Jonnie," he replied.

"And where are you from?"

"Auckland."

"Where? Don't mess with me. You were found in the river, so unless you had an unhappy accident in South Feasgar, I wonder whether you may have come downriver from the north?"

Jonnie didn't say anything. He felt confused, and even though he was feeling good, like *really* good, he was aware enough to know that he'd been given something potent from the vial and needed to be careful.

"So, do you come from North Feasgar?" the man demanded.

"I've been there," Jonnie mumbled, "but it's not where I come from. I come from Auckland, in New Zealand."

He couldn't see the man's face through the black mesh, but he could hear frustration in his voice as he spoke to the other man.

"Enough of that. I'll question him when he wakes up later. You're not to talk to anyone about this. You've not seen or heard anything strange. Do you understand?"

"Of course I do, sir," the man said, "I live a quiet life here on my own. I only see people when I go to the market."

"*Hmm...*" the man in black muttered. "No, this is too important... You *will not* talk to anyone!" He extended his left forefinger towards him and Jonnie could see some sort of ripple pass through the air, a strange disturbance, and then the man was clutching his throat, his face bright red as he tried to speak, but nothing emerged from his mouth other than the raspy sound of his terrified breath escaping. He'd been muted. Jonnie tried to sit up, protesting, but found himself struggling against an incredibly weird, sluggish feeling. He was going fuzzy, his head was spinning and filling up with cotton-wool. He fell back on the couch in a deep stupor.

The next time he woke, it was to a bright light that attacked his eyes like shards of glass. Screwing them up tightly again, Jonnie gradually opened them to a slit, letting them get used to the brightness. Once he could see properly, he found himself in a stark white room with bright lights above and sun streaming through a large window. He tried to shade his eyes so he could see outside, only to find his hands were strapped to the side of his bed. He attempted to move his feet, but they too were tied down. He reared his body in panic, straining against the straps, but they wouldn't budge. His heart was pounding and his breath caught in his throat as he struggled uselessly, until someone who must have quietly entered the room put a hand on his shoulder.

"It's okay, just calm down and I'll undo the straps for you," a male voice said. Jonnie took several deep breaths to get his racing heart back to normal. When he'd relaxed, he felt the restraints on his feet being released. Looking down the length of the bed, he saw a figure wearing a white headdress and a green gown that stopped at the knees with white baggy pants beneath, moving towards his left arm. He was lying on a narrow bed, a bit like a massage table, but bent in the middle so he was on an incline. Maybe a bit like a dentist's chair? He didn't like going to the dentist! Another person came in wearing the same clothing and untied his other arm. This person spoke with a woman's voice and was obviously the other person's superior. She told him to wipe him down (he'd been sweating in terror), then to go and get Argin and tell him the boy was awake.

Addressing him directly she said, "Just lie quietly. We had to tie you down while we healed your leg. It's important you don't move until the bone has knitted properly." She moved behind him out of his vision and, after wiping a cool cloth over his brow, the male figure nodded at her and left the room.

It was very quiet. All he could hear was the background murmur of people's voices in the vicinity and soft footsteps in the corridor outside his room. He realised he couldn't hear any traffic or other noises from outside, though he assumed he was in a hospital in a city. After about fifteen minutes a tall, black clothed figure swept into the room, covered from head to foot so he couldn't see his face other than the vague shape of eyes behind black mesh. With a start, the memory of Burqa-man in the cottage came back to him and he could feel his body respond by stiffening into high alert. The probable-man stopped at the foot of his bed and pointed to the woman with an imperious finger that he then flicked towards the door, through which she abruptly retreated.

The probable-man moved closer to him.

"What's your name?"

Definitely a man then. His voice was deep and commanding. He tried to speak, but only a croak came out of his mouth. The man beckoned to the woman hovering just beyond the door, who approached with a glass of water that she gave to him to sip through a straw. What an odd straw – it wasn't plastic, metal, or even bamboo. He had no idea what it was made of, though it was smooth and cool to his lips. He managed to take a couple of sips before whispering, "Jonnie." The man dismissed the woman again with a flick of his hand and she left the room quietly.

The man proceeded to ask him questions – a lot of questions, like an interrogation. Who was he, where was he from, where was New Zealand, how had he got into the river? Jonnie didn't know how much to say. He didn't think he knew anything of use to the man and wondered why he was so interested in him, but he instinctively didn't like him and felt wary. He tried to keep his answers short and factual, starting with how he'd gone to the mountain with Willard on the orders of some strangers and how they'd fallen into the river while they were inside the mountain. Something told him not to mention Kayla or the others. The man seemed to be mostly interested in whether they'd entered the mountain from the north…

"I guess… but I'm not too sure where I am now, whether we're even talking about the same mountain."

"There is only one near here, Greyvyn. So, you somehow found yourself in North Feasgar, went into Greyvyn, fell into the river and now you're here… If you're not from North Feasgar, how did you get there from your world?"

"I don't know. They told me it was through something they called a rift. It's happened to some others too."

There was a long pause. If he could see his face, he reckoned he'd be looking thoughtful, or maybe sceptical…?

"So where is this… Willard now?"

"I don't know. I lost sight of him while I was being swept along inside the mountain. I don't know if he could swim."

He walked over to the door.

"Ragus," he barked, "send some men to search the river from the city back to the barrier. You're looking for a stranger to these parts, a man who goes by the name of Willard. Boy," he said, turning back to Jonnie, "what does he look like?"

Jonnie did his best to describe him. The man turned back to the doorway. "He's tall, greying hair and likely to be either dead or unconscious… And silence anyone who's come across him."

"Why do you need to do that?" Jonnie asked. "The man who found and cared for me was muted…"

"And so?... He would only have been one of the peasant class and it won't stop him from doing his work. We can't have gossip and fear spreading amongst the uninitiated about people from the north appearing in our country. He was lucky he was spared his life!" he responded curtly. "I haven't finished with you – I'll have more questions for you later. No leaving here. I can silence you too if you create any trouble for us. You'll be safe while you're useful, so don't do anything stupid!" The man had moved behind him as he spoke, doing something while he was out of sight. Jonnie tried to relax on the bed – his whole body felt tense like a tightly strung instrument. The man then moved to the foot of the bed, watching him intently. Jonnie felt like all the bravado he'd worn like a cloak in North Feasgar had deserted him. He felt vulnerable and confused. And something else… He started to notice a kind of a clouding around the edges, and as he dropped into a fuzzy state of half sleep, he had time to wonder if he'd been sedated again, before he slipped further down into a deep state of unconsciousness.

***

The return of awareness approached slowly, fragment by fragment, blurrily approaching then retreating, interspersed by an unravelling. Snatches of moments from his past presented to him in a painful, nightmarish, unrelenting series of frames, broken up by his desperate attempt to wake. A sense of shame about his actions and decisions grew inside him as he dreamed, but was immediately extinguished on his waking realisation that here he was, in an unknown and dangerous situation, that right now he had no means of escaping. He was left with an unease and dread but couldn't remember where it came from... A headache was hanging, jagged, around the edges of his consciousness.

"What did you give me?" he mumbled thickly to the white, shrouded figure beside him, his tongue feeing too big for his mouth.

He must have dozed off again, because next he realised with a start that someone was leaning over him. Opening his eyes fully, all he could see were eyes watching him out of the cross-hatch of the white head covering.

"You're wake. Would you like some water?"

He recognised the voice of the young man, one of the healers. He wasn't sure whether that meant a doctor or a nurse. He nodded his head, feeling completely disconnected from the reality of the room around him. He took a couple of sips.

"How are you feeling? Do you have any pain in your leg?

We thought it was best to sedate you while it healed, but you've been asleep for a long time. You were really knocked out for a lot longer than we expected!"

He felt like he was trying to fight his way to the surface of a container filled with cotton wool – it was filling his ears and mouth and brain, still partly lost in his waking dream and profound sense of dread. The only time he could remember feeling anything like this before was when he was little, maybe about six or seven, when his mother had got really angry with him and locked him in the cupboard under the stairs. It was dark and stuffy and once he'd got past his anger and frustration he'd got bored. It was a storage cupboard that had been used to dump anything that didn't have a place in the house. There were boxes of papers, implements like the iron, ironing board and vacuum cleaner, shelves stuffed with rags, bottles, shoe polish and batteries. The cupboard was very dim, only lit by a few slithers of light coming in through cracks in the boards making up the door. After fossicking around for a while, he'd picked up a bottle that had liquid in it that smelt good and tasted good, so he'd drunk a lot of it and had passed out. When his mum eventually got around to letting him out, she'd found him lying on the floor and had panicked, rousing him enough to make him drink water and forcing him to walk around and around the house until he started to come around properly. She'd never thought to ring an ambulance – probably knew they'd question her about how he'd got hold of a whole bottle of cough syrup.

"Are you thinking that we've drugged you?" the healer asked.

"What?"

"Your thought pictures were linking your experience as a child with how you feel now."

42

"My thought pictures? What do you mean?" When the healer didn't reply, he tried again. "Can you read my mind or something?"

"No, not really, I can just pick up images associated with your emotional memories."

"That's weird. How do you do that?"

"It's just a Gift that I've always had."

"So how come that man has to ask me questions? Why can't you just tell him what I'm thinking?"

"I already said, I can only 'see' visual memories and at the same time some feeling impressions. And anyway, people in the Healing Order are bound by an oath of confidentiality. We're a small community – we live together, keep to ourselves and work hard. We don't all have the same Gifts, so people like Argin wouldn't know to ask me."

"What's an Order?" Jonnie asked.

The healer hesitated, as if unsure how much to say.

"It's the structure we live by in South Feasgar. Those in white, like me, have been initiated into the healing arts. We use our magic in the service of medicine."

"Magic?" Jonnie broke in, looking sceptical.

The healer continued, "Yes, magic – it takes different forms. Those in black are the Mages, initiated and trained in the use of magic for leadership, organisation and control. They're the authorities everyone has to obey. Those in dark blue, the Guardians, carry out their orders and keep the population under control, by force if they need to. The fourth Order wears brown. They're the Artisans, like engineers, architects, builders and craftspeople. Those with no headdress, the uninitiated, are the uneducated class. They have service or peasant roles." He stopped speaking and quickly walked around behind him to do

43

something he couldn't see. "Are you all right? You've become pale. Are you in pain?"

Jonnie was feeling confused and overwhelmed. Too much had happened in too short a time. Well at least it felt like a short time, but it seemed he'd maybe been in this place much longer than he knew anything about.

"No, my leg's fine. It's just all so strange. And yes, I do feel like I've been drugged. Do you think that man in black might have given me something? He went behind me like you did just now."

"I've been adjusting your drip. We've had to feed you through your veins while you've been asleep. I suppose he could have introduced a sedative through it…"

Jonnie looked at his arms. He hadn't been aware of it, but there in his left arm was a needle connected to a tube that passed behind him out of his sight. "But I can't feel it – I didn't even know it was there."

"We can remove your pain while you heal, but it does also remove some of your body sensations."

"How long have I been here for?"

"You've been with us for more than three weeks now; long enough for your leg to stabilise. Healing this way halves the normal recovery time for a bad break like yours."

Jonnie took a while to digest this. Three weeks seemed incredible, when he could only remember a few moments of it. And a bad break? He couldn't feel anything!

"So, what's your name? I can't keep calling you White Burqa man."

"It's Linden. What's a burqa?"

"That thing on your head. Why do you wear it?"

"We call it a krill."

44

"I think I've heard that word before, at school, something to do with the ocean."

"Well for those of us in the Healing Order, wearing a krill helps to shield us from all the bacteria and viruses we might come into contact with. We could keep from infection by using our healing gift, but it's better not to drain ourselves in that way, so we can keep our power for bigger things. Like your leg – knitting bone together takes a lot out of us. I'm not sure about the purpose of the krill for the other Orders, although we're told that wearing it helps us to focus our magic by keeping a stronger personal field, though I sometimes wonder whether it's more to do with power in a different sense. I mean, if you can't see someone it makes them more mysterious, and in the case of the mages, more scary. Maybe that gives them more control."

"Yeah, that Argin guy is scary, and the guy who brought me here… he was cold and… cruel," Jonnie shivered just thinking about the way the man who had found him had been muted. During the pause in conversation, Linden started tidying a trolley near the bed. When Jonnie started to ask him another question about how his healing worked, Linden cut him off.

"Not now. I'm finishing my shift. Now that you're awake, someone will bring you some food and I'll be back in the morning. I think you'll find that you're quite tired for now, but tomorrow we'll start trying to move your leg with some simple exercises." He left the room and Jonnie, in the quiet, realised that he felt weary – not the kind of drugged tiredness that took him to oblivion, but an almost calm kind of weariness. He wondered whether Linden had somehow put that into his mind, or whether he just knew bodies much better than he did. It kind of didn't seem to matter, because he could sense that Linden wouldn't be doing anything that was bad for him. Even without seeing a person's face, he realised he could somehow sense the decency or malice in them.

***

Sleep this time was just sleep, deep and restorative. On waking, he found the woman healer, who Linden had called Sarraphin, at his side. She told him she was stopping the pain relief that had been dripping into his veins and that they would observe him over the day to make sure he could manage as his body sensations returned.

Over the next few hours he experienced the very odd feeling of his body returning to life. It was a bit like the pins and needles he'd had after falling asleep on an arm and having it wake up again, an itchy, partly painful tingliness. He wondered about how little he'd noticed before all the extraordinary things that went on in a human's body moment by moment. Like the gurgle from his stomach, the prick of the needle in his arm when he flexed it, the butterfly feeling of his eye twitching. There was no real pain though. His injured leg felt sort of tight, like the muscles were a bit cramped, and nerves seemed to flicker and twitch. He realised he could feel his toes, sleepy and distant beyond the break.

The next time he saw Linden alone, he asked him again about how his healing magic worked.

"I'm not really supposed to talk about it. I don't know why – people either have the gift or they don't. No one can 'steal' it from us... I can't tell you exactly what I do though, just because it's hard to put into words. I sort of centre myself and focus my mind on the two broken ends of bone. I send blue lines of energy to the site with my mind, building up a cross-hatch over the injury line by line. It creates a matrix across and around the bone ends to hold them in place, a scaffolding that I then send filaments of new bone along to grow and knit the two bones together over time. It accelerates the healing process. By now your leg will have pretty much mended, but it's still important to keep your weight off it for a little longer to allow it to become really strong. It's a lot more effective than putting on an external immobilising device."

***

For the next twenty-four hours Jonnie didn't see Linden. People came and went, bringing him food and drink and a woman started him on simple exercises for his leg. He didn't feel any pain, but when he put it to the ground it felt kind of heavy and dull, like he was dragging a heavy blanket around with it. She told him that it was to be expected and as he started weight-bearing the nerves would heal a lot more rapidly. He was now allowed to get out of bed and go to the toilet, so long as he used crutches and kept his full weight off his leg for another couple of days.

He took to sitting in a chair by the window as a change from lying staring at the unmoving ceiling. The city he was in, Scathach he was told, looked incredible, like nothing he'd ever seen before. The hospital seemed to be located on a hill, surrounded by a green belt of trees. Beyond that though lay a sprawling city, with higgledy-piggledy houses made of wood or stone clustered along winding streets that all seemed to lead towards a city centre, like the spokes of a wheel. Stone buildings about three or four storeys high, gathered around the central square, unusual in that many of them seemed to be standing crookedly, leaning in towards each other, as if they had to huddle to keep them upright. Overlooking the city from its position on a slight rise, was a dominating and menacing building, if you could call it that. Was it a castle, or a palace? It was made of deeply reflective black stone that looked like shards of glass, with great spiky towers reaching jagged into the sky, above walls that were all flat planes and sharp edges. It gave him the creeps. It was a monstrosity – beautiful in a stark way, but it reeked of power and control; control of the city. When he looked more closely he could see that the highest tower, rising like a needle from the centre of the building, had a purple-hued light surrounding it. Maybe coming out of it? It wasn't uniform, it was kind of undulating, but not smoothly, more sort of warped and crackling. It was like a fizzing energy that wasn't quite contained.

Seeing something so strange made him feel even more confused and out of sorts, a bit like when he started high school and went on a school camp when he didn't have any friends. A sort of home-sickness even though he didn't like home. Maybe the unknown brought up feelings about not belonging, not having a place to be himself. He left the window to lie down on his bed again, pulling a blanket up to his neck in an attempt to find comfort. He wished Linden was around – at least he was someone friendly to talk to. The rest of the staff were very efficient, but didn't really talk to him. It was as if they just had to make sure his body was okay and who he was as a person didn't matter. He could feel lots of very old emotions stirring in his stomach and chest. Normally when he started to feel bad, he just did stuff so he wouldn't have to think. Like seeing his friends, hanging out, smoking or drinking. Though he always felt guilty drinking – he was terrified of turning into an alcoholic like his mum. Generally, though, being a smart arse deflected from the crap he was feeling. Now he could feel it creeping up on him, festering inside. He felt really vulnerable and couldn't do anything to stop it.

He had a sudden memory from when he was younger, when he was about ten and his mother started bringing men home. They were noisy and drunk most of the time, with his mum being really stupid and flirty, the men getting loud, with their hands all over the place. Eventually they'd go upstairs to her bedroom. He felt so confused then. Such a mix of abandonment, and being scared, yet somehow protective towards his mum, because he knew the men often turned nasty and made her do things he couldn't imagine her wanting to do. But most weirdly, he also felt kind of jealous. It was like they were getting his mother's attention, and she didn't even see that he existed. A big blob of blackness had formed inside him that he hadn't known how to pull apart – this was probably the first time he'd ever had to face it properly. Oh god, he suddenly remembered the time one of the men had lurched down the stairs in the evening when he'd still been up watching TV and had sat down on the couch beside him, stinking of alcohol, and had leered at him and tried to put his hand on his dick. Gross! He'd whacked his hand away and got up quickly, but then he worried even more about having to keep an eye on Kayla whenever there was a man in the house.

Kayla. She was the one good thing in his stinky life, and he hadn't listened to her; he'd let her down. He'd pretended he was the big man, getting along with Willard, being included in a way he never had been before, and he'd treated her like she was just an annoying kid sister. He didn't want to be like his mother, but with no dad, just crappy men, there was a big vacuum until Willard paid him some attention. He knew Willard wasn't a good man, but he couldn't stop himself wanting to be noticed, to be good enough, so he'd had to try out being tough to get approval. He realised now that he'd been jealous of Tom and Arthur's relationship and had made out that they were lame, when it was something he desperately wanted himself. Not just that they were lame, but that goodness was lame. He'd scoffed at them. What a jerk! He was so embarrassed... and so angry with his mother, with the circumstances of his whole life and who he'd become. It wasn't who he wanted to be. His eyes welled up with tears and he could feel his breath sticking in his throat.

He didn't notice Linden hovering at the door. He'd picked up on some of Jonnie's emotional images and stepped back to give him space, realising that maybe it was the right time for him to face them. About five minutes later he walked through the door and over to the bed in time to see Jonnie collecting himself, wiping his eyes and taking deep breaths.

"So, who's the girl?" he asked.

"The girl?"

"Yes, the one you really care about. I could see her. Dark hair, very slender."

"Oh, my sister Kayla."

"You're worried about her," Linden stated.

"Yes, I've really messed up. I left her and did some stupid stuff and I don't know if I'll ever see her again to try to put it right."

"Look, you nearly died. Give yourself a break – you're feeling emotional, but that's a good thing. It's okay to make mistakes so long as we learn from them. You know, sometimes we have to try out who we don't want to be so we can work out who we *do* want to be..."

Jonnie was quiet for a minute, but, deciding he'd had enough for one day, got Linden talking to him about South Feasgar instead.

"What's the black stuff that huge building across the city is made of? It looks like glass."

"It is a kind of glass. It's called obsidian, and comes from volcanos, I guess from the one north from here."

"The one I came from? Greyvyn?"

Linden had a strange look on his face. "I don't know about that, but maybe." He didn't seem to want to say any more, so Jonnie changed the subject and asked him about the Orders and how he trained to be a healer.

"It takes seven years for someone introduced into an Order to train. We have to show some aptitude when we're at school if we want to be chosen. In the first three years, we're Apprentices. We have some classes – for me, to learn about the body and how it functions, and how to focus magical energy, but mostly we watch until one of the Affiliates lets us try."

"What's an Affiliate?"

"Second stage. When we pass the Apprentice stage, we become Affiliates. We have to reach a safe standard before we're initiated as an Affiliate, then it takes another four years, which are more about magical healing, working on our own under the guidance of a Master. I'm just finishing my Apprentice training – I only need to have another two cases after you before I go into the Affiliate initiation ceremony. Then I get a month off to visit my family, who I haven't seen since I started when I turned eighteen!"

"Where do they live?"

"On a farm in the north west. I was singled out for training when I was at school and I'll be a fully qualified Master when I'm about twenty-five. It's been really hard not seeing them – we're a close family and I'm the only one who's been selected for training, so my brother and sister have their lives mapped out running the farm and caring for my parents as they get older."

"Can't they decide what they want to do?"

"Not really – we get prepared at school. My sister's really clever and should have been chosen for something where she could keep learning, but she was ill in her last years of school and didn't get noticed."

"That doesn't seem very fair. There must be a way for her to start now."

"Well probably, but I don't know anyone in the other Orders and neither does she. Someone needs to represent her to them. How does it work where you come from?"

"We just decide what we're interested in, and choose to go to university, if we can afford it, or get a job. It's usually just a matter of doing what you know about unless you have parents who encourage you."

"What do you want to do?"

"No idea," Jonnie replied shortly.

"Did your parents not encourage you?"

Jonnie abruptly changed the subject. "I just don't get the magic part…"

"What do you mean?"

"We don't have magic where I come from, and a girl I know in North Feasgar wants to be a healer, but that's just using herbs and medicine and things."

"Where?"

"North Feasgar."

"Where's that?" Linden demanded, his voice suddenly taking on a strange tone.

"Up north of the mountain, where I just came from…"

Linden blanched and whispered "Sshhh…" as he walked over to the door and looked around down the corridor. Seeing that there was no one around, he returned, saying quietly, "Don't talk about that place. We're forbidden, and if anyone hears us they'll silence us. I'll talk to you later sometime when it's safe," before turning abruptly and leaving the room. Jonnie's mind went straight to the man who had found him on the side of the river, silenced because, somehow, he'd seen something he shouldn't have. Why were they trying to keep North Feasgar's presence a secret from their people? He didn't want to get Linden into any trouble, so he'd better be careful what he said.

The next day when Linden came on duty, he talked to him instead about how he'd been chosen to be a Healer.

"We're chosen at school, depending on what our abilities show we'd be good at. I remember a teacher watching me fussing over a bird with a broken wing, trying to calm it so I could strap it down while it healed. I took it home with me in a box. From then on, she kept giving me things to read and learn about healing, and I guess it all started from there. What are you good at?"

"Dunno, nothing really. I've never thought about it."

Linden raised an eyebrow, "Why's that?"

"Always had too much else to think about."

"Like?"

"I guess everything that goes wrong, like my mum, stuff at school, having to look out for my sister... Anyway, why are you asking me these things? You're supposed to be healing my leg."

"So, who says that healing is only about your body?" Linden replied as he walked out the door.

Jonnie was acutely aware that he'd talked more to Linden than almost anyone else, ever, in a completely different way to the short, half conversations he exchanged with his friends at home. He seemed to get pulled in somehow – it wasn't just that he had nothing else to do. He lay there and thought for a while about what he'd like to do if he had a choice in this land. He'd probably end up as one of the uninitiated – that was probably all he was good for. But another part of him played around with the idea of the four Orders. As he mulled on them, he remembered that the one time he'd really enjoyed school was the year he got to do a subject they called 'hard materials', where he got to try out making things with wood or metal. He'd loved woodwork and had made his mother a really cool bedside table that his teacher had raved about. He'd felt really proud! He took it home and gave it to his mother. She didn't say anything! A few weeks later, when it was still sitting in the middle of the lounge where he'd left it, Kayla had picked it up and taken it to her room to put beside her bed – she loved it, but he'd never gotten rid of the sour note it left in his mind that he'd tried so hard to do something nice for his mum, and not only that she couldn't accept it, but that she'd completely ignored it. The story of his life! Still… maybe it was something he'd be good at now? He knew deep down that it wasn't right that his mother got to dictate how he was for the rest of his life. He knew he and Kayla were both scarred – maybe being in this strange place was where they could find out who they could really be…

After a couple more days of walking carefully with his crutches and sticking to the exercises he'd been given, Sarraphin told him he could try walking unaided. It felt a bit weird; his leg felt vulnerable somehow, but it didn't hurt. He wondered what would happen to him once he didn't need to be in hospital. The man, Argin, hadn't been back to see him, but he guessed it was just a matter of time. Linden now had two new patients to work with, the last two he'd need to work with intensively before he could graduate, so he didn't get to see him as much. Mind you, he didn't really need the attention of a healer any more, but he really missed having him around to talk to. Linden had visited him briefly the evening before as he went off shift and they'd talked about what they were taught in the south about the land north of the mountain. According to their teachers, the north was lawless, a place of disorganised chaos, where people lived hand to mouth, in a much more primitive way than they did in the south. The barrier had been put there for their protection, to keep out people who would try to take what was theirs. "What? That's madness," Jonnie exclaimed. "The people there are perfectly ordinary, good people, just like you and me. Well, they're probably much better than me! They say that the barrier was introduced by them to try to keep out the black magic of the south!"

"Well that'll be why they don't want any of us to know anything about the north. Somehow it must serve their purposes to keep us afraid and unquestioning! Many of us are concerned about what the Mages are up to and how they try to control the population. There are good people here, but they're kept compliant by the Mages and the Guardians."

Linden hadn't known anything about what would happen to him now, and thought Jonnie needed to be really careful how much he said to Argin about North Feasgar and the people he'd met there in case he gave them information they could use to cause harm. Last night, when he was alone again, he'd been left feeling really anxious, and in the light of day today, that hadn't dissipated. He looked out the window at the black building, the Shard. It looked dominating and ominous – a good daily reminder to the people who lived in Scathach to be afraid and to behave!

Suddenly Jonnie noticed a flurry of activity outside his room. Several people walked past his door wheeling a trolley with someone lying on it.

"We have him!" a man's voice exclaimed.

Another voice that sounded familiar, maybe Argin's, asked where he'd been found and the first voice replied that he was being looked after in a village by a retired healer. They moved down the corridor out of his hearing, but Jonnie was left with the sick feeling that they were talking about Willard.

Chapter III

Confusing Feelings

Tom was sitting in the sun on the back steps at Riverstone, trying to work out how to fasten a metal clip to a piece of wood, when a fast-moving ball of fur rocketed down the path and leapt into his arms, knocking him backwards, unbalanced with his arms out to hold her.

"Hermione! What are you doing?" he asked as he righted himself. She tucked her head under his chin, rubbing herself against him happily.

"She's back!"

"She?"

"Sarah! She called for me. She's walking from the turnoff to Morwyn's tree house, down the main road towards us."

Tom was having trouble focusing on what Hermione was saying. A part of him had thought he'd never see Sarah again, maybe so he wouldn't need to hope or feel disappointed, but she was here!

"Well hurry up, we don't have all day!" Hermione admonished.

Hermione jumped down as Tom got to his feet. They'd have to take the motorbike, which they'd brought back from Willard's after Sarah had returned to England, because Arthur and Mary had taken the truck on an errand. They'd be back soon, but he didn't want to wait for them.

Tom set off along the road on the bike, Hermione balanced on the back behind him, her whiskers twitching as the air rushed past her. After about ten minutes she sent him a thought message that Sarah was close by, and peering into the distance he spotted a small dot on the side of the road. Sarah too, must have picked up a message of their approach from Hermione – as they rapidly drew closer, she resolved into a figure who had moved to the middle of the road, and was standing there waving her arms excitedly.

Easing off the throttle, Tom brought the bike to a halt a short distance from her. Jumping to the ground, he didn't stop to let himself feel awkward – he ran to her and caught her up in a huge hug. It felt like they'd been waiting for this for so long! They stood, pressed together, chest to chest, hearts pounding strongly, until a "what about me?" from Hermione made them reluctantly move apart. Sarah bent and scooped Hermione up in her arms, burying her nose in her soft fur and running her hand down her back.

"Oh Hermione, it's so good to see you! And you too of course, Tom," she said blushing. She felt flushed and fluttery and wasn't sure where to look.

Tom wanted to ask her a million questions, but instead he just looked at her – it felt like he was drinking in six months of missed opportunities. She was looking gorgeous. A light flush was spread across her pale skin. *Of course, it must be winter in England at the moment,* he thought. Her fair hair was longer and tied back in some sort of complicated looking braid, and her blue eyes were a bit crinkled at the edges from the sun and, he hoped, her happiness at seeing them. His questions could wait – better to get her to Riverstone so she could tell them all about how she came to be back.

They rode back with Hermione squished between them, nestling into Sarah, with her head tucked under her arm, purring happily. When they arrived, Hermione jumped down as Sarah got off the bike, and Tom took her backpack from her. Walking up the path, she had time to notice how inviting the millhouse looked nestled into the countryside, the sun shining warmly on the stone of the house and reflecting a myriad of glitters off the river. The next minute the door flew open and Mary rushed down the steps, throwing her arms out wide, exuberantly whirling Sarah around in a circle. When they stopped, Sarah drew a deep breath.

"Wow, that was an amazing welcome! I'm so happy to see you!"

"And us you, dear girl. I was so hoping you'd be able to come back."

A minute later Arthur appeared at the door looking puzzled, wiping his dusty hands down his work apron.

"Mary, what's going on? I'm trying to get back to work, but Hermione wants me for something – I can't work out... Sarah! Oh my goodness. It's really you! Come here girl – let me take a look at you." He gave her a big hug and then held her at arms' length. "You're looking pale and drawn – and I'm pretty sure you've lost weight! Wait, don't tell us anything yet. Let's just go inside first. There's plenty of time."

Sarah followed him up the steps with Mary and Tom trailing behind. Walking into the millhouse, Sarah had the feeling that she'd never been away; it felt really familiar and so much like home. Tom headed for the stairs with her bag and she went to follow him, but hesitated, flushing pinkly. Mary, noticing, drew her aside.

"I'm sure this is all very confusing for you Sarah. You're likely to feel a bit awkward for a while, especially with Tom, given how you'd just got to know each other properly before you left." Sarah blushed more deeply. "Of course we knew what was happening," Mary continued, "and we think you're just right for each other, but new relationships are always prickly things. Just take your time."

***

As Sarah had come to know and expect, they all sat down at the table to catch up and talk over food and a cup of tea. It was so nice, all sitting together – she felt like she belonged. Even Hermione was on one of the chairs beside her, sitting with her head swivelling from side to side as she intently followed the conversation.

"Why don't you tell me first what's been happening," Sarah began. She didn't quite know where to start for her part of it. She was still feeling a bit bewildered from her sudden arrival and needed to catch her breath.

"Well," Mary began, "we've been checking regularly on Galawand and Kayla, and they're doing really well together, keeping the barrier strong and they're really good company for each other. Kayla seems settled and is learning really quickly from Galawand."

"The only thing that worries her is that she can't help thinking that Jonnie has somehow survived. She keeps worrying about him," added Arthur. "It's been six months now and there hasn't been any sighting of him."

"Yes, she can't let go of thinking about him – it's the not knowing that gets to her," Mary continued. "She's much better in herself though – she's losing that frightened look she had."

"She's not so skinny now either. She's turning out to be

60

really pretty," Tom chipped in.

Sarah felt a jolt of the old jealousy she used to experience when Tom spent time with Kayla. She hated it, but didn't seem to be able to stop it. Mary and Arthur exchanged a glance and Arthur jumped in quickly to continue the story.

"Willard's disappearance was a topic of local gossip for a while. Some versions linked it to the strangers, but over time they seem to have disappeared. Something to do with the barrier being strong again we've been thinking. And now everyone seems to have forgotten they were ever here."

"Yeah, those two boys haven't reappeared at school either," Tom added.

"So, everything seems to have turned out well, and yet…" Mary's voice trailed off.

"And yet?" Sarah asked when nothing more was said.

"Well… I just have a feeling something's brewing but I can't tell you what."

"It doesn't *feel* right," added Hermione, "It's like I can smell an agitation but I can't put my paw on it." Sarah smiled at her use of paw instead of finger.

"Galawand agrees," said Tom. "She thinks it's coming from south of the barrier; that there's a growing sense of something preparing, getting ready, but she doesn't know what for. She says it's like an increase in psychic pressure."

Sarah had turned to look at Tom as he spoke. He seemed so much more confident than before… And he was so good-looking! He was gazing steadily at her, one hand brushing back the bit of hair that always stuck up on his head, a remembered gesture that made her heart lurch. She felt such a confusing mixture of attraction and awkwardness that she didn't know what to do with it. Instead she blushed again and looked away.

61

"How about you, Sarah, what was it like when you got back?" Arthur asked.

Sarah paused and drew a breath, trying to build up her courage to talk about things that were still so painful for her.

"My grandad…" she began, but couldn't carry on. There was a huge lump blocking her throat that her words couldn't get past. She swallowed and suddenly blurted it out. "My grandad saw me and saw the photos – he was so excited to know what I'd said had really happened – and then he died!" Big tears were rolling down her cheeks and Mary moved over to put her arm around her.

"I'm so sorry, Sarah," she said, "that's awful. You must really miss him."

"He had a heart attack just before I went back," she gulped. "My gran got angry that he'd helped me and broke the plate, and he panicked that I wouldn't be able to get back and got cross because she didn't trust us and had called my parents. He seemed to be okay for a little while, until I'd seen him, then he died," she managed to say in a rush before collapsing onto her arms on the table, sobbing.

"And none of that is your fault," Mary said, rubbing her shaking shoulders.

"But if I hadn't come back here he'd still be alive," she said in a very small voice.

"Well, no one knows that," said Arthur. "A heart attack can happen at any time – and look at how much pleasure you gave him by showing him that North Feasgar actually exists. It's really important to know that there is more than what we can see and prove with our senses."

"I feel so confused." She wanted to be back with them all, but was feeling worried about her parents and a bit sick about the decision she'd made, and that she might never see England and her friends and family again. Then there were her confusing feelings for Tom. And, gnawing away at her underneath all that, her deep sense of loss and confusion about her grandad. She didn't really know how to talk about it – she didn't want to worry Mary and Arthur, and it all seemed such a jumble that she couldn't really put it into coherent words. She felt selfish about being angry with her gran, when she'd lost her husband. And selfish for leaving her parents. All she'd been thinking about was herself and how bad she was feeling, but... She was in such turmoil she couldn't even complete her thoughts. "I don't know what to do. I'm so sorry to blurt it all out at you like that," Sarah said, sounding breathless and overwrought as she spoke. She was biting the corner of her nail, her old habit when she was stressed.

"I think you've been really brave, but now that you're here your whole body is reacting to six months of stored up feelings. And you'll be tired from travelling. I think the best thing for you would be to have a good sleep. It'll all feel different tomorrow. Come on," Mary took her hand and guided her away from the table and took her upstairs to her bedroom.

***

Tom needed to think. When Sarah had gone upstairs with Mary, he decided to go for a walk. Outside there was a light breeze ruffling the trees in the garden and he could smell the lavender and the slightly fermented scent of plums that had fallen and squashed into the ground. He wandered through the gate and over the field to the river listening to the soothing sound of the water slowly flowing down to the mill... This is where they'd first met three years ago – somehow both an incredibly long and short time depending on how he thought about it. In one way it felt like he'd always been here in North Feasgar – he'd managed to rid himself of his nightmares of Gerald, and even his mum and Leah had faded into the background. He loved it here, with the Birches. They were more parents to him than his mum had ever been. And Sarah... how did he feel about her? Could he say he loved her after the short time they'd actually spent together? Yet something in him knew she was right for him and he needed to try to be grown up about owning his emotions and finding a way to let her know how he felt. He heard soft footsteps behind him and turned around to see Arthur making his way towards him over the field. He was amazing – he'd obviously picked up on his turmoil and wanted to make sure he was okay.

"How're you doing, Tom? I bet it's good to see Sarah again..." There was a long pause.

"I don't know. It was fantastic to see her when she first arrived, but then everything got awkward. It's like there's her and me and a great gulf between us. How do I get over it? How do I know whether she likes me like I like her?"

"I think it's pretty obvious she likes you; she's just confused and overwhelmed by so much happening to her so quickly. She's feeling guilty about leaving her parents, sad about her grandfather, and in the midst of her anxiety about getting here, thinking it wouldn't happen, suddenly she was through the rift. She must feel very disoriented."

"So, what do I do? I don't want to push her, but she might think I don't like her if I don't say anything."

"Look lad, trust your instincts. There's no hurry. At the right time you'll know. The early stage of a relationship tends to be excruciating, so you're not alone with your uncertainty, but you're both good kids and you'll work it out. When Mary and I met, at about your age, Mary had just moved to the town I lived in, and at the time I was a bit stuck on a girl, Laura, in my class. She was a real looker. She was gorgeous! She had all the boys hanging around her like moths to a flame. I didn't really even notice Mary, other than that we had a new girl in the class. When I looked back later I realised it must have been hard on her coming into a bunch of people who'd known each other most of their lives and were quite cliquey. She felt very alone. Anyway, the annual school dance was coming up and I was in agony over whether I should ask Laura to go with me. I guess that was probably the hot topic in all the boys' brains, but I wasn't going to talk to any of them about it. I waited and waited for the right moment when she was alone, until one day I happened to walk home past her as she came out of the newspaper shop. I didn't see her group of friends waiting for her. I plucked up courage and hesitantly asked her if she'd go with me. I'll never forget her look of disdain. "You?" she said. "Why would I go with you? I'm going with Duncan" – the most popular boy in the school. She turned away laughing, and when she joined her friends she made sure I could hear her saying loudly that I'd asked her too, and she wondered why on earth I thought she'd go with a farmer-boy. I was so humiliated I didn't know where to put myself."

"That's awful. So what happened? How did Mary come into it?"

"Well, the next day, at school, every time I went near Laura's little posse of girls, they laughed and looked me up and down, whispering and sniggering. My friends wanted to know what was going on and when I told them they laughed. Later I realised it was because they couldn't believe I'd done it – they knew much better than me what she'd be like if any of us lesser mortals dared to ask. I was a bit naïve I guess, but at the time I felt let down by them and terribly embarrassed. I took off by myself at lunch time and went to the trees at the edge of the playing fields to feel sorry for myself. Mary was down there, reading a book and we struck up a conversation. She was so 'normal'. She was clever, more by far than the other girls in the class, and down to earth, and, well, kind. I never felt the uncertainty with her that I did with Laura, but of course there's always that awkward stage of moving on from being friends to being more than friends. Something about crossing a physical barrier that's really difficult unless you're one of those people who get physically close with anyone who'll let you. We went to the school dance together and dancing helped us to get over that and we never really looked back. Well of course, we had our ups and downs, but there was never anyone else for either of us – we were mad about each other by the time we went through the rift and found ourselves here, and we've been together ever since." Arthur squeezed Tom's shoulder. "Let's get back, I'm hoping you'll come with me in the morning to Hunterdale to pick up some garden supplies, so we'll need to get up early."

***

Sarah fell asleep the minute her head hit the pillow. She was exhausted physically and emotionally. Mary checked on her later in the evening and saw her lying on her back as if she'd been completely flattened. She felt the need to check that she was breathing and chided herself afterwards for being anxious about her. Hermione had gone upstairs with her and jumped onto the bed, stretching out along the length of Sarah's body.

"Take care of her Hermione, she's in a lot of turmoil."

Sometime in the small hours of the morning, Sarah woke up, for a moment wondering where she was. Before long, her mind kicked in, playing over and over all her tumultuous feelings from the day before. She couldn't let go of them and replayed all her thoughts and everything she'd said; not just yesterday, but at all the difficult times over the past six months. She started to get the horrible stressy feeling that made her chest feel tight and her breathing blocked in her throat, and tried to make herself take deep breaths. She had a bad feeling in the pit of her stomach. There was a small thump as Hermione jumped up onto the bed and made her way up to her chest, nuzzling her nose in under her chin.

"You're awake. You were dead to the world before, so I went out for a hunt."

Sarah couldn't even respond, other than putting her arms around her and holding her tightly.

"I'm picking up a whole jumble of overwhelming feelings from you. You'll make yourself ill with worry."

"Hermione, I don't know what to do. I'm really scared. I feel so awful, and I can't breathe properly and I feel sick in my stomach. I feel really panicky!" Her breath was shallow and ragged. Clutching Hermione was all she could do to keep hold of some sense of connection.

"It's okay, Sarah, just take a deep breath in… now breathe out. And again, in… and out. Everything's going to be all right. Keep breathing, in… and out. Now imagine yourself somewhere you love to be, somewhere in the countryside maybe. You're walking through some fields with your grandad beside you." She spoke slowly and quietly, "You can feel the warm sun on your skin and you can hear birds in the trees and the sound of your breath, in… and out. As you walk you can see the grass around your feet and in the distance some more trees and a stream winding lazily between them. A cool breeze wafts across your face. I wonder what you can smell…?"

"Honeysuckle," Sarah whispered.

"You can smell honeysuckle, sweet in the clean air, and as you walk, the smell of the grass crushed under your feet. Your footsteps are muffled except when you step on a twig – it gives a little cracking sound. You're really aware of your grandad walking beside you. He's holding your hand in his large, warm one, and he's strong and solid. His voice is soothing as he points out trees and plants, naming them for you. He will always be there for you, he's inside you, he's safely in your heart. As you continue walking, keep breathing in… and out, nice deep breaths. Each time you breathe out, let go of your worries and relax." Hermione's voice was soft and slow and soothing, and as Sarah relaxed, it turned into a rhythmic purr. She was lying on Sarah's chest, her head just below her chin. With her arms around her, Hermione felt like a warm, vibrating, comforting fur rug, and it didn't take long before Sarah slipped off quietly into a deep sleep. Hermione waited for a while before slipping out from between her arms and going downstairs.

***

When Sarah woke in the morning, she lay for a moment wondering where she was before remembering everything that had happened the day before. She gasped and sat up, her eyes roaming around the room, fixing on the familiar things around her, like the jars of herbs and the books she'd brought back from Morwyn's, so long ago now. In some ways it seemed like yesterday, yet three years had passed and so much had happened. She could hear voices downstairs, but she wasn't ready to talk to anyone yet – she still felt really vulnerable after her panic attack in the night. Sitting on her bed wondering what to do now, she heard Tom call out goodbye to Mary. She walked over to the window and looked down on the side of the garden bordering the drive and the road. The sun was well up in a cloudless sky and it was going to be a beautiful day. She heard the truck doors slam and saw it slowly moving to the road, where it turned left towards Hunterdale. Tom must be driving, because she could see Arthur's elbow resting on the open window frame of the passenger door. She'd forgotten how quiet the steam-powered vehicles were here – it was almost inaudible as it drove off.

Maybe a bath would help – she ran the water until it was really full and immersed herself in it, feeling like she was being enveloped in a warm and soothing cocoon, until the water became cool and her fingers and toes turned wrinkled and pruney. She'd tried not to think too much, rather to relax and soak in her new surroundings. She wrapped herself in a towel to walk back to her room, pausing when she went past the bookshelf. The book with the Anam Cara symbol on the spine pulled at her attention. Taking it from the shelf, she curled up on the bed with it. She loved the soft leather and the gold lettering – it felt so luxurious as she ran her finger-tip over the symbol. She'd left a slip of paper in the book the last time she'd read it and she went to the page to remind herself about what the writer said about the Anam Cara. She stopped at a statement that said:

Have courage, stand tall, and when the Anam Cara is aligned within and without, then you'll find your true power.

Sarah read it out aloud, the words having a strong impact on her, though she didn't know why. She felt like straightening her shoulders and standing up taller, feeling a point in the centre of her chest expand – tears came to her eyes...

Feeling quite a bit better, Sarah dressed and went downstairs quietly. There she found Mary in the kitchen. As soon as Mary saw her, she walked over and put her arms around her, giving her a squeeze. She felt so familiar and comforting that her worries about having left England started to melt away. Breakfast was waiting for her – dark, stewed plums from the garden, with their sweet, crimson juice bleeding into the thick and creamy yoghurt, topped with crunchy nuts and seeds. Yum! Her stomach rumbled as she carried her bowl out to the front steps. On an impulse though, she continued from the landing around the corner to the steps on the other side that led down to the river, where she'd first arrived from her grandparents' place all that time ago.

Sitting on the top step looking down at the river stones where she'd arrived in North Feasgar, she shivered even though the day was mild. If that hadn't happened, how would things be different now? Maybe her parents would have split up permanently, maybe she would have gone to the local school and never have met Jas and Lara. Her stomach gave a lurch – she'd completely forgotten to tell them she was going away. She felt sick. Even a lie about where she was going would have been better than just disappearing! What sort of a friend was she? And Hannah too – she didn't see her as regularly, but she'd still be worried. She forced her mind away from them – she felt too wobbly to go there right now, and she couldn't change what had happened. One thing was for sure, she wouldn't have met Tom and the Birches if it hadn't been for that fateful day and she wouldn't have had the chance to grow up the way she had. She was proud of the way she'd learned so much and stopped being a girl afraid of her own shadow. Or maybe she was somehow destined to meet them and it would have happened anyway, just another way? The tarot cards seemed to be pointing her towards experiences somehow destined to happen, if she chose to see it like that, or at the very least being open to explore what was presented to her.

Her thoughts were abruptly cut off by a screeching noise from above her. Looking up she saw a dark shape approaching in the sky, arcing across the trees beyond the river, swooping down towards her.

"Ryder!" she yelled, standing up to wave her arms excitedly in the air. Gliding on a current of air, he dropped lower and lower until he drifted to an elegant landing beside her, extending his beak to nibble at her outstretched hand before rubbing his soft, downy head on her arm. Sarah put her arm around him, gathering him in, squawking a bit, to lean against her body. He let her caress him for a minute before shrugging himself free and stretching his great wings.

"I'm so glad to see you're completely better Ryder," Sarah laughed, knowing there was only so much human contact he could tolerate. She had to listen really hard to tune into his speech again. Funny, given how it was just instinctive with Hermione and she hadn't missed a beat with her. Through his scratchy sounds she picked up how happy he was to see her and that he had news for all of them.

"Tom and Arthur have gone to Hunterdale, but they'll be back soon I think. Let's go inside and find Mary."

Sarah walked back into the house with Ryder, and as they sat in the living room together waiting for Tom and Arthur's return, Sarah quizzed Ryder about what he'd been up to over the past six months since she'd last seen him, and about whether he'd checked recently on the elixir.

"About two moons ago I flew there and it was safe. No one would ever go there to come upon it."

"So, what would we do if ever anything happened to you

Ryder? What if we urgently needed it for something?"

"Tom and I have thought about that – I've told Hermione where it is, and even if it was difficult for her to get to herself, I'm sure she'd find a way to get it back."

"It sounds like you respect her Ryder – so much for her being 'just a cat' or potential prey for you!" said Sarah laughing.

As if she'd heard her name, Hermione appeared shortly after, jumping nimbly up onto the table, looking haughty and twitching her tail.

"Hermione, Ryder was just telling me how clever he thinks you are. What do you think about that?" Sarah said teasingly.

"Well he's quite smart for a winged creature," Hermione retorted, "but I won't say anything else about his bird brain because of those lethal talons of his!"

Ryder made a scratchy noise that could have been a laugh and made a pretend swipe at her twitching tail with his beak.

"Come on you two, anyone can see you're good friends," Sarah laughed.

"You're sounding a lot better today, Sarah," Mary said.

"I guess it's starting to seep into me that I'm surrounded by my friends and what a special place this is. I'm lucky I was able to find my way back... Listen, I think they're back."

Footsteps could be heard coming up the steps. Tom appeared at the door and looked straight across the room at her. Her heart gave a lurch. *You idiot!* she thought as her cheeks went pink, cross with herself that her feelings were so obvious. She managed to notice Tom's attempt at nonchalance though. Sarah smirked inwardly to herself – so he was feeling as awkward as she was!

"What's up, Ryder?" Tom asked, "We didn't expect to see you for a few days."

"Galawand has sent a message for you all."

"What's he saying, Tom?" Arthur asked.

"We need to sit down – Galawand has news and from Ryder's tone it sounds important."

"Gosh, Tom, you've got good at understanding him," Sarah exclaimed, "I'm having to get used to his speech again."

"Yeah well, when you left I spent a lot of time with him while his leg was healing to make sure I could in case anything important happened… So, tell us, Ryder."

"I visited the mountain on my usual weekly circuit and met Kayla at the entrance. She gave me a message for you and said it was very important that you got it immediately." He extended one leg and Sarah reached over to unroll a small piece of parchment-like paper rolled around his leg and tied with a crimson thread. Sarah read Galawand's hand-writing aloud:

Hello all of you. We're picking up a strong magical presence at the base of Greyvyn, interfering with the other side of the barrier. We need you as quickly as you can get here – that includes Hermione this time. If the old stories are correct, Sarah will have been summoned by now and will hopefully arrive soon. Be prepared to be away for a while.
Love, Galawand

"Perfect timing, as ever Sarah," remarked Tom.

"What does she mean, summoned?" Sarah asked. "I thought I chose to come here… though I guess I did get a strong feeling that it needed to be now, or possibly never!"

They all looked at each other silently as they considered the impact of the note.

"So," Arthur broke the silence, "here we go again!"

"Remind us what the 'old stories' say that you and Galawand have talked about before, Mary…?" Sarah asked.

"We don't know much. They've been passed down through the one hundred years since Feasgar was divided; that at a time of crisis a young boy and girl would appear in North Feasgar to save us, and when Arthur and I looked in the labyrinth pool we could see that it had something to do with us too."

"No pressure then!" exclaimed Tom. "I thought we'd done our bit when we helped to get the barrier strong again."

"Well it looks like something much bigger is happening now. If anyone's going to know more, it will be Galawand – she's been maintaining the barrier since the beginning. I wonder how she keeps going at her advanced age – I suppose so long as Kayla is there to help her stay strong… but sometimes she must want to stop and see out her days with some comfort, and daylight! Maybe we've been a bit complacent over the last six months, knowing that the barrier is strong again and that the strangers seem to have gone," said Arthur.

"Actually, I don't know that they have," Sarah chipped in. "When I arrived through the rift I was near the forcefield they put around the treehouse. It's still there – I nearly walked into it. Maybe they've just been keeping a low profile for six months – if they needed to get anything from outside no one other than us would be able to see them anyway."

"It sounds like you've plenty to tell us, not just about yesterday, but about the past six months – how about we have some lunch while you talk to us, then we can work out what we're going to do next."

While they were eating, Sarah talked to them about what had happened since she saw them last; about her parents and Singapore, about her school, and then how she came to realise

74

she needed to return to North Feasgar. When she got to the bit about visiting Mary and Arthur's old town they asked so many questions, looking dumb-founded when she described what it was like now. At the mention of Jack Houghton, Arthur wracked his brain for a minute.

"Oh, of course, he'd be getting on a bit now! He was a friend of my father's. He was a hard case! What did he say about my family?"

"Not much, just that your mother died a while back and your father lives with your eldest brother. He said they'd be happy if you visited..." Sarah decided not to say anything about him supposedly breaking his mother's heart. "I got away as quickly as I could after that because I didn't want him asking me any tricky questions."

When she said how guilty she felt about leaving her own family and worrying about whether she'd done the right thing, Arthur just said, "What's done is done. If you'd stayed you'd always have wondered how it, and you, could be different. I know you're feeling bad for now, and it will get better..."

"So you're saying to suck it up."

"No, I'm saying to let it out, talk to us and let us care about you. Let yourself feel vulnerable. We all love you and want you to be okay."

"What do we need to take this time?" Arthur wondered, once Sarah had finished talking. "There seems to be some urgency, but I think we need to take our time and make sure we're well prepared."

"It sounds like you need to take me, and I'm not much pleased about that!" Hermione sniffed. "You know I don't want to go into that mountain."

"But cats can see in the dark Hermione, and you have such

a good sense of direction. You don't get claustrophobic, do you?" Sarah asked.

"Claustrophobic?" Hermione snorted. "Don't be silly! So long as I don't have to go anywhere narrower than my whiskers," she shuddered at the thought. "I just don't like the feeling of all that rock above and below and around me!"

"Isn't that a kind of claustrophobia, even though you're not worried about not being able to breathe or getting stuck?" Tom asked, fascinated. "Sarah worries about that, but she was okay inside the tunnels."

Hermione just swished her tail and didn't deign to reply.

They couldn't think of much they'd forgotten the last time they'd gone into Greyvyn, but Mary suggested they pack more clothes and said she would make sure they had enough food to last a few days. And this time, she'd make sure she had some first aid supplies!

"We'll leave early this afternoon – there's no point messing about wasting time. Are you okay with that Sarah, or do you need another night to get your bearings?"

"I'll be okay. It's probably good for me to have something to do."

"All right, if you're sure, you two get your packs sorted, then maybe you could help Mary with the food and other supplies – leave some room in your packs to add food and water so we don't have too many bags to carry. I'll sort the ropes and lighting."

Tom and Sarah went up to their rooms. Sarah unpacked everything she'd brought with her and arranged it in her room. She laid out the clothes she would wear, plus a change and a warm jumper just in case it got cold inside the mountain. This time she decided on two pairs of sturdy walking shoes, placing one pair in the bottom of her pack. As she put them in she noticed that a tarot card had escaped from its black cloth wrapper and had lodged itself against the lining of the pack. *What's with my tarot cards? They keep jumping out at me!* Turning it over curiously, she saw that this time it was The Tower. She put it back with the other cards and placed the book that went with them on her bed to remind her to look it up later. Wondering how Tom was getting on, Sarah wandered across the corridor to his room. He'd just finished putting his clothes in his pack (not very neatly, she noticed!) and turned to smile at her as she stood at the door. She walked towards him and the next thing she knew he was standing right in front of her, one arm around her waist, the other on the side of her face so she had to look into his green eyes. He drew her into a kiss, their lips lightly touching at first, then more deeply, as if they were both reaching down into the depths of each other's souls. Neither of them had ever experienced anything like it. It was full of a yearning and meeting and love that left them both weak-kneed and happy. At Hermione's "*Hmmhmm*", they pulled apart, Sarah feeling giddy; Tom unable to even think for a moment – disorientated and trying to pull himself back to reality against a force of attraction that felt like a strong magnet.

"Well at least you can't tell the others anything Hermione," Sarah said when she'd gathered herself again.

"What makes you think I need to – they'll see it written all over you!"

"What do you mean?" she demanded.

"Yesterday you were tired, confused and despondent, now both of you are glowing."

They looked at each other, Sarah's fair skin still suffused with pink. At the question in her expression, Tom took her hand and squeezed it.

"I'll go down first while you finish your packing it won't look so obvious if we go down separately."

Tom left the room and made his way downstairs. Sarah found herself in her room, pretending she still had packing to do, when in reality it only took her a couple of minutes to finish putting her clothes tidily in her pack on top of her shoes. She wasn't in the right mood to look up her Tarot book right now, so she stored it in her pack and wasted a few more minutes looking at the books on her bookshelf from her first visit to North Feasgar, before feeling sufficiently calm to go downstairs.

When she entered the living room, all their eyes seemed to suddenly be on her.

"What?" she asked. She saw Mary and Arthur glance at each other.

"Nothing," Mary replied, "it's just nice to see you looking a little happier than yesterday. Why don't you come with me and check on the food and supplies I've put aside to take with us?"

In the kitchen Mary had laid out a mixture of fresh and dried food on the bench, along with water bottles and a knife.

"I haven't put utensils and plates in, because they'll make the packs too heavy. I thought we'd just keep it simple."

"How about we take tea-towels to use as towels? They'll be much lighter and pack up smaller, and we can dry them more easily," Sarah suggested.

"Good idea," Mary replied, getting three clean ones out of the cupboard. "I presume you've both put a toothbrush in with your clothes?"

"I did, but I'll check with Tom – his pack looked a bit random." She smiled at Mary.

"Now over here I've put aside some basic first aid things. Not much, but bandages obviously. Remembering back to my ankle injury last time you were here, it would have been incredibly helpful to have been able to bind it properly. Some creams for sunburn, insect bites and common injuries like cuts and scrapes…"

"Did you make these?" Sarah asked looking at their hand-written labels with interest.

"No, I got them in Hunterdale at the market. Are you still interested in that sort of thing?"

"Yes, I'm really keen to learn more. I was looking at the things I brought back from Morwyn's when I was in my room this morning. My grandad thought I'd make a good doctor, but I still think I'd like to learn how to use natural plants and herbs."

"Maybe you could do both? I know medicine in England has quite strong boundaries about what is and isn't acceptable, but maybe here you could make your practice work for you and what your patients need in a different way…" Sarah just nodded – there was plenty of time for her to think more about that later, and right now she had enough occupying her mind, between the warm feelings about Tom that seemed to be trying to side-track her, and the practical things they needed for their journey! She pulled her attention back to what Mary was saying.

"I'm not sure what else we need. Something we can make a tourniquet with maybe? I don't know what we're going into, but for some reason I'm thinking of a… a conflagration?" Mary was looking for the right word for something that might be catastrophic. "It feels like maybe this time something really big is going to happen that's been a hundred years in the making."

Sarah was quiet for a bit, thinking… "Mary, if it could be something really serious and people could get hurt, should we be taking the elixir?"

"Well, there's a thought. I think a small amount is supposed to have incredible healing powers."

"And surely we have to have found it for some purpose other than Morwyn's vanity and desire for power. None of us wants it to prolong life or to make us super-strong, but at the same time I remember how kind of seductive it was – it had some sort of pull tempting me to 'just try it.' I think it's quite dangerous…"

"Maybe Ryder could keep it unless we need it," suggested Mary.

"But Ryder won't be in the mountain with us," Sarah said, pausing for a moment to think, "… but Hermione will! I wonder if we could make something to put it in that hangs around her neck. She might not be very happy with that idea, but she'd certainly make sure we couldn't use it unless it was really necessary. She'd probably get quite bossy with us!" She smiled at the thought.

They met up with Arthur and Tom again when they'd finished checking the ropes, grapple hooks and the other tools they thought they might need, and Mary put the idea to them.

"I think it's a good idea, but I can't imagine Hermione tolerating it around her neck – it's big enough that it would make walking and climbing very clumsy for her," Arthur said.

"I know…" Tom said, "it could be like the harnesses that dogs sometimes wear instead of a choker collar. My next-door neighbour in Auckland used to have one. If we could make one out of leather, could we make some sort of basket to attach to the harness to hold the elixir?"

"Great thinking. Come with me to the workroom and we'll see what we can do."

While they were working on the harness, Mary and Sarah packed supplies into the top of each of the packs. The other gear would need to go into a fifth pack, which Tom and Arthur would take turns carrying. Sarah went outside to see if she could find Ryder – they'd told both he and Hermione to be at Riverstone by mid-day. She found Hermione sunning herself on the path, and Ryder hovering in the sky, circling expectantly. She called to him and explained what they needed him to do and told him to meet them on the road between Riverstone and Greyvyn. He shot off towards the mountains, leaving Sarah to plead their case to Hermione, knowing that she'd at least pretend that she didn't want to be burdened with the elixir. True to form, she made her statement by putting her nose in the air and objecting to being used like a packhorse. It was clear that in doing them such a favour they'd have to be very, very nice to her, but at the same time she let Sarah know that she'd take the job seriously.

"Yes, I told them you'd be bossy with it," Sarah laughed, "and that's good because none of us want to be tempted by it, and we certainly don't want it to fall into anyone else's hands!"

Hermione twitched her tail and minced up the steps and inside to see what sort of contraption they'd designed for her.

They found Arthur and Tom back in the living room, having fashioned a leather harness out of straps from the mill, with a buckle attached to hold it in place so it wouldn't come undone. On the top, they'd crafted straps that crossed, forming a small latticed basket to hold the box with the elixir in place. Tom fitted it onto Hermione, who strutted proudly around the room – it didn't seem to impede her movement at all.

"Well, I'm glad she's decided to be proud rather than put out," Mary whispered to Sarah.

"Harrumph, I heard that," Hermione said snottily, swishing her tail.

Sarah bent over to give her a pat at the same time as Tom, and their hands brushed together. It was like a jolt of electricity running between them. They jumped apart, Sarah suffusing with pink again. Hermione gave every appearance of rolling her eyes and they were both too embarrassed to look to see whether Mary and Arthur had noticed. They checked once more that they hadn't forgotten anything, picked up their packs and went out to the truck. Tom and Sarah clambered up onto the back deck, while Arthur and Mary got into the front, with Mary driving. They were on their way again, totally unsure how long it would be before they saw Riverstone again.

Chapter IV

Finding Friendship

"Linden, was that a man called Willard who was brought in yesterday?" Jonnie asked when Linden came into his room on his next shift.

"Yes, I was going to tell you that your friend has been found. He hasn't suffered any serious injuries like you did, but he's a lot older than you and he was lucky that a healer found him, although she wasn't able to stabilise his chest condition. He's quite poorly at the moment, but we're keeping a close eye on him."

"He's not actually my friend, just someone I know. In fact, I'm not sure that he's what you'd call a decent guy, I think he's a bit shady. I just got caught up with him when I had nowhere else to go."

"It sounds like he's been a handful since he was brought in. He evidently gets angry and abusive, so he'll probably be kept sedated for a while. I already asked if you could see him, but they want to talk to him first."

"What – to see whether we both tell the same story?"

Linden looked uncomfortable. "Well, I guess you're probably right," he mumbled. "It doesn't sit well with me that people from my city are corrupt, and I can't put my head in the sand – I think you're possibly in danger if you don't, or can't, give them something they want."

"The Mages?"

"Yes, with the Guardians to help them do their dirty work... If I was ever caught talking to you like this, I think I'd disappear and never be seen again!"

"So why do you?" Jonnie asked.

"Good question. I think because from what I can see inside you, you've had a difficult life so far, but you have a good heart. I'd not like to see that goodness squashed in you, but it's so easy to turn the wrong way if no one believes in you."

There was a long pause before Jonnie spoke. "I've never had anyone believe in me, except maybe Kayla, but now she's seen the worst of me. I've done all sorts of crazy shit to make myself feel better, but I've never set out to hurt anyone." His voice was croaky with emotion and Linden quietly put his hand on his shoulder without saying anything further.

Later in the afternoon before he left for the day, Linden debriefed his shift with Sarraphin. When he asked what was going to happen to Jonnie now that he was almost ready to be discharged, there was an awkward moment, her body turned away from him, and she paused as if she was weighing up what to say. Eventually, in a flat tone of voice, she said that she didn't know yet. He then risked asking her about Willard. As he wasn't one of his patients, strictly speaking this was against protocol, but she'd offered what he'd heard about Willard previously without him asking, so he thought it was okay to try. When he asked though, she just looked at him, accompanied by an unfathomable silence. Had he done the wrong thing in asking, or did she know something she wanted to keep from him?

"What do you know, Sarraphin? Is there something you're not saying?" he asked.

Eventually, she broke the silence: "As your superior, I need to say to you that I think you have become too involved with your

84

patient Jonnie." At Linden's look of dismay, Sarraphin continued. "However, as your mentor, I'm not at all surprised. You're my most talented apprentice and you have gifts of human connection that make it entirely to be expected that you'd make friends with someone like him. You have a goodness within you that allows you to empathise and do what's best for your patients," she paused. "So unofficially, what I'm saying is, I think you need to prepare Jonnie to get out of here at a moment's notice. I don't know what will happen, but the Mages will either want something from him, or they'll want to dispose of him, neither of which will have a good outcome. So be prepared, get him walking again as much as possible, and think about how you might get him out of the hospital."

Linden felt stunned. This was Sarraphin, the person he most respected in the world, and she was telling him to do something at odds with what the Mages would want.

"Linden," she added, more gently, "sometimes you have to do what's right; what your heart tells you is right, not what the law says. I suggest you start taking him for walks in the corridors in the evenings. The south wing doesn't have any patients at the moment, so you won't be seen. You need to strengthen his leg for when he has to leave. Tell Jonnie to limp whenever there are people around so no one thinks to recommend his discharge too quickly. We need all the time we can get to plan his escape."

"But how will I get him out of here unseen?" Linden asked, still feeling shaken.

"If he's wearing healer clothing, no one will be able to tell that it's him. He's taller than you, so I'll bring you a spare set of my clothes – they should do for him. We'll need to get our stories straight, because I may need to back you about where you were if they're questioning who may have helped him to get away. We can talk more about that later. If they're planning to move him, they'll have to go through me. Just be ready to move at a moment's notice."

"Where will I take him?"

"I've been thinking about that – I think you should take him to your hostel and keep him in your room until we can make plans to get him out of the city... And Linden, sometimes doing what's right means questioning your own morals. What I'm saying is that you might have to lie about where you've been and what you've been doing. Make sure you rehearse what we decide so that if you have to, at least it sounds real!"

"Why would you help us, Sarraphin? If we get caught it would ruin your career."

"So why are you taking that risk? Ask yourself the same question. We'll talk more later."

***

Over the following forty-eight hours, Linden took Jonnie for long walks in the evening, when most of the staff had left the hospital. Up and down the dark, unused corridors, at first feeling endless and like torture to Jonnie, but his walking rapidly improved, though he remembered to make his limp more pronounced whenever they came across others. On the second day there was a flurry on the ward, with a lot of movement to and from a room further down the corridor. Sarraphin later told Linden that Argin had insisted on Willard being woken so he could question him. She had attended this meeting, saying that Willard's health was too precarious for him not to be accompanied by a senior healer in case his condition regressed. Willard had willingly talked to Argin. In fact, he seemed eager to ingratiate himself, telling him about North Feasgar and all he'd done to help the strangers. When asked about Jonnie, he'd been dismissive, implying that he was inconsequential and didn't have anything to offer them, that he'd merely been hanging onto him to feel like he was part of the action. As Linden related this to Jonnie during their evening walk, Jonnie experienced a mixture of anger and relief. It was clear that Willard was out for himself – what a total jerk! At the same time, he felt quite relieved to no longer be involved with him and not to be seen as anything like him. When he expressed this to Linden though, he was surprised at how worried he seemed.

"What's the matter?" he asked.

"Well, if you're inconsequential to the Mages, they won't have any reason to keep you. You probably know too much about the north and pose a threat to their propaganda if you talk. I think that puts you in a very vulnerable position. I'll talk to Sarraphin on my way out – I think we may need to push forward with our plans to get you out of here rather than waiting for her to hear about their plans for you. She's important in the hospital, but they may over-ride her authority and just take you!"

When Linden left, Jonnie was left with a growing sense of apprehension. He was in this country completely on his own. He didn't really know where he was, or what was going to happen, just that there were bad forces that seemed to be out to get him, even though he hadn't done anything wrong. Linden was the only person he knew a little and would have to trust. He unaccountably felt like crying, but he stifled it, choosing instead to think about what he'd learned so far about the south and how much he'd changed in the short time since he'd fallen in the river. And how he hoped sometime to make things up to Kayla!

***

Sarraphin agreed that they needed to get Jonnie out as quickly as possible. She'd brought a spare set of clothes the previous day and, after checking they were alone, transferred them from her locker to Linden's.

"I think the best time would be to wait until the end of your shift, and during the changeover, take him out, as me, and I'll wait until the coast's clear before I leave. If anyone asks us later, we stick to the story of leaving together. Thank goodness they don't appear to have a guard on the hospital entrance, though they'd be unlikely to realise it's 'me' who has left twice. When you get to your hostel, speak to no one – hopefully it will be quiet, but there will be other staff returning. If you have to, keep up a pretence that I'm not well and speak for me. Once he's safely in your room, he must *not* leave for any reason until we've planned his next move."

"Thank you, Sarraphin. I don't know what to say… The fact that you're helping me is scary in itself, because it means all my own uncertainly about what's happening in the city is suddenly more real – it's not just my paranoia."

"Indeed it isn't. There are a lot of people feeling the same way, but only a few we trust enough to talk to about it. That's how powerful people keep control. Split us off from each other so we feel isolated and then we'll be too afraid to do anything on our own! Go well tonight…" She briefly touched him on his arm and left her office, leaving him to follow, trying to decipher his complicated feelings of fear, tinged with something like excitement that something unusual was happening. He had the premonition that nothing would be the same again.

"Go ahead of me and look confident. When you get out the door, turn directly right and keep walking."

"Sarraphin?" a colleague called from down the corridor as Jonnie stepped through the heavy wooden doors, obviously registering the gold braid at the bottom of his tunic, designating a Master. Linden turned.

"Leave her be. She's had a hard day and has a headache." The person nodded and moved on down the corridor. Linden hoped Sarraphin would keep herself somewhere out of the way until the night shift was settled in and she could make her way out unseen. As he pushed through the door after Jonnie, it briefly crossed his mind, with a flicker of warmth and pride, that in a few weeks he may be able to add the Affiliate's silver braid to his own tunic.

As Jonnie exited the building he was enveloped by the warm, dark air, settling on him like a fine blanket of silk, dropping gently over him and moulding itself to his body. He could appreciate the quiet noises around him, which seemed far from the hush of the hospital: the occasional call of night birds in the trees; the faint rumble of vehicles in the city; the soft sound of wind on the leaves of the trees nearby; a creature scurrying through the undergrowth. His nose wrinkled at a pungent smell coming from the trees – maybe animal shit? In contrast, a sweet smell hung heavily in the air – a flower? Not Jasmine, but a bit like it – strong and heady. He remembered picking some from the side of the road for his mother when he'd just started at school, and how upset he'd been when she'd thrown it out. It wasn't as if it was something like onion weed that smelt bad even though it looked pretty! Pulling himself back to the night in front of him, he thought it was as if all his senses had been starved in the hospital, and now he was hypersensitised. If he'd come out into the busy daylight it could have been overwhelming.

Linden caught up with him and hurried him along the path, wanting to get them away from the hospital as quickly as possible.

"That was close!" he exclaimed. "How's your leg?"

"It's fine for now. How far do we have to walk?"

"Not far. About five minutes." They walked in silence, the only person they encountered being an old man sweeping the street with a small motorised cart, circular brushes whirring against the curb. He doffed his cap in the air as they passed, with Linden responding with a kind of half salute in acknowledgement.

Their brief walk was uneventful. When they arrived at the Healer's hostel, Linden put his palm up against a glass panel that registered his palmprint. This was a standard safety measure all the hostels used that meant only people staying there, or their guests, could enter. They didn't encounter anyone directly inside either, although they caught sight of a few people coming and going. The ones returning from their shifts would be tired and heading as quickly as possible for their beds, and those heading to the hospital would already be preparing themselves for a busy night. It was really only in the dining and lounge areas that they had much to do with each other. Once in the hostel they no longer had to wear their krills, but often left them on until they got to their rooms and could change and relax, so it wouldn't be considered odd that they were still wearing them. It may be seen as odd though, that a Master was accompanying an Apprentice to his area of the accommodation, so he walked quickly, trying to think up a reason in case they were stopped.

Arriving at his room, Linden unlocked a solid wooden door and entered ahead of Jonnie. It was larger than Jonnie had expected. At a first glance around the room he noticed all the basics he imagined would be in a hostel – a bed, a desk, a couple of comfortable-looking chairs and a small table. When Linden dropped his work bag on the bed and gestured to him to sit in one of the chairs, he moved further into the room. From the chair he could see an open door in the wall facing him that looked like it led to a bathroom and toilet, and he started to notice things about the room that made it more personal to Linden, like a hand-crafted woollen cover on the bed, woven in deep reds and blues. So, this was to be his home for the next while. When Jonnie turned his attention back to Linden again, he got a real fright. Linden had removed his krill and he was looking for the first time on the face of a young man, maybe a few years older than himself (or at least he calculated he would have to be if he was about to finish his Apprentice training), with a youthful face, flawless skin that had obviously not seen the sun for some time, and light brown hair pulled back into a short pony-tail. His eyes were a vivid blue and even though he wasn't tall, he had a sort of presence about him that he'd felt even before he could see his face. Seeing Jonnie's surprise, Linden smiled, which lifted his face right from his mouth up to the corners of his eyes. Jonnie couldn't help but respond with a smile of his own.

"That must have been weird for you – I've known what you look like all this time, but you've only known me by my voice."

Jonnie found himself suddenly tongue-tied. He didn't know what to say. Everything was too confusing. Instead of replying, he got up and wandered over to the desk, looking at the pin-board on the wall to hide his uncertainty and give himself something to do. It was crammed with pictures of the human body. Drawing pins were stuck into body parts, with different coloured yarns stretching out to join with hand-written notes arranged around the sides of the board.

"That's how I learn. It helps me to be able to visualise the parts of the body: where they are and their size and shape, so that when I'm treating someone I can visualise where I'm sending my energy to. We don't all do it the same way. Some of the others do it by touch."

Jonnie didn't say anything. It was like he was closing in on himself and couldn't find any words. He was suddenly desperately tired and just wanted to blot everything out for a while.

"Come on. I think you're tired and overwhelmed and need to sleep. The bathroom is over there." Linden pointed to the door in the wall. "You'll find a spare toothbrush and towel already in there, so take a bit of time to wash and settle in and I'll find you something to wear to bed. We'll have to share the bed, top and bottom I'm afraid, until we work out something better."

The minute Jonnie's head touched the pillow it was as if he was snuffed out like a candle. He fell into a deep sleep of overwhelm and exhaustion, only waking vaguely in the small hours of the morning to hear a light tapping on the door and Sarraphin whispering to Linden about having found a bedroll in the hostel storeroom. He immediately fell asleep again. When he woke in the morning, he was alone. A thin mattress was rolled up by the desk and a note had been propped up against a jug of water on the table, accompanied by a plate containing fresh bread, butter, cheese and some sort of spread that he didn't recognise.

He picked up the note:

Jonnie, I didn't want to wake you – you were in a very deep sleep. I've gone to work. My shift today is 7-4, so I'll be gone until at least 4.30. Don't open the door to anyone other than me.

I managed to get a bit of food for you from our dining room, but I had to be careful that I wasn't drawing attention to myself by piling it up too much. I hope that's enough until I get back. I'll work out something better with Sarraphin when I see her. She brought us a bedroll in the night, so at least we'll have more space for sleeping. Hopefully you can keep yourself occupied with reading or writing or drawing for the day. You'll find paper etc in the desk draws. Please help yourself to anything you need.

A whole day to himself and stuck in this room! No TV, computer or phone to occupy him. It was the first time he'd thought about his phone – he must have lost it in the river, but it would have died from the water anyway. He couldn't think of a time at home where he'd stayed in one place, on his own, without some sort of device to occupy him. The idea of a day with nothing to do filled him with dread.

After showering and changing into the clothes Linden had left for him, he ate some of the bread. The spread turned out to be an unfamiliar taste – he couldn't work out what it was: savoury, not sweet, some sort of heavy taste, maybe like dead mushrooms. Not bitter, just odd. Maybe the taste that he'd heard of called 'umami'? He wasn't at all sure he liked it. By then he'd used up an hour. Now what? He did a few exercises – push-ups, stretches, sit-ups. Another thirty minutes. With the whole day stretched out in front of him, some of the thoughts he'd been pushing aside started to crowd in on him.

What was he going to do? How would he ever get back to the north? And if he didn't, where would he live and how would he survive, especially if he had to hide out from Argin's mob? Everything was unfamiliar and he didn't really know where he was, other than south of the mountain. Maybe he could find a map in Linden's things – that would give him something to do for a while, and if he found one, at least that would orientate him a bit.

It wasn't going to take long to search the room – there wasn't anywhere much to store stuff. He started with the draws in the desk. There were four, two each side. Everything in them was arranged incredibly neatly. Paper, pens, drawing pins, a few letters. Didn't look like much else. He randomly picked up an envelope, expecting to find a letter inside, but it contained photos. Black and white, of people. They must be his family, because Linden was in one with people old enough to be his parents, and a younger girl. *Hold on a minute*, he pulled the photo closer to his face. She looked so much like Kayla, not as skinny, but definitely a strong similarity. How weird!

He put them away and moved on to the bookshelf. No obvious maps among the books. They were mostly on anatomy, physiology or pathology. The ones that stood out as being different were a bit odd. One had something to do with stars and constellations that looked a little like astrology maybe? Another called 'Heralding: The Art of Divination.' Flipping through it, he thought it looked really flakey. Stuff about reading signs in cloud patterns, something called scrying, dream interpretation, geomancy? There were a few novels at the end of the shelf, but even they looked fairly serious. Linden didn't have much time for fun then!

The only other place that could store anything was the wardrobe. He opened it to reveal clothes and shoes nearly arranged in racks. Beneath them though, when he rummaged through some of the lower-hanging tunics, he spotted a large, slightly battered-looking cardboard box. He tugged on the side facing him – it was heavy, so he squatted down and grasped the ends with both hands and pulled. The box reluctantly moved towards him and he kept pulling until he had it positioned in front of the wardrobe. Sitting cross-legged on the floor, he opened the flaps on the top. Inside there were several small canvases and sketchbooks at one end, and jars of paint at the other. Brushes were stored along one of the sides. He pulled out a sketchbook and flipped through it. *Holy crap he's good at drawing!* The sketches were mostly of people, birds and animals, along with a few strange looking symbols. He recognised instantly a sketch of Sarraphin bending over a patient. The likeness was incredible.

Putting the book back, it caught on something that stopped him pushing it right down to the bottom of the box. As he shuffled things around to move what was obstructing it, he saw a smallish wooden box. Pulling it out, he slid the lid open, finding to his surprise that it was filled with seashells. Beautiful shells of different shapes and colours – some that looked remarkably like the paua shells he knew from New Zealand – iridescent blues and greens that shimmered in the light as he turned them over in his hands. A small scallop shell maybe? Was that twisty one called a whelk? He'd never been very interested in knowing about them. He wondered why the shells would be among the few belongings he had with him in Scathach. Putting them back in their box, Jonnie returned it to sit amongst the paint jars, then pushed the cardboard box back into its position in the wardrobe. No map then!

With no luck finding a map, Jonnic was thrown back on his thoughts again. He felt SO alone. What made it worse was that the one person he kind of knew, Linden, was putting himself in danger for him. That made him feel doubly dependent on him and somehow responsible for anything that happened. He couldn't get his head around an uncomfortable mix of worry and gratitude. He'd never been able to depend on his mother – he'd had to grow up fast and take care of her and Kayla, yet at the same time he'd run away from that and avoided feelings of responsibility by doing stupid stuff with his friends; distracting himself so he didn't need to think about, or feel his confusion. Now there was literally no one other than Linden, and what he'd thought were feelings of boredom were actually covering up something much deeper. It was like a desperation, like being tossed about at sea clinging to a bit of debris without a lifebelt… But how could he trust Linden? No one had ever been kind to him for no reason before. Why did he want to help him? No one ever did things without wanting something in return – what did he want from him? What if he was right now telling the Mages where he was? Or what if they'd arrested him and were making him tell them? What if they muted or even killed him? With his thoughts spiralling, he was feeling increasingly panicky – his stomach was in knots, his chest felt tight and he had a lump in his throat. Drinking some water helped a bit, but then he thought he might throw up.

He was sitting on the floor with his arms around his knees and found himself shaking and making little keening noises, a bit like a trapped animal. Noticing it though allowed him just enough space from his feelings to stop and take some deep breaths. He started to think about Kayla and how he would try to put things right with her if he ever saw her again. That started another spiral, this time of shame at how he'd responded to the kindness of Sarah and Tom and to Arthur and Mary – how cocky he'd been. What an utter jerk! He wanted desperately to be able to do their arrival in North Feasgar all over again, but maybe he'd never have that chance. And if he did, he'd feel so stupid and small and squirmy. He'd screw it all up again if he couldn't get past himself!

**

Linden walked into his ward and immediately picked up an atmosphere of tension. Everyone seemed to be going about their jobs as usual, but they had their heads down, and were being super-efficient and quiet, their unsaid thoughts crackling silently in the air. He saw Sarraphin, who merely nodded at him in greeting as he hurried to see his first patient.

He'd not been working for long before he was summoned by Sarraphin to go to her office. As she walked him there, she murmured quietly, "Just stick to our story – they've already spoken to me."

Two black-robed figures were in the room when they got there. One of them nodded abruptly to dismiss her.

"We want you to tell us about your movements last night for the hour before you left your shift." Argin's voice emerged from his krill, his dark eyes penetrating from behind the mesh.

"Why? What's happened?" Linden asked, sounding bemused.

"Never you mind. Just answer our questions."

"Well, I checked on my three patients over the last hour – they all seemed fine and well settled. Then I had my end-of-shift debrief with Sarraphin. She wasn't feeling well – she had a hcadache, and we left together about fifteen minutes after my shift ended."

"Did you see anything unusual as you left, or did you speak to anyone other than Sarraphin?"

"… No, I don't think so. One of the other staff called to Sarraphin just as she was walking out the door, but I told them to leave her alone because she was feeling unwell. Some of the staff never give her any peace – she's too good at her job."

"Did you go straight to your accommodation?"

"Yes."

"Did you see anything unusual when you were outside?"

"No."

"Did you see anyone at all?"

"Only the street sweeper."

"Did you talk to your patient Jonnie before you left?"

"Well yes," Linden replied. "He's my patient and one of the three I checked on before the end of my shift."

"Tell us what you talked about."

"Oh, I'm not sure… let me think…" Linden paused. "I remember he asked me how much longer he'll be in hospital for. He's become impatient for his leg to heal – I don't think he likes being cooped up in the hospital. He also asked after his friend Willard."

"Did he say they were friends?" This question was the first to come from the other Mage, another male.

"Yes, I think they know each other well," Linden responded, watching the two figures exchange a glance.

"Would he be capable of walking to Willard's room to speak to him?"

"Yes. He still has a limp, but he's been practising walking in the corridors when we have time to accompany him."

"So, did he talk to you about what he planned to do when he was discharged?"

"No, but Sarraphin discourages us from too much conversation with our patients. She's taught us that it's not good to get too involved with them. I got the impression that he and Willard are going to do something together when they get out."

Telling him that they may wish to speak to him again later, they dismissed him and he went back to his patients, choosing not to speak to Sarraphin until they came across each other on the ward, where he made sure to ask her about Jonnie's empty bed space within the hearing of other staff. He didn't get the opportunity to catch up with her properly until they were on a break and managed to find a quiet spot in the cafeteria.

"What did they ask you?" Sarraphin asked. Linden filled her in. When he got to what he'd said about Willard, she interjected: "Good thinking. I'm sure they know that Willard is in it for himself and will probably lie about anything that makes him look good, so you've raised a bit of doubt for them."

"Yes, I wanted to give them something to think about other than us!" Linden responded. "Sarraphin, why are they so focused on Jonnie – he's just a teenager a long way from home – how can he harm them in any way?"

"I suppose if they think he and Willard have deliberately come here from the north they may imagine they're up to something? Or at the very least they won't want them talking to any of us about what the north is like. They hold their power not just by magic, but by making people believe what they tell us, to keep us in their control."

"Well thank goodness, they don't have the type of magic that can read our thoughts!"

"No, but we must still be very careful. They'll have to try to trick us to see whether our stories are true. They may believe Willard and Jonnie have been talking and plotting, but if anyone was to help Jonnie to get away from the hospital, it would be likely to be you or me, as we were the only ones who really spent time with him."

"How might they do that?"

"I've been thinking that they might try to split us off from each other. Like, maybe say something incorrect to one of us about the other to see what we do. Maybe something like telling you that I overheard you plotting something with Jonnie? We need to keep on trusting each other whatever is said. And don't forget that they're supposed to be able to shapeshift! I don't know whether that's true or not, but if they can, they could either pretend to be me to see what you'd say to me, or the reverse; or I suppose they could be even more direct and pretend to be Jonnie. Either way, they could hope to flush something out with one of us."

Linden felt a bit sick. "So what can we do about that?"

"I imagine if they're going to do anything it will be today or tomorrow, because they can't risk him getting too far away or it will be much harder to find him. Don't talk about Jonnie to anyone at all, and in the future, when we meet, we need to use a password of some sort in case they pretend to be one of us. I imagine that we'd pick up a fake quite quickly because they don't know how well we know each other... Work out something with Jonnie too, just in case, though if they present to us as Jonnie and we know he's safely in your room we'll know not to fall for it. Do you have any ideas about what might work?"

"How about something simple like a colour. If it's you I'll slip the word green into the conversation – your eyes – and for me use the word blue. I think I'll probably know though, because

I'm used to your pattern of thought images... Maybe I'll suggest to Jonnie that if ever we come upon him outside of where we're expecting, say if something goes wrong and he has to get out of the hostel room, that he asks if I've seen Kayla, his sister."

"Okay," Sarraphin was nodding in agreement. "I feel a bit better about that now. Look, I'm going to go – we don't want to draw any attention to us talking together. I haven't seen any Mages around other than the two who've taken over my room, but over the next few days, as they continue to not find him, they're going to have their eyes everywhere. Just stick to our story – if we trust each other we'll be fine."

***

The day proceeded normally, other than for the steady trail of people who were summoned for questioning. Linden noticed the Healer who'd tried to stop 'Sarraphin' leaving the night before emerging from the interview room, and hoped that the person hadn't suspected anything, or at least wouldn't want to say anything to the Mages. The Healers were mostly loyal to each other and Sarraphin commanded a lot of respect, but of course there were always the jealous ones who were out for themselves. At the end of the day, Linden reported at Sarraphin's office for the usual end-of-shift debrief and found one of the Mages still present. He apologised, indicating that he was looking for her and backed off. He found her talking to another healer and she simply asked him if there were any issues with his two remaining patients, then told him he could leave.

As Linden walked out of the hospital entrance with a group of his peers, he drew the fresh air into his lungs and saw the sun shining, wishing as he often did that he could rip off his krill and feel it on his skin. He was glad to be on day shifts again – he was always rostered to whatever shift Sarraphin was on. As an Apprentice he only got to work with his assigned Master. When he graduated as an Affiliate he would start being rostered with two other Masters as well so he could deepen his learning. He'd been so lucky to have her – they weren't all as talented, or as fair and considerate as she was. Day shifts also meant he got to mix more with his peers on the way to and from the hospital. There were two in particular he had a lot in common with – Ailesh and Hamlin. While he was walking down the steps he heard someone call him from behind.

"Linden? Is that you?" It was Ailesh. When the Apprentices knew each other well, they could kind of guess by height and weight who was who, even with their uniforms on. He turned and waited for her. By the time she caught up with him, the group had spread out, with small clusters walking together along the path towards their hostel.

As they walked, Linden bent his head towards Ailesh, listening intently as she spoke to him about one of the patients she'd just started seeing.

"It's quite confusing. When I put my hands on him I feel something like a wave of deep pain, but it has within it such a mix of abandonment, desperation and aggression that it almost swamps me. Even though he's come in because he's physically unwell, I'm thinking that most of his problems stem from some sort of psychological trauma. I'm not sure what to do to help him, or even if he wants me to try to heal anything other than his stomach problems." She paused for a minute. "I wonder whether you could come and find me tomorrow and see what you can pick up from him?"

They quite often shared their gifts. She was particularly

good at picking up on a person's problem by touch. It was as if they could look at a patient with different lenses, and while they didn't have a way yet of developing the other's talent, they still learned a lot from each other.

"Linden, I think someone's calling you," Ailesh suddenly said, pulling him away from his immersion in their conversation. He looked over to the bushes she was pointing at and saw someone partially hidden from view.

"Linden, is that you?" Jonnie's voice asked. So, this was it then, what he and Sarraphin had thought might happen. As he looked more closely, he could see that the person had every appearance of being Jonnie. He wondered how the Mage had recognised him out of a bunch of other Apprentices all wearing the same uniform. He doubted that even Jonnie, who knew him reasonably well now, would be able to pick him out of a group.

"Hey, I'd better go and check – I think it's Jonnie, that patient who disappeared last night," he said to Ailesh.

"Oh, was he one of yours?... Do you want me to stay?" Ailesh asked.

"That would be great, thanks," he replied, thinking it might be useful to have a witness to whatever happened next.

Walking over to the bushes, 'Jonnie' whispered to him that he wanted to see him on his own.

"It's okay," Linden replied, "Ailesh is a friend. What are you doing there? Where have you been?"

"I told you I needed to get out. I need you to help me."

"What do you mean? You said you were bored, but you're not yet well enough to leave the hospital. You need to be really careful with your leg to make sure it mends properly... Look, come out of the bushes and Ailesh and I will take you back to the hospital. You'll be much better off there and Sarraphin and I can

103

help you to plan what you're going to do next. I imagine you've been feeling quite lost wondering where you'll go." He reached out a hand to him, and helped to pull him to his feet. "We've been really worried about you!"

He and Ailesh walked either side of him back the way they'd come. As they walked, Ailesh drew him into a conversation about how long he'd been in the hospital and how he'd injured himself, giving Linden the opportunity to tune into his emotional images. They made him catch his breath. They were black and twisted, not so much even images, as sensed impressions of desire and anger... no, more like rage! Of hunger for power, mixed in with frustration; an image of being thwarted and having to fight for control; another image of being ridiculed, accompanied by a seething fury... All about striving for something and not quite achieving it, and a turmoil of unsorted emotions, blotting out any goodness that might have once been there. What could have happened to a person to twist him like that? And how important it was to keep out of his way!

Arriving back at the hospital, they took him to the ward, where Linden found that Sarraphin was still working, sorting some handover documents for the next shift. They explained how they'd found Jonnie and then settled him in his bed. Sarraphin told them they must go and report it to the Mages, who were still occupying her office. The one Mage remaining there was Argin, who listened carefully while they explained what had happened. He thanked them curtly and they were dismissed.

***

By the time Linden got back to the hostel it was an hour later than the time he'd indicated in his note. Opening the door, he found

Jonnie pacing the length of the room.

"I was worried about you!" he exclaimed when he saw him. "You're much later than you said – I thought maybe you'd been arrested or something."

As Linden boiled some water to make herbal tea, which was the most they could cater for themselves in their rooms, he explained everything that had happened since the morning. As he talked about seeing him in the bushes, Jonnie started looking more and more incredulous.

"What do you mean, they can shape-shift?" he demanded. "How is that possible?"

"I don't know how they do it – I wasn't even sure that the rumours were true until today. But it happened! And it means we have to be very, very careful. I don't know how long it lasts for either, or what they'll do about the Jonnie who's now back in your hospital room. I guess he'll just disappear again when they've tested him out against the other staff like Sarraphin. We've worked out a way though of making sure the three of us can tell if we're real or not." He outlined their plan to Jonnie, noticing that he was almost at the end of what he could absorb for now, so he then switched the topic by pulling out some of the cafeteria food he'd saved for him and asking if he was hungry.

When Jonnie had calmed down a bit, Linden asked him how he'd spent his day.

"Well doing naff-all of course. What else is there to do?"

"You're feeling angry because you're cooped up. I understand that, yet you need to get past it if you're going to manage the next few days until we've made a plan. You have a choice – you can spend your days being angry and belligerent, or you use them to work out who you want to be!"

Jonnie frowned. He wasn't used to anyone being direct with

him in a well-meaning way. Part of him wanted to hit him, but a deeper part of him knew he was right.

"Sorry…" he said grudgingly, "I did some exercises, then looked through your stuff for a map, which I couldn't find. Then I felt like shit for a while until eventually I felt a bit better and started reading a novel. I've never really read one before, only the bits we had to for English at school. Kayla reads all the time, but normally it feels like something's going to explode inside me if I stop in one place, other than to sleep."

"Which one did you choose?"

"The one about the fisherman looking for his son… They're all a bit heavy, aren't they? Nothing easy or full of action!" Jonnie complained.

"Everything written here is censored. People who remember things being different aren't allowed to write about them, and fantasy is out. The Mages won't tolerate anyone writing anything about magic, or about anyone trying to overturn authority. I've read a few banned ones passed down through my family, but I wouldn't dare keep them here. Anyway, did you enjoy it?"

"Yeah kind of, once I let myself. I like the way Brin is just an ordinary guy, not all perfect and knowledgeable, but good at what he does and he sticks at trying to find his son even though everything is against him."

"Do you think that could be like you?" Linden asked.

"What do you mean? I'm no fisherman!"

'No, but you could learn to accept who you are and be determined to keep on going no matter what."

Jonnie muttered something unintelligible, then got up to go to the bathroom and shut the door. Linden sighed – he was trying to help him to re-frame his negative thoughts and build up his sense of who he was, but it was hard-going. He'd obviously been through a lot in his past – his thought images indicated much disturbance, but he'd have to be careful – he didn't want to come across as patronising or he'd lose his trust.

When Jonnie came back into the room, Linden thought he'd try once more before leaving the topic for the evening.

"Look Jonnie, I don't know what's going to happen, and you could be here for a while. Your thoughts are taking you down – that needs to happen so you can make sense of them, but maybe we need to think up some sort of structure for your days so you don't go mad."

"You always seem to be so calm. Don't you have stuff that bothers you?"

"Well of course, everyone does. But it really helps that when we start our apprenticeship they spend a long time teaching us how to focus our minds. We can't heal people unless we're calm and centred as we connect to another person's energy field. Some of the things we're taught might help you too."

"I bet I've done much worse things than you ever have!"

"From the impressions I've picked up from you, you've had a much tougher life than me. But remember, who you've been and what you've done doesn't need to define you for the rest of your life."

Jonnie just nodded, so Linden changed the subject thinking that was enough for now.

***

That evening, as they sat eating the dinner Linden had brought back from the cafeteria, some sort of strange, grainy, nutty salad and chicken, Jonnie asked him about his family. He found out that his sister was called Anika who was about his own age.

107

When he mentioned her resemblance to Kayla, he was surprised that Linden seemed to take that lightly, merely saying "Well maybe we're all linked somehow."

"What do you mean?" Jonnie asked, thinking that people in this place had much whackier thoughts than where he came from.

"I've come to accept the unexpected as being about something bigger than what I currently know," was all Linden replied, leaving the conversation hanging in the air. He did, later though, talk more about his training and what it was like living in Scathach. Jonnie listened, letting the words wash over him, gathering the impression that there were lots of rules that controlled their lives. It didn't seem that they were free to move around much – Linden mostly seemed to spend his time between the hostel and the hospital, with his only friends being from within his Order. He didn't really seem to have much reason to go into the city, other than where he walked for exercise, so he didn't mingle with people from outside. The thing he seemed to find the most difficult though, was not being able to go home to visit his family. Jonnie wondered what it must be like to be so controlled. Even though he'd felt so stir-crazy at home, at least he'd always had the freedom to go out, to do pretty much anything he wanted, or at least anything he could afford to do!

"At least you have a family to go home to, who want to see you," Jonnie commented bleakly.

"I can see the sadness in your memories of home. I'm sorry it's been so hard for you. We all deserve a good family."

"Perhaps I don't!"

"You have a good heart – I can feel it."

"No, I'm full of shit! That's why I ended up following Willard. Maybe I'm no better than him... Anyway," he tried to change the subject, "it sounds like you spend most of your time doing things to help other people. When do you have a chance just to be you, to muck around and enjoy yourself?" he asked.

"I enjoy helping people..." Linden responded.

"But you're always having to give to people. And what stops you going mad when all the time you're picking up our thought pictures?"

"I don't really pick them up all the time. It's a bit like when you go somewhere like a market where there are a lot of people. There are voices all around you, but you don't get overwhelmed with everything they're saying because you don't 'listen' to each voice, they're just kind of in the background. If you want to listen to any one of them you have to focus on it to hear what's being said. With thought images or emotions, it's the same. I can be aware that they're there, but I have to actually tune in to them to bring them to the foreground... Do you realise that even asking me these questions means you're not like Willard?"

Jonnie looked at him questioningly.

"Well, do you think Willard has any interest in anyone other than himself? Do you really think he'd be thinking about me?" The question was left unanswered, sitting between them for Jonnie to ponder on that night when he went to bed.

Before they turned in for the night Linden talked to him about how to focus his thoughts, trying out some techniques with him. The one he liked best was the one where he paid attention to all the parts of his body. He could have dropped off to sleep in the middle of it but Linden kept him awake long enough to get him to come up with ideas about what he'd do on his own tomorrow. He wanted to read more of the novel, but also thought he might try writing down everything that had happened since he went through the rift, to try to make sense of it.

It was quite late when they got into bed. About ten minutes

109

after they turned out the light, they heard a light tapping on the door. Linden walked over and said "Hello?" After hearing Sarraphin's soft reply, he opened the door and let her in. She walked over and sat on the foot of the bed, looking closely at Jonnie.

"How are you?" she asked.

Jonnie mumbled something unintelligible, so Linden responded, "He's bored and a bit afraid about what happens next, but his leg is good."

She nodded. "We need to catch up about the day and then think together about how we'll get you out of here safely Jonnie."

Sarraphin outlined how Argin was maintaining his interviews with staff and how 'Jonnie' was still in the hospital. She'd been to see him and had had a stern conversation with him about trying to leave and how important it was to limit his movements until his leg was properly healed. She wasn't sure how they thought he would fool either her or Linden, because although he looked the same, he was a bit like a cardboard cut-out – he didn't know them well enough to be able to talk to them convincingly. She'd just bustled in and out without much discussion, keeping it like business-as-usual. She imagined that he would disappear again as soon as their interviews were completed. Maybe they'd want 'Jonnie' to talk to Willard too, to see how Willard reacted to him.

"Have you had any ideas about what happens to Jonnie now?" Linden asked.

"Well yes. So long as 'Jonnie' disappears again, you have just two patients to discharge before you've completed your Apprentice training. I checked on them before I left today and I think we can discharge them this week. Ailesh and Gronin have also completed their training, so we could hold your graduation towards the end of next week. That means that you'll be due your month's leave. If we can find a way to get both of you out of Scathach and into the countryside that would be much better for Jonnie. Do you think your family would be willing to have an extra guest?"

"I think so, but I couldn't lie to them. I'd have to tell them that he would be in hiding and why…"

"Could you trust them not to talk to anyone about him?"

"Absolutely. They're really good people."

"Do you know anyone who comes regularly to Scathach who you could trust enough to give your parents a message?" Sarraphin asked. "I don't think you should contact them in any way that could be intercepted or overheard by the Mages should they be watching you."

"Two people from our village come to the produce market each week. I wouldn't want to ask the man who brings the meat, but the one with the vegetable stall is a close acquaintance and would carry a letter without opening it…"

"Good. You should be okay to get to the town square on Saturday since we're not rostered to work. You'll need to be very careful that you're not followed and that no one sees you giving him the message. Don't say too much in the note, just that you'll be graduating next week and you expect to see them by the end of the weekend, and that you'll be bringing a friend with you. You'll need to talk to them about him when you arrive. We'll need to think about an alternative in case they're not happy, but not tonight! Jonnie, do you think you can manage being in hiding here for another ten days?"

Jonnie nodded glumly – yes, he could manage, but then, he didn't have a choice, did he?

Once in bed, he turned his thoughts to Willard and the way

111

he'd been attracted to his brutish maleness, as if somehow, in the absence created by not having a dad, this was the way he'd decided real men needed to be. Linden was showing him something completely different... As he finally drifted off to sleep, an old memory surfaced and dropped into his mind, as if teasing him, wanting him to make a connection. He was little, maybe in his second year at school. He'd hurried through the school gates and didn't notice a gang of boys from the next year up waiting for him. They'd cornered him, teasing him about the shoes he was wearing – ones he hated, that his mum had got from a second-hand shop. He'd tried to walk right past them but one of them had put out his foot and he'd sprawled on the hard ground, grazing his chin and his palms and knees. When he pulled himself up so that he was sitting on the ground, he found he was shaking, all over, whether from the shock of falling, or from the taunts still ringing in his ears, he wasn't sure. He picked some of the gravel out of the spongy parts of his hands, trying not to cry. Then he'd felt someone squatting down beside him. It was his teacher, Mr Green.

"You know, they're not strong, they're just bullies. You're a much better person than they are. Here, let me help you up. Do you want me to call your mother?"

He recoiled violently. The last thing he wanted was his mum turning up, reluctantly, making it all about her and sucking up to Mr Green. He didn't even need to say anything, Mr Green just seemed to get it.

"That's okay, let's go and let the nurse take a look at those grazes." He pulled him to his feet gently and walked with him, an arm around his shoulders. He was remembering the warm feeling he had of being cared for by someone he admired and looked up to as he slipped into sleep...

Chapter V

Escaping the City

Stepping briskly away from the hostel on market day, a note for the man from his village in his pocket, Linden breathed in the fresh air – it still carried with it a cool bite, but the sun was out and held the promise that the days were starting to get longer. From the hostel, it was a twenty-minute brisk walk to the city centre, the streets rapidly becoming more densely populated after leaving the leafy area around the hospital and the residential area surrounding it. The streets fanned out from the central city, with the market place at the hub in the centre. The street Linden was walking along radiated inwards, in a direct line to the market.

It was as he crossed the ring road that delineated the central city from the outer areas that he started to feel the back of his neck prickling. Was someone watching him? Was something about to happen? He rotated his head and raised his shoulders, trying to shrug it off. It didn't work; he couldn't dispel a sense of strangeness, malevolence even, that clung to his shoulders like a cloak. He stopped and casually looked around him, under the pretence of adjusting his tunic. There wasn't anything suspicious; all he could see were a few people nearby. A mother with two young children; someone from the Guardian Order, which wasn't unusual, as they always maintained a presence on the streets of the city; a teenage boy leaning against a fence. He kept walking, but the feeling was persistent, so he stopped again to look in the window of a bookshop so he could surreptitiously glance behind him again. Nothing unusual, *but* the Guardian was still the same distance behind him, also stationary, looking at a poster on a wall. Strange. Why would he be being watched? Maybe any of the healers heading from the hostel to anywhere other than the hospital was being followed? Or was it more personal, given that he'd been looking after Jonnie? Although, how would anyone know it was him with his krill on? Only people who worked with them a lot could tell them apart by size and mannerisms. Maybe someone from the hostel was keeping an eye on him? Whichever, it meant they'd have to be even more careful about their movements when it came to getting Jonnie out of the hostel. He decided to head off the main road by turning left into a maze of criss-crossing smaller streets between the ring road and the central city. He could check out whether he really was being followed and it would make it easier to lose the man if he had to.

It was almost like stepping into another world as he left behind the main road, with its abundance of vehicles, to make his way along a narrow, winding street parallel to the one he'd been on before. Motorised bikes wound their way around clusters of people who were on foot, meandering past shops and stalls and cafés with outdoor tables and chairs. There were benches laden with household goods; men's trousers in piles, socks nestling together on trays; women's skirts, scarves and dresses hanging outside windows, colourful fabrics shifting in the breeze; umbrellas and hats; and as he got closer to the central market, food. Every kind of food imaginable, from brightly coloured fruit, to dried apricots, figs, spices and nuts, vegetables, baked goods, large sacks of rice and lentils and flours... It was bright, colourful, bustling, noisy – and yes, the man was still following!

He dawdled. A detour into a shop; the inspection of a tray

of quilled pens; the slow selection of fruit after turning and sniffing as many as he could before an irate shop owner moved him on; and a long, drawn-out coffee sitting in the sun outside a café. That would test his follower's patience. He was unshakeable though, sticking to him like a leech. Why did he think he wouldn't notice him, or maybe he didn't care? The morning was marching on and Linden knew he needed to get to the market soon to make sure he could meet his acquaintance and pass on the note before the market ended, so while he was drinking his coffee he hatched a plan, and a backup plan just in case.

He knew the streets well between here and the market. Since he didn't have family in Scathach, or many friends outside of his Order, he tended to walk a lot on his own, to get out of the hospital environment, get some exercise and de-stress. He turned into the next street, then quickly ducked into a doorway that led to a private garden before the man reached the corner, thinking that it would be a good start to see what happened. There was enough bustle in the street for the man to think he was still up ahead, just temporarily out of sight amongst other shoppers. The one thing he didn't want to do was to try to lose him by running. At the moment, he was obviously of interest to the Guardians – well, the Mages – in that they were probably checking on anyone who could have helped Jonnie to escape, but they had no reason to be suspicious of him. If he ran, they'd know he was up to something. And, the Guardians were trained to use magic to arrest movement. He'd had to treat a patient who'd been stopped by their spell and hadn't come out it. The effect had been brutal! He'd had to use his healing matrix to bring him back. Maybe he could use the same principle on himself to ward off the spell if he needed to? He could possibly surround himself with a matrix that wouldn't allow the magic to work. But he'd prefer not to have to put that to the test if he could help it!

Linden watched from just inside the doorway until the man walked past. He waited for a moment, and was about to put his head out to check whether the way was clear when someone ran past, responding to a shout. Another Guardian! There were two of them! The situation suddenly seemed much more serious. His heart was hammering in his chest as he wondered what to do now. Damn his white krill and tunic for being so conspicuous! He'd have to resort to Plan B if they spotted him. He put his head out and looked to his right. It seemed clear – they must both be occupied searching for him further down the road. He stepped out hesitantly, trying to look casual in case they spotted him. They wouldn't know exactly where they'd lost him. If only he could get to the next small lane that ran between the main arterial route and the road he'd been walking up towards the city centre, he might just miss them. He didn't want to go back, because if they spotted him, they'd know he was trying to give them the slip. Or maybe he was overthinking it. He just didn't know any more. His head was whirring with possibilities. If they saw him now and he kept his cool, they still might think they'd just lost sight of him amongst the shoppers.

He tried to stroll nonchalantly. So far, so good. Reaching the lane, he turned into it. It was even narrower than the last one and he slipped between people and bicycles, walking as calmly as he could towards the market. He was just starting to relax when he heard a shout from behind him. He tried to keep up the appearance of strolling calmly, but used the excuse of stopping to avoid a dog to check behind him. The two men were running towards him, weaving their way between people, the one in the lead rapidly closing the gap. Without thinking, he turned and started to run. That was really stupid, but too late – they'd know now that he was onto them. It was only a short distance to the end of the lane. The last shop before it spilled into the market place was a shop that he'd been to in the past to buy clothing. It had an entrance from the lane, and another into the town square. As he ran, he concentrated hard on building up the lines of healing matrix inside him. They cross-hatched his body, becoming denser with each second that elapsed before the Guardian in front cast a stopping spell on him. It was hard work, trying to keep his focus, while at the same time dodging people and obstacles in the lane.

Linden felt the spell reach him when he wasn't far from the shop. It was like a dragging on the skin down his neck and back. A bit like when a cat picks up her kitten by the scruff of the neck and its skin stretches backwards towards her. He could feel the pull, but it didn't arrest his movement. His own magic was working! As he reached the shop, he ducked through the door. He didn't have long. He vaguely knew the girl who worked there, so he grabbed a brown, woven tunic from a hanger and raced to the curtains that created a changing cubicle at the back of the shop, signalling to the girl to follow him. When she got there, he thrust some money into her hand and quickly told her that two Guardians were about to come into the shop. He asked whether she could tell them he'd run through the shop and out the other entrance into the marketplace. When she left, he quickly took off his krill, rolling it up into an untidy bundle, and pulled the tunic over the top of his white one. He was transformed – no longer from the Healing Order, he looked just like an ordinary peasant guy, though rather too pale. He hoped no one would be interested enough in him to notice. He thought he'd heard them head straight through the shop, and leaving the changing area, the girl

117

confirmed that they'd gone and handed him a paper bag he could put his krill in. Thanking her, he left through the side door back into the lane and mingled with the other people moving towards the market.

He felt totally drained and exhausted. Keeping up the healing matrix, while trying to get away from his pursuers, at the same time as thinking his way through what he needed to do, had been almost too much. He sat down for a minute to get his breath on a bollard that had been placed at the end of the lane to stop vehicles getting through. Looking around, he could see a sea of people meandering around the market stalls. All the wares were being sold from mobile wooden trolleys that could be wheeled away in the afternoon when the crowds dispersed, as opposed to the more permanent shops located in the lanes leading to the central square. It was a melting-pot of colourful shade cloths, goods on sale, people of every shape and size, noises and smells. A sensory experience that threatened to overwhelm Linden every time he visited, after the ordered and quiet life he lived between the hospital and hostel.

He couldn't see the Guardians, so he wandered casually into the market square and mingled with the crowd, strolling past stalls, chatting to stall-holders about their goods, heading for the vegetable stall run by the people from his village. Before he got there, he saw one of the Guardians run into the centre of the square where he could slowly turn, perusing the crowds, searching for a white krill. With an inward smile, Linden turned his back to him and picked up a sketch of the marketplace that was on sale, along with other drawings and water-colours. He wished he had more time to draw himself – these were very good, and seemed to fetch a good price. By the time he put it down, with a smile to the stall-holder, the Guardian was again out of sight. He reached the vegetable stall without noticing either of them again.

Linden's acquaintance was surprised to see him, especially without his Healer clothing. Everyone at home knew that his training was why he was in the city. After asking after the man and his family, and about news of the village, he broached what he needed.

"I'm not meant to be here today," he remarked with a wry look on his face, "so I decided to leave the hostel in my ordinary clothes so I didn't stand out in town… I wonder if you could please take a note to my parents – it's a private matter, so I'd really appreciate it not falling into anyone else's hands." The man seemed to take it in his stride – their families had known each other for generations, and slipped it into a pocket under his apron. He smiled at Linden, encouraging him to help himself to some produce, before having to turn away to serve other customers.

As Linden meandered through other parts of the market, he realised it would be better to change back into his Healer clothes to return. His business was done and once away from the crowds, he didn't want anyone to see him and his pale skin heading towards the hostel. In his krill, they couldn't be sure he was the same person they'd followed, and anyway, he wouldn't be doing anything wrong. In a lane on his way back to the arterial road, he nipped into an alley-way, pulling off the brown tunic and bundling it in the bag, swapping it for his krill. Covered again, he resumed his walk back to the hostel, without seeing the men.

***

Walking to work the following morning, Linden felt a huge sense of relief at being away from the hostel. He'd returned the previous day to find Jonnie feeling stir-crazy, bored and agitated after being cooped up in such a small room for so long. He was looking for a fight, and wasn't interested in what had happened to Linden at the market, so Linden had gone off in search of Sarraphin and had off-loaded on her the events of the day and his worries about what needed to happen next. Now, as he recalled her calm manner and reflected on what he had lined up for the day, rather than being anxious, he felt happy to be heading back to work. The whole sharing a room thing with Jonnie was starting to wear really thin. He was the sort of person who needed space, while Jonnie was so bored that the minute he walked in the door, he needed to be entertained. He couldn't blame him – it must be really hard, but it was time for them to move on, and yet they still had until the end of the week to go.

Arriving at the hospital, he went again in search of Sarraphin, finding her in the utilities room, checking supplies. He entered the room and closed the door behind him. He'd been thinking overnight about the possibility of fake-Jonnie and Willard meeting up and wondered if it was a good idea. He imagined the Mages would want to check out Willard and his story before he was discharged, and they'd already checked out all the rest of the staff who'd been involved in Jonnie's care. He talked this through with Sarraphin and they decided they wouldn't try to control it in any way, they'd simply hold to their story of not being involved. The other thing that had been bothering Linden overnight, was about how fake-Jonnie and the Guardians had known who he was when he had his krill covering his face.

"*Hmmm…* I'm not sure. I don't think the Mages have the power for that kind of knowledge. Wait… I imagine you used your palmprint when you exited the hostel to go to the market?"

"Yes," Linden replied, "I had to, to get out."

"I wonder whether the Guardians have access to that data? If they could access who was arriving and leaving, that would be an obvious way of keeping track of people of interest."

"I guess so, but what about fake-Jonnie. How did he know?"

"Well, I'm not sure, but think back. What happened? Did he call out to you?"

"He'd been calling my name, and Ailesh told me. Oh… I wonder whether he knew our group had left the hospital and called out, knowing that eventually I would hear and respond?"

"That would make sense, wouldn't it?" Sarraphin said. "It does highlight that we need to be incredibly vigilant though. Let's take keeping an eye on fake-Jonnie in shifts today. Hopefully he'll find Willard quickly and then just disappear. You go first – check in with him, then I'll pick up the watch a little later."

Linden made his way to the ward. First, he checked his other two patients who were due for discharge. They were progressing well and would be ready to go home within twenty-four hours. He then moved on to the supposed Jonnie. He was sitting in his room looking out the window, a bored expression on his face. At Linden's approach, he turned and asked, demandingly, when he was going to be able to leave.

"The weekend staff tell me that your leg is well mended now and there's no reason to keep you here, so I imagine Sarraphin will discharge you today. Where will you go?" Linden asked.

"Argin has arranged somewhere for me," he responded. "He has work for both me and Willard, so I need to see him before I go. Which is his room?"

"I can't arrange that, I'm sorry. We don't encourage our patients to mingle. You might ask Sarraphin when she comes to see you – I'm only an Apprentice, so I can't change the rules for you."

'Jonnie' looked annoyed, and rather than have any further conversation with him, Linden left the room, making a point of busying himself with duties that would allow him to see the corridor outside his room. Sure enough, a short while later, 'Jonnie' left the room, looking in both directions down the corridor before heading to Willard's room. Linden quickly went to find Sarraphin, who made her way to the room, pausing outside the door in time to hear Willard's first words.

"What do you want, boy?" Willard growled, his voice still gravelly from his chest condition, underlaid by his usual belligerence.

"Argin wants me to work with him and you when we're out of here. I can help you, like I did in North Feasgar. He said I have to check with you."

"Help? You're just a kid who ran some errands for me. We don't need you meddling in important work."

"But what am I supposed to do? I've got nowhere to go," 'Jonnie' said pleadingly.

"Not my problem. Go on, clear out!" He brushed him off with a wave of his hand, just as Sarraphin walked in the door.

"What's going on here?" she demanded.

"Jonnie is just leaving," said Willard dismissively.

Sarraphin walked 'Jonnie' back to his room and told him she'd come back later to discharge him, but by the time she returned there was no sign of him. A cursory look around the hospital didn't reveal him, so she filled in a report saying that a patient had discharged himself, but was well enough not to pose any danger either to himself or anyone else. This was standard protocol and she wanted to do everything by the book. She hoped that that chapter of the saga they were involved in was out of the way.

***

With all three of Linden's final cases discharged, he had completed his clinical requirements and was eligible to graduate with the other two Apprentices on Friday. Everything was arranged for Ailesh, Gronin and him to present themselves to the panel of healers who would recommend their graduation, followed by a small ceremony attended by the other Apprentices and those from their year who had recently become Affiliates, and their teachers. While he was waiting, he carried on working with new patients, and back at the hostel, tried to keep Jonnie's spirits up. Now that he knew his confinement was almost over, Jonnie had become incredibly irritable and impatient. Linden understood what was happening, but it was the last thing he needed after a long day of work. In the time he spent with him, he encouraged him to try various activities, like drawing and reading. He'd been making progress with them earlier, but now seemed to have given up and it was like he was revelling in feeling sorry for himself.

On Thursday he set Jonnie the task of tidying up the room and packing his belongings, which, between him and Sarraphin, had grown considerably during his stay, as they'd found for him the things he needed. In the evening Linden pulled out a backpack himself and stuffed some clothes and other necessities into it to last for the time he was going to be with his family. To Jonnie's surprise, he pulled out the box from the bottom of the wardrobe, fossicking around, looking for something. Eventually he pulled out the box of shells.

"What're they for?" Jonnie asked.

"They're for my sister. I've only been to see the ocean once and she's never been. I picked them out for her, and now that she's stuck, not able to do what she really wants to do, I thought maybe they'd remind her of freedom. If you shut your eyes and smell them, it's like they can transport you to a place far away…"

Jonnie held the box and buried his nose inside it, closing his eyes and breathing in. Something nudged the back of his mind. He breathed out, then in again, deeply. Suddenly he was back in New Zealand, at the beach, smelling the surf and the sun, mingled with memories of his friends and Kayla. It was so powerful that tears came to his eyes and he jerked himself upright, thrusting the box away from him towards Linden.

"Yeah, that's cool, it smells like the sea," he managed to mutter, embarrassed.

Linden didn't say anything, although he'd picked up on the thought pictures the shells had brought to Jonnie's mind. This was a guy who felt things deeply, but didn't know what to do with them. Maybe the things happening to him at the moment were there for a reason; maybe he would learn how to deal with his past by facing the dangers they were heading into…

**

The graduation on Friday was both deeply moving and a lot of fun. Surrounded by people he liked and admired, Linden was full of gratitude that he'd had the opportunity to pursue what he'd dreamed about his whole childhood. He knew he'd worked hard for it, but at the same time he was much more fortunate than most – for his gifts, and for being chosen, and was determined to make sure he helped other people to find a way to be who they were meant to be, whether that meant Jonnie finding safety and a direction, his sister being able to use her talents, or his patients becoming well enough to enjoy living.

Before he left for the hostel at the end of the day, Sarraphin called him aside, on the surface to congratulate him and admire his Affiliate braid, but really to double-check their strategy for getting Jonnie away from Scathach. He and Jonnie were to leave in the morning with his peers and their supervisors, seemingly to have some time to relax, exploring the market as a way of celebrating and unwinding. They hoped that as part of a group, Jonnie wouldn't be noticed, and that they could avoid identification at the exit by everyone tail-gating Sarraphin as she checked out, being the most senior person. Once in the city, the group would break up and he and Jonnie would catch a mopas to his parents' village. The others in the group only knew that they were going to the market, and if questioned, wouldn't have anything more to tell. The only problem would be if Ailesh or Hamlin wondered who Jonnie was, so Sarraphin said she'd walk with him – two Masters together wouldn't be approached or questioned by his friends.

After a broken night's sleep, where Jonnie and Linden were too wound-up to be able to relax properly, they set off. They'd decided their backpacks would be too obvious, so they'd layered on their clothes, just carrying a small bag of essentials around their necks under their tunics. Hoping the day wouldn't be hot, they joined the rest of their group at the front door to the hostel, with Jonnie walking out confidently immediately behind Sarraphin. As they anticipated, they were soon picked up and followed by a Guardian, but they arrived at the market without noticing any more, and the group broke up into pairs and threes as they explored the market stalls. When Jonnie and Linden split off from the group they waited and checked for any sign of being followed, but the Guardian seemed to have attached himself to two who had bags and were headed towards a place where they could hire bikes for the day. They imagined he must have been kicking himself at being alone and having to choose who to keep an eye on.

"Okay, let's head to the Mopas Centre," Linden said.

"What's a mopas?" Jonnie asked, puzzled.

"The omnibus."

"Omnibus? You mean a vehicle that carries lots of people?" Linden nodded. "Where I come from we just call it a bus. What does Mopas stand for?"

"Mobile Passenger Service. What do they call them in North Feasgar?" Linden asked.

"I don't know. I only ever went to Hunterdale, which is just a small town. I guess I didn't even think about it, because I don't recall seeing any, just cars and trucks and bikes," Jonnie responded.

Linden led Jonnie towards the central hub that the mopas left from. After purchasing tickets and food for their journey, Linden climbed aboard and led the way to their seats, which were towards the back. He sat down by the window, with Jonnie joining him in the aisle seat. The mopas slowly filled up with other passengers. Five minutes before their departure time, there was a flurry of activity outside. They could hear people's raised voices and the driver climbed down from her seat and went out to see what was happening. More raised voices, and Jonnie could see her gesticulating at someone in front of the mopas. She returned shortly after with a Guardian, announcing bluntly to the passengers that they would all need to produce their identity cards and tickets, but because she didn't want to run late, the

Guardian would travel with them to the first stop. The last passengers climbed aboard and took their seats. The driver abruptly started the engine and swung out of the transport hub, causing the Guardian to lurch in the aisle and grab hold of one of the front seats before plonking down into an empty one in an attempt not to fall down the front steps. The driver aggressively drove off, turning abruptly at cross-roads, clearly angry at having her routine interfered with, and appearing to want to make his job as difficult as she could. It was clear that the Guardians were not popular with the general population.

Linden and Jonnie looked at each other, suddenly fearful. Linden had his identity card, but they hadn't even thought to get one for Jonnie. Their multiple layers of clothing were far too hot. That, and fear, were creating rivers of sweat that trickled down their backs and they were unable to think properly about what to do. As the Guardian managed to get to his feet and start checking the cards of the people in the front, they felt more and more anxious. Fortunately, the Guardian's progress was very slow, as the driver seemed to be relishing the chance to make his life a misery by erratic driving that threw him around in the aisle.

"It's not far to the first stop," Linden whispered. "Hopefully he'll get off and we'll be okay."

Jonnie just looked at him, his mind racing. The Guardian was now only two rows in front of them and he was feeling really panicky. He was breathing too quickly – thank goodness no one could see the sweat trickling down his face – it would be a dead giveaway that he was stupidly, and suspiciously, anxious.

"How far is it between the next two stops?" he asked suddenly, as the bus started to slow and pull over to a bus shelter – he realised he couldn't think of it as a mopas – what sort of stupid name was that for a bus anyway?

"Not very far. They spread out once we leave the city," Linden replied. "It takes about two hours to get to my village, but a lot of people just use the city part of the route."

The mopas had pulled to a stop. None of the passengers were getting off and the Guardian was obviously determined to check them all before he did, but a couple were making their way on board. As they found a seat up front and the driver started to close the doors, Jonnie quickly got up, muttering to Linden to come back and find him, raced up the aisle and slid through the almost closed doors. He stepped onto the pavement and sauntered off down the road, trying to look nonchalant and completely unconcerned. Linden looked out at him, his mouth open in surprise. He hadn't seen that coming, but it was a perfect move. The Guardian continued to check the rest of the passengers, including him, and would probably get off at the next stop. He'd get off there too and make his way back to Jonnie. They'd have to wait a while before the next mopas, but he hadn't told his family what time they'd be arriving anyway. More than likely the next one would be checked at the Mopas Centre before leaving, or by the first stop, so they should be okay for the next part of their journey. Their driver really had unknowingly been on their side by trying to make it difficult for the Guardian!

At the second stop Linden got off the mopas after the Guardian, and watched as he crossed the road to wait at the shelter to catch one returning in the other direction. It was hot walking back the way he'd just come with all his layers of clothes and it seemed to take forever before he caught sight of a figure in white sitting on a low wall near an intersection. He assumed it would be Jonnie; there was no reason for Healers to be in this part of town, and when he tuned in he could pick up confused and messy thought images – he must have been anxious even though he'd made himself look so relaxed when he got off the mopas. Linden raised his arm to identify himself and Jonnie stood up at his approach, crossing the intersection to meet him.

"Am I glad to see you! I wondered if I'd done the right thing, but it was all I could think of."

"You absolutely did the right thing. I was scrabbling about in my mind wondering what to do and you just acted in the moment. You were great!"

"Sorry I didn't walk any further, but I wasn't sure if the bus would turn or go straight ahead at the intersection."

"That's okay," Linden responded. "There's a park near here anyway and since we're going to have to wait for a couple of hours, we might as well go there. This is a popular mopas route, but they don't all go as far as my village. I don't think we should stay here and invite the Guardian to be curious about us if he notices two Healers on his return to the city!" He led Jonnie a short distance along the road to a pathway that ran alongside a fence, with a sign indicating the direction to Serpentine Park.

"Why Serpentine?" Jonnie asked.

"The park has been created around a winding river. Look, you can see it up ahead." The path had opened out onto a beautiful vista. The river slowly wound its way between green lawns, flower beds and shady groves of trees. A walkway meandered along its banks, with benches regularly placed so people could sit and enjoy the view. They found one in semi-shade under the canopy of a tree that looked a bit oak-like to Jonnie, and made themselves comfortable, to talk and wait.

***

Four hours later, their mopas drew into a village in the

129

countryside, discharging Jonnie and Linden outside an old, grey, stone building that looked like a general store. Jonnie noticed fruit and vegetables stacked in boxes outside the front doors, and a dim interior cluttered with shelves of food on one side and, at a quick glance, a conglomeration of implements and household goods on the other. He didn't have much time to take it in though, because Linden had already set off down the road and was waiting for him, impatiently pulling off his krill while stepping from foot to foot as if he had fiery ants crawling up his legs.

"What's up?" Jonnie asked.

"It's been so long – I suddenly can't wait a minute longer. Come on, let's get going. You won't need that krill on any more either."

It was the first time Jonnie had felt the fresh air on his face in South Feasgar. He'd always been either unconscious, or inside, or covered by a krill. He stopped for a moment just to breathe and feel its coolness, before hurrying after Linden. They walked quickly through the village and up a hill. Ahead of them Jonnie could see a small cluster of low stone buildings: a house, shed, barn and some smaller outbuildings off to one side of the barn that might be a woodshed, or maybe shelter for small animals or farm implements. On the other side of the barn there was a fenced area that looked like it was used for holding cows or other animals. The buildings were nestled in front of a line of trees, beyond which a grassy hill extended to the skyline, small white dots indicating grazing sheep or goats. It all looked idyllic, but Jonnie knew from conversations with Linden that it was actually hard work.

As they walked up the path, Jonnie saw the front door of the farmhouse open and a girl ran out, dressed in a brown tunic, with a scarf flying behind her as she made for Linden. She flung herself into his arms and pulled him around in a circle with her until he gently stopped her.

"Linden! I've been waiting all day! What took you so long?" Without waiting for a reply, she turned to take a look at Jonnie.

"Anika, this is my friend Jonnie. Jonnie, my sister Anika."

Jonnie saw a slight girl with brown hair, with quite a likeness to Linden except that the colour of her eyes was much darker, almost violet, and her fair skin was lightly tanned with a smattering of freckles across her cheeks. She had less resemblance to Kayla in person, but there was still something... She looked to be a similar age to him and was studying him with a very intense, curious look.

"Jonnie... hello, it's nice to meet you. We haven't met any of Linden's friends before, and you haven't even told us about them," she said, turning to Linden with an accusatory expression in her voice. "But then, you haven't really even written to us much about anything except what you've been learning. Anyone would think you've had the most boring three years imaginable!"

Linden just smiled at her and held out his hand, taking it to lead her towards the house.

"So where are the others?" he asked.

"Mum and Dad are in the barn, tending to a sheep that's poorly. Ardon is up in the high field mending a fence. He won't be back until dinner time. It's my turn to cook dinner and do some housework."

"You mean, have a chance to catch up on some reading!" Linden retorted, smiling.

Anika blushed. "I know there's no point..."

"But there is! You love it – it's part of who you are to keep wanting to learn."

Anika looked stricken.

"I'm sorry," Linden apologised. "I know how hard it is for you, but we'll find a way to get you into an apprenticeship. Come on, Jonnie and I are going to take off our layers of clothes and head to the barn so he can meet Mum and Dad. And... I might be able to help them with the sheep."

As they walked to the barn, Linden explained to Jonnie that he and Anika shared their mother's passion for learning. She'd chosen to marry for love and to live a farming life, but it was different for Anika, who desperately wanted the chance to study but was prevented from joining an Order because of the system they had to follow.

"They're not controlled in that way in the north, from what I've noticed," Jonnie said. "Anyone can choose to go to university, but they don't seem to be as technologically advanced as here in the south, and they don't have Mages or Guardians to control people."

Linden wondered how he'd explain where Jonnie came from to his family. He wanted to tell them the truth, but at the same time didn't want to endanger them because of their knowledge. He'd probably have to though – they weren't stupid and would ask questions. He didn't want to lie to them.

They found his parents in a pen in the barn, sitting down on bales of hay, Linden's father stroking a sheep that was lying on its side, flanks heaving and its whole body trembling. When they saw them enter the barn, they stood up quickly, wiping their hands down their aprons.

"Oh, Linden, it's so good to see you, and we're so filthy we can't even give you a hug!" his mother said, holding out both hands to grasp his, his father clapping him on the back with a large hand. Linden introduced them to Jonnie and they self-consciously shook his hand, embarrassed that they were smeared with spit and diarrhoea from the sheep. The smell was really bad!

His father nodded at the sheep. "She's got a gastric bug – she can't keep down any fluids and she's dehydrated – I think we're losing her," he said helplessly.

Linden sat down on a hay bale and centred himself, blocking out their presence, letting his emotional field connect with hers. He quickly felt her distress, and a deep, pervading unease, a sickness, churning through her guts, rolling and agitating so strongly that he felt his own stomach heave. The further he moved into her core, the more turbulence he found, until he came to the source. A cluster of disturbed cells, hot and festering. Reaching into them with his healing magic, he circled them, building a matrix of blue energy with more and more filaments, closer together, until he'd completely separated them off from the healthy tissue surrounding them, drawing his noose tighter until they were completely cut off and asphyxiated. They shrivelled and died. As Linden retracted his energy from the site, he spread a cooling energy over her intestines to calm them down. By the time he emerged from his trance state and re-joined his family, the sheep was already less agitated and was breathing more easily.

"Linden, what did you do? That was incredible," his mother exclaimed. They'd never seen his trained gift – he hadn't been home since he'd begun his apprenticeship. Linden flushed, partly proud and pleased to be able to help, but also feeling awkward. It was as if something in their relationship had changed – he'd always looked up to them, and now they were looking at him in wonder.

Jonnie watched on with a strange mixture of envy at the way they cared for Linden, and their obvious pride in him, and at the same time in awe at what Linden could do. His mother looked a lot like Linden and Anika, though she was showing her outdoor life with the fine wrinkles around her eyes and tanned skin. His dad, on the other hand was much chunkier. He looked like a farmer, strong, weathered and tough, but with a kindness that Jonnie suddenly wished he could be a part of. They turned to him then, smiling inclusively at him and drawing him into their conversation, Linden's dad putting his arm around his shoulders as they walked back towards the farmhouse.

Chapter VI

Returning to Galawand

Compared to the last time Sarah made the journey to Greyvyn, this time it passed in a flash. She and Tom leaned companionably against each other on the deck of the truck, their backs propped up against the cab. Hermione was stretched out, sphinx-like between their legs.

"Are you chaperoning us, Hermione?" Tom had asked her when she jumped onto the back rather than going to her customary place in the front. She just gave an inscrutable cat look and started grooming her face, not deigning to reply.

"Nah, she just doesn't want to miss out on anything. And, I hope, she wants to spend time with me to make up for the past six months." Hermione licked her on her leg. "See?" said Sarah, stroking her.

As they drew near to the base of the mountain, where they would turn off to park, the truck slowed down and Arthur stopped on the side of the road. They turned to look questioningly through the cab's back window, as Mary got out and came around the side to talk to them.

"We thought it might be a good idea to call at Greyvyn Village on our way. We've met some of Galawand's friends there and I think we should warn them about what's happening, even if we don't know much yet."

"Okay, but will that make us too late to get to the mountain's entrance before dark?" Tom asked.

"I hope not, but if it looks like that might happen we could either stay with one of them for the night and set out early tomorrow, which doesn't sound like a bad idea when I think about it, or we could camp out somewhere on the track. It's warm enough and the weather seems settled."

Getting back in the front, she shut the door and Arthur started the truck again. As it moved forward, Tom remarked,

"You know, I feel so safe with them. That's something I've never had before. It's like I can feel sure of myself and brave because I've got them backing me, if you get what I mean."

"Like the three musketeers, circling with their backs to each other, facing out to their enemies... I feel that too. Though I haven't spent much time with them yet, I completely trust them."

"And there's you too of course," Tom added. "I'm still working that out, but it's just like we belong together." He took her hand, feeling strangely vulnerable, wondering what she would say. Would she be embarrassed? She squeezed his hand in response and when he dared to look at her, he could see tears glistening in her eyes.

They remained silent driving to the village. As they neared it, the first impression was of grey. Grey stone houses, walls and cobbled lanes, with the grey mountain looming as a backdrop beyond it. But when they entered the village, they could see bright painted doors and window shutters, with flowers cascading riotously from boxes hanging beneath the windows. Gardens were packed with herbs and vegetables, jostling comfortably between shrubs and flowers – greens and purples and reds and yellows blending together hazily in the sun. In Sarah's imagination she added bees bumbling between flowers and cats sunning themselves on doorsteps – it looked so peaceful.

But where were the people? When she commented about this to Tom, he told her that they'd all be at the market, held twice a week, where they sold and bartered their goods and livestock, mostly grown and bred on the land beyond the village that ran along the river to the base of Greyvyn. A little further on they began to hear the hum of voices and clatter of carts being pulled over the cobble stones, getting steadily louder until they could see the village square ahead. Their way was blocked by carts and market stalls, so Arthur stopped the truck and backed it back until he found a side road where he could park without restricting the main road into the square.

"What are you going to do Hermione?" Tom asked. "Wait here or come to the market with us?"

"I'll wait in the truck – there might be too many smelly animals for my liking!"

"Go on, you just want a snooze!" Tom teased, as he rubbed her under her chin before she jumped up into the cab and curled herself up in a ball on the passenger side.

As they made their way on foot to the square, the noises of the market grew until they could make out a loud mix of voices calling attention to their wares, children laughing, dogs barking and the strident sound of a gong being beaten. Stepping between stalls, they were suddenly swept into a hive of activity. It was very different to the Hunterdale market. This was a working farmers' and market gardeners' place for trading. Huge bins of every vegetable imaginable; honey still in its natural honeycomb form; cages of chickens squawking noisily; pigs tethered in a make-shift pen; a pony taking children for a ride around the square, led by a squat, heavy-set man in overalls and a farmer's hat; the most gigantic pumpkins they'd ever seen, one of them boasting a first prize garland... It was bustling and interesting, and Sarah and Tom felt like their heads were on swivels trying to take it all in. The gong noise they'd heard was coming from the far side of the square where people seemed to be throwing a ball at a metal plate, trying to hit it with enough force to win a prize. Children jumped up and down, shouting gleefully each time someone succeeded.

"Those are weird," Sarah said, pointing at a pen of unusual-looking sheep with a wide band of darker, brownish wool around their middles.

"See those jumpers for sale at the stall next to them?" said Mary. "That's what happens when both colours of their wool are spun together. Interesting, aren't they?" The jumpers looked thick and luxurious, with shades of colour blending in a way that almost created the perception of movement in the wool. But Sarah's attention was diverted to a stall of herbs and she wandered over to it. Fresh and dried, some hanging in fat bunches, some in posies or stored in jars. A woman, probably in her sixties, with crinkly grey hair was behind the counter and smiled as Sarah approached.

"Can I help you?" Her voice was quite deep but soft, with a lilt she didn't recognise.

"Is it okay for me just to look? Everything looks wonderful! What do you use these for?" she asked, her attention drawn to a brown box with partitions that separated small packets of dried herbs into compartments, each one with a different letter stamped onto it.

"These are my medicinal herbs," the woman replied. "Here, you can have this if you like." She handed her a sheet of paper with a descriptor for each letter. The ones I've pressed into a cream base are over there," she indicated the other side of the counter.

Sarah smiled, "Wow, this is great, thank you. I used to know someone who did this."

"Oh?" the woman said questioningly.

"Someone from near Hunterdale called Morwyn." She saw a shadow briefly cross the woman's face, wiping away her smile, and she turned away abruptly to tidy some of the bunches of herbs behind her.

"Deantra!" Mary's voice called out from behind her. The woman turned, smiling with welcome as Mary approached.

"Lovely to see you, Mary. It's not often you find your way to our village. What brings you here?"

"A chance to see you and Kollin, and Saraya and Darthin if they're around. I see you've met our Sarah," she said putting her arm around her shoulders. Deantra looked quizzically at Sarah.

"Ah, the girl had me wondering. What's with her knowing Morwyn?"

"Well, you could say that she got on the wrong side of her and is lucky to be alive. It's a long story – I'm surprised that you haven't been told it by Galawand."

"Oh… that girl! And there's a boy too isn't there, staying with you? Galawand says they've helped her greatly already and have more to do with her yet. Welcome Sarah, it's nice to meet you."

"Hi," Sarah responded, feeling a little overawed that people here knew of her.

"Deantra, we came here hoping we could find you. We need to talk to the people in Galawand's network when the market's over."

"That sounds intriguing," Deantra replied. "I'll gather people together at my place when we've packed up. Shall we say about four? Do you remember where I live?"

"More or less. Vinegar Lane, isn't it? Remind me which house is yours."

"The one with the blue door and shutters, lavender out the front in boxes, on the left side of the lane if you're travelling away from here."

"Excellent, thanks. We'll see you in a couple of hours." Mary turned and led Sarah away to find Tom and Arthur.

They found them watching a wood chopping contest. Several men and a couple of women with rippling muscles, were swinging heavy axes into huge blocks of wood to see who could chop through one first. Each whack with the axe biting into wood, was accompanied by a grunt, droplets of sweat spraying around them, their shirts drenched and skin taut and shining.

"You wish!" said Mary, nudging Arthur in the ribs. "We're off to find something to eat. We've spoken to Deantra and we're meeting up at her place at four."

"Why don't we go to the pub by the river – it's a nice spot," said Arthur.

After eating, they wiled away the time by the river, talking and watching the deeply flowing water, coursing its way between steep banks towards Greywyn. Sarah shuddered, remembering how scary it had been when she capsized three years ago, on her way to this very destination. She didn't want to navigate the River Dearth again in a hurry.

The early afternoon boat from Hunterdale arrived and discharged a handful of passengers onto the jetty, one making his way to the pub, the rest heading towards the market.

"Doesn't that guy look kind of familiar?" Tom asked, indicating one of the men walking towards the market.

"I don't know – it's hard to tell," Sarah replied.

"I think it might be a stranger!"

"What? Oh my goodness, so that might be why his appearance is sort of slippery, blurred around the edges. It's a bit like when I try to focus, the image of him dissolves – it's freaky," said Sarah.

"What man?" Arthur asked. "Which one do you mean?"

"That one lagging a bit behind the rest – he's walking past the fruit shop."

Mary and Arthur glanced at each other, then at Tom. "We wouldn't have noticed if you hadn't said anything. We can see him, but he's kind of hazy."

It began to sink in what that might mean. Were the strangers about again? What was he doing in Greyvyn Village? There wasn't anything they could do for now, though they'd have to warn Deantra and her friends later. Meanwhile, it was a warm day, quite still, with light puffy clouds drifting almost imperceptibly across the sky. Despite their heightened anxiety, they sat under an umbrella, away from the sun, feeling increasingly sleepy as the effects of food and the local brew saturated their bodies. Eventually they made their way to the shade of a tree and stretched out on the grass, dozing their way through the afternoon until Mary roused them just before four.

On their way to Vinegar Lane, Sarah and Tom noticed several more people, all heading in the same direction, towards the other end of the village. It was really creepy and changed the atmosphere from a nice day with the suggestion of an adventure ahead, to a much more serious sense of apprehension. They tried to make light of it by checking out the interesting things in the village as they walked, but underneath, both Tom and Sarah felt quite jittery and anxious. As they got close to the house they detoured past the truck and woke Hermione from her position curled up on the seat in the sun.

"Hey, lazy bones," Sarah said, "have you been asleep all this time?"

She just looked haughty, but as they walked towards Vinegar Lane she told them that she'd seen some of the strangers and had decided to keep her head down in case they sensed her watching them.

"I wonder why it's called Vinegar Lane?" Tom mused as they turned into the street.

"This village has always had a strong artisan presence in North Feasgar. I'm guessing that way back one or more people in the street made and sold vinegar?" Arthur responded.

"Well, I'd choose to live in an apothecary street, or maybe Honey Street," contributed Sarah.

"Or Pumpkin Alley!" said Tom.

"This looks like it must be their house." They'd arrived at a tidy, detached stone house with blue shutters. Over the stone wall surrounding the property, they could see a riot of plants tumbling together in the garden.

Arthur knocked on the door and they were let in by a tall man with a little pointy beard and his hair pulled back in a scraggly ponytail.

"Kollin, nice to see you again. It's been a while. You know Mary of course, and this is Sarah and Tom."

They all shook hands and Kollin led the way down a narrow corridor, which opened into a large, light-filled kitchen and living area at the back of the house. Doors opened onto the garden, creating a first impression of green – there were plants, lots and lots of plants clustering in every available space. Indoors, a large frame was suspended overhead from the ceiling, from which herbs hung in various stages of drying. Masses of them, along with bunches of dried flowers. Seedlings sprouted in rows of pots on the floor inside and outside the doors, and the whole garden seemed to be a jungle of herbs, flowers and vegetables, with a narrow path bisecting it to lead towards the back fence.

Deantra welcomed them from the kitchen where she was assembling a tray of baking to bring to the table, where two others were already sitting. Kollin introduced them as their friends Saraya and Darthin. When they were all seated around the table, Deantra told them that no one else would be joining them.

"We thought that rather than inviting all the others, we'd meet with you first, then get word out to the rest of the network. Too many of us finding our way here at once might look a bit odd, and even though we have no reason to think there are people in the village out to harm Galawand, our priority is still to keep her existence and the important work she's doing a secret."

"Very sensible," Mary remarked, "especially since Tom picked up the presence of the strangers in the village today. Several of them, all making their way to the far side of the village. We think that indicates that what we came here to talk to you about is gathering momentum, and that we have cause to be both alert and cautious!"

They started by telling them a little about how Sarah and Tom came to be in North Feasgar, their encounters with Morwyn and Willard, and then later, six months ago, how they were all involved with helping Galawand to restore her power to hold the barrier in place.

"Kayla's another one of you, isn't she?" asked Saraya. "We owe her so much for staying with Galawand. She couldn't have managed much longer without her."

"She came here a couple of years after us, with her brother," replied Tom.

"Where is he then?"

"We don't know if he's even alive." Arthur decided not to say anything negative about Jonnie – he was just a kid who'd been caught up with a scheming man. "He and Willard fell into the river in a scuffle when we were inside the mountain. They were both swept away and we've heard nothing from them since."

They went on to talk about Sarah's recent arrival back again from her world, the idea that she'd been summoned to fulfil an old prophecy with Tom, and how that had coincided with Galawand's message calling them to her in Greywyn.

"That'll be no coincidence then," Deantra remarked drily. "Galawand still has plenty of tricks up her sleeve despite most of her magic being used for the barrier."

They discussed the sighting of the strangers and how problematic it was to keep tabs on them when they could hide their presence. Knowing that they were still in North Feasgar and that they seemed to be making a move towards Greyvyn at the same time that Galawand had detected an incursion on the barrier from the south, was enough to make them wary.

Saraya and Darthin accepted the task of talking to all the people they could trust in the village, while Deantra and Kollin agreed to go to Hunterdale and rally supporters there. Even if people didn't know how they could contribute yet, they needed to be ready in case they were needed.

"Oh, please make sure you see Corrin and Gwynn first," Sarah suggested. "They'll want to be involved."

"Yes, we know them – they often come to sell their leatherware at our market. They're good people."

"Please say hello from me and tell them I'm back and hope to see them soon. They helped me so much once when I was in a difficult place and was feeling very alone." Sarah felt a rush of emotion, partly fear from remembering what had happened to her, and partly gratitude towards Corrin and Gwynn. She felt flustered as she tried to listen to the others as they continued planning their next steps.

"I'm worried about how we make people aware of potential danger from the strangers when they can't see them," Kollin said.

"I think we have to remind them of how unsettled they were six months ago when they knew something was going on and yet couldn't quite grasp it. They were holding community meetings in Hunterdale that they'll recall. Remind them that the strangers will show themselves if they need something, otherwise they're able to cover themselves from sight. Even if people do get an impression of them, they find their details slip away and they're left with a feeling of fear. Just because they've been keeping a low profile since then doesn't make them less dangerous," said Arthur.

"Maybe that makes them worse," Sarah suggested. "They had to withdraw when the barrier became strong again, but they've had six months to plot their next move. I wonder how South Feasgar communicates with them? Does anyone know?"

"It would have to be some form of divination to get beyond the barrier," Deantra said.

"But what can anyone actually do?" Tom burst into the conversation. It was all very well talking about 'being ready', but being ready for what? "What happens if they breach the barrier? How on earth can we stop them when they have magic and we don't, other than Galawand?"

There was a long pause as they all considered such an immense unknown. Sarah felt a jolt of fear with the thought of everything they knew tumbling down and being destroyed. She suddenly remembered the tarot card.

"Hold on a minute, I need to get something." She went to where she'd left her pack and pulled out her tarot book. "I found a card on my way here and I think it's important – it's called The Tower. I didn't get a chance to read about it before." She skip-read quickly through the story of the destruction of the labyrinth and the Minotaur by Theseus, then read parts of the last section out loud.

"On an inner level, the god-struck Tower is an image of the collapse of old forms... and is a representation of structures, inner and outer, which we ourselves build, like Minos, as defences against life and as concealment to hide our less agreeable sides from others... On a divinatory level, the Tower augurs the breaking down of existing forms. This card depends a great deal upon the attitude of the individual in terms of how difficult or painful it is to deal with... It seems that the Tower will fall anyway, whether we are willing or unwilling, not because some malicious external fate decrees it, but because something within the individual has reached boiling point and can no longer live within such confines." [1] pp.67-68

"So..." began Mary after a long pause, "we may need to think of what's happening for North Feasgar as an opportunity that we walk towards rather than something we fear and try to avoid... I don't know what it will mean in reality, but let's trust in the solidarity, good will and determination of the people of North Feasgar." She thought for a bit longer, then added, "The barrier has given us freedom from the black magic of the south, but if it does come down, maybe it will give us the freedom to create a new country. The shadow side of having the barrier has meant that we're cut off from anything from the outside, not all of which is bad, and maybe if we defeat the Mages we can begin again in a different way."

They were silent for a while, letting her words sink in. When Deantra spoke, it was like she broke a spell, bringing them back to the present.

"You've got a lot ahead of you to deal with tomorrow. I think you'd be best to stay in the village for the night and set off fresh in the morning. If Sarah and Tom are happy to share a room – you can change in the bathroom – could Mary and Arthur stay with you Saraya?"

"Yes, of course, we've got a spare bed and we'd love to have you both."

"Are you okay with that Tom, Sarah?"

They both nodded, while internally wondering what it would be like to have a whole night together and what that might mean. Sarah noticed Mary looking at her questioningly – she flushed, but smiled and indicated that she was okay with that.

"What about you, Hermione, where will you stay?" Sarah asked.

"I'll stay here to chaperone you," she replied with a smirk.

"Hermione!"

"You act as if you're having a conversation with her," remarked Saraya.

"They both do – they can thought-share with her," said Mary. "It makes me wild that I can't, but we have an understanding, don't we Hermione?" Hermione strolled over and head-butted her on her leg. "See?"

"That reminds me, what about Ryder?" Tom said.

"Oh, of course. He'll be okay – when he sees we're not there he'll scout around a bit and likely find a perch for the night to wait for us."

"Ryder?" asked Kollin. "Who's this then?"

"A hawk. A fabulous hawk!" replied Tom. "We can talk to

him too, though not quite so easily."

"Weird," said Kollin, "wonderful, but weird!"

"Hey I wonder whether we could get Ryder to bring you messages if we need to, to keep you in touch with what's happening," Tom suddenly thought out loud. They decided to put a piece of red material on a pole in the garden as a marker for him, and put several small pieces of paper and ties in their packs to attach to his leg if they wanted to send a message.

***

By the time Mary and Arthur left with Saraya and Darthin, it was past six in the evening. Kollin started to prepare a meal, while Deantra took them out to show them the garden. While it looked like a riot of plants, it was actually methodically organised. As they walked down the central path towards the back of the property, Deantra pointed out areas designated for herbs; for flowers that co-existed well with herbs, like marigolds to keep the bugs away; flowers for drying, like roses and strawflowers; flowers just because she loved them and thought they were beautiful; edible flowers; vegetables and, at the back, a fenced-off area with a locked gate.

"What's in there?" Tom wanted to know.

"Well, I don't grow any of the poisonous herbs, but I do have a few that are useful in small doses, but could be dangerous if used incorrectly. Like valerian to help with sleep or anxiety – some say that it can be toxic if someone takes too much; or comfrey can be bad for the liver even though it's so good for many illnesses. So I keep them in there so I can make sure whoever I sell them to knows about the risks. I always make sure they're labelled for correct use."

"Morwyn tried to sedate Tom by giving him belladonna, but she kept giving him more and he could have died," remarked Sarah grimly.

"Yes, she called herself a healer, but we all know she was twisted. I wouldn't sell her my herbs and I'm not sure where she got them from. She wasn't a grower. I'm the opposite – I cultivate and prepare them, but I'm not a healer."

"I want to be a healer, though it would be cool to know how to grow them too!" Sarah said.

"You could do that for yourself on a small scale, but as soon as you start to cultivate as much as we do it's very time-consuming."

After dinner they made their way to their bedroom. Sarah was going to sleep in the single bed and Tom on a mattress on the floor. It was still early, but they were tired and were being woken at six in the morning so they could have breakfast, meet Arthur and Mary and be away by eight. The room had a kind of rush matting on the floor that Hermione sharpened her claws on until they told her to stop, after which she made a big deal out of kneading the pile of Tom's clothes on the floor, then circling until she found a comfortable position to curl up in, closing her eyes.

"Why is it, do you think that Hermione's chosen to face us, Tom?" Sarah said teasingly. Hermione opened one eye to a slit, twitched her whiskers and closed them again.

They both felt awkward – nothing to do with Hermione's presence, just the slight barrier between them of not quite knowing what to do, who should make the first move, and what might happen. Tom sat down on the edge of Sarah's bed and held out his hand. She took it and sat beside him. He then lay back on the bed, pulling Sarah down to his side. They stared up at the ceiling.

"Why is this so hard?" Sarah began. "I mean, knowing how to be when we're together, even though we know we both like each other – a lot!" After a moment's silence she continued in a whisper, "What are you most afraid of?"

"Maybe… maybe that you'll get sick of me and leave, or that you don't want me, you're just feeling alone here and know there's something we're meant to do together? I've learned to trust Mary and Arthur, but being with you – that's a whole different story! I mean, why would you like me?... What about you? What are you afraid of?"

"Well," she said quietly, "that you're just being nice to me, that I'll end up being too needy and you'll be too nice to tell me you don't want to be with me any more?"

"What? Like your parents?"

"Oh! I hadn't thought of that! Yes, with Mum being sick and all that, I think Dad was fed up having to do everything for her, but he didn't leave after that first time I came here. Maybe he'd have been more honest if he had!"

Tom turned towards her on the bed. "So how about we try to experience things in the present rather than getting anxious about the future? You know, one step at a time. How about we make a pact to leave our families and our pasts behind – I don't mean not to talk about them or anything, but…"

"You mean, draw a line in the sand?"

"Yeah. And let's be honest with each other. Surely there's nothing we can't fix if we keep talking," he added, squeezing her hand, which she squeezed in return. They lay there for a while, quiet with their own thoughts.

"Tom?"

"Uh-huh?"

"Have you ever, you know, done it before?"

"Um, no. I haven't even met anyone else I like since I've been here. What about you?"

"What, at a girls' school? Boys are all they ever talk about, but it's all talk, I think, unless they have a secret supply of boys I don't know about…" she paused, "I'm a bit scared about it – knowing what to do and all that…"

"We don't have to do anything until we know it's the right time – probably not in the house of people we don't really know, just before heading off into something unknown again!"

Sarah felt relieved – she was so glad she'd said something.

"You can stay here though can't you, I mean for the night?" His arms tightened around her and she snuggled into him. Before long they fell asleep comfortably entwined, both feeling the safest they could remember they'd ever felt before.

***

Tom woke first in the morning, with a feeling of calm and happiness suffusing through him that took a while for him to realise was related to the warm body curled up against him. Actually, two warm bodies; Sarah on his right, and a furry body on his left. Hermione had taken over half the pillow and was twined around the top of his head – he could hear a gentle rumble coming from somewhere inside her soft abdomen, so close that if he turned his head he'd have a face-full of fur! He reached an arm up and stroked her gently – her response was to start kneading the pillow, with her purr growing louder.

"Ouch Hermione, that hurt!" he exclaimed, as a kneading claw caught the side of his head.

"What's happening?" Sarah sat bolt upright, woken out of a deep sleep.

"It's okay, it's just Hermione pretending I'm her mother. Who'd be a cat's mother with all those sharp claws?... Hey Sarah, I had a dream last night."

"But you said you never dream!"

"Yeah I know. Anyway, I've got no idea what it meant, but it was scary!" Tom said. "I was somewhere dark, inside, or maybe in a cave or something and I was being chased by a presence that felt evil. I was running and running – it wasn't catching up with me, but I couldn't get away from it either. My heart was pounding and I was really afraid, but I realised I could see a pinprick of light ahead of me that got bigger as I ran towards it. Then I woke up."

"Wow, so there's light at the end of the tunnel!"

"Oh, I guess so – I didn't think of that."

"Have you ever felt anything like that before?" Sarah asked.

He hesitated before replying. "Well, I guess the worst evil I've felt coming after me was Gerald..."

"I read a bit about dreams back at school because of the ones I had about being here. I think everyone dreams; they just don't always remember them. I bet it's a good thing you've remembered one, even if it was scary, because then you can kind of put it out there and talk about it. Maybe when you get to the end of the tunnel and out into the light you can leave all that old stuff behind? Maybe you've been running for a very long time?"

"Yeah... I didn't think of it like that. And I guess, even if it's about something that's going to happen here, in the dream I'm alive and there *is* that light at the end..."

"Is it time for us to get up?" Sarah asked.

"I think so. I can hear someone in the kitchen. I'll go to the bathroom first if you want a minute longer."

By the time they finished breakfast, Mary and Arthur had

arrived, and after a last-minute reminder about what they were to do in Hunterdale, Deantra and Kollin wished them well and sent them on their way with more food and wishes for a safe return. The drive to the base of Greyvyn was short. They left the truck in the clearing at the start of the track, hefted their packs onto their backs and set off, Tom in the lead and Arthur bringing up the rear. Twenty minutes into their hike they heard Ryder's distinctive cry and looked up to see him circling above them. They waved, relieved that he'd found them, and trudged on, grateful that the weather was overcast and not too hot as they managed their heavy packs.

For Sarah it was only the second time she'd made this trek, and compared to the last time it seemed to pass in a flash. She remembered back to how agonisingly slow it had been trying to make their way with Mary's injured foot. They'd also been really anxious about the unknown ahead of them. At least this time, although the future was still unknown, they were no longer new to the mountain. She didn't need to be afraid of being claustrophobic, and they were all looking forward to seeing Galawand and Kayla again. The other three had made this journey once a month while Sarah had been away and it was very familiar to them now.

Arriving eventually at the platform in front of the tunnel entrance to the mountain, they dumped their packs, stopping to get their breath and have a snack. As they gazed at the vista open in front of them, they could still see the barrier glowing towards the south – that was a good sign surely! They could make out a dark dot heading towards them through the sky and before long Ryder sank down to alight on the rock beside them. He had the container grasped in his talons, which he released as he landed. They told him what they'd been doing in the village and how they'd suggested he might carry a message to Deantra and Kollin if necessary.

"Ryder, if you're willing to stay around the mountain keeping watch it would be really helpful – you can be our eyes and ears out here and let the others know what's happening," Sarah said to him, explaining their thoughts to him about the red marker in Deantra and Kollin's garden. He inclined his head towards them in agreement.

Before he flew off, Tom asked, "Out of interest Ryder, how high up does the barrier go?"

"I don't know – as far as I've ever flown I think. They'll not get anything over to breach it that way," he replied.

When he'd gone, Tom picked up the container and attached it to Hermione's harness. She didn't resist as it was strapped on her, but Sarah picked up a strange, slightly panicked look in her eyes.

"Hermione, are you okay with this?"

"Yes, but I'm not happy about being in the mountain… I'll feel very small in there," she admitted reluctantly.

"Would it help if you were to ride in the top of my pack? Then you'd be close to me, at least until you get used to it." Hermione rubbed herself against Sarah's arm, so she repositioned the food sitting in the top of the pack and created a layer of clothing on it. Leaving the fasteners open, she pulled the pack onto her back and got Tom to lift Hermione and place her in it – she circled to make herself comfortable and settled into the nest Sarah had made, with her head wrapped around the side of Sarah's neck.

Just inside the entrance, Arthur and Tom picked out two brands and lit them, the flames fluttering for a moment, briefly flashing with a whoosh, before steadying into an incandescent glow. They caught a waft of the pungent smell given off by the burning fuel wrapped around the top of the brand, then, since they were carrying the extra packs, they passed the brands to Mary and Sarah to hold before heading into the first cavern. In the sudden silence that enveloped them with its cool, clear and very ancient fingers, they felt like they'd entered a different world. With involuntary shivers as the coolness trickled down their backs, they made their way, Mary and Arthur in front, to the passage on the far side of the cavern that would lead them to Galawand. As they entered the narrow passageway, Sarah felt a moment's lurch of fear and breathed deeply to steady herself, then felt her hand being picked up and squeezed by Tom, his hand feeling like an anchor in the underworld.

It didn't seem long before they reached the first fork in the passage – they took the left one, without needing to worry this time about whether they were going the correct way. After the second fork they were forced to slow down as the floor became increasingly uneven and began to descend more rapidly. They ended up walking in single file, which meant, Sarah remembered, that they weren't far off the cavern that the river traversed. Thank goodness – she was just beginning to feel the edges of panic with the space more enclosed and no longer being able to hold onto Tom. He was behind her though and seemed to sense her anxiety, touching her on her shoulder regularly. Mary, who was in front of her, also turned often to make sure she was okay.

"How are you Hermione?" Sarah whispered. It somehow felt wrong to talk out loud in the hush of the passage.

"Fine. Maybe better than you I'm thinking." She rubbed her head against Sarah's and started purring rhythmically in her ear to soothe her. Just as she was starting to relax, Hermione stopped purring and gave a single, plaintive meow. The earth suddenly lurched far below them, with a loud rending sound that pierced the air, accompanied by a deep, grinding rumble. It was as if the dense rock around them was briefly tossed into the air and then released. It felt primal and gut-wrenching, and left them literally reeling, clutching at the rough walls to maintain their balance. Mary fell into Arthur, who just managed to hold both their weights by gripping a sharp outcrop of rock. They felt small and inconsequential, just dots inside a great piece of rock that could obliterate them in seconds. The total silence that followed was ruptured by an unearthly yowl from Hermione.

"Are you all okay?" Arthur asked shakily. They grasped for each other, hearts pounding, relief that they were all right competing with the desire to run and get out as quickly as they could. Sarah's breathing was shallow and ragged, but she managed to put an arm up to her backpack to comfort Hermione, stroking her head. Somehow soothing her helped her own shattered nerves so that she could just manage to agree when Tom said they were almost there and that they had to keep going to make sure Galawand and Kayla were okay. They shook dust from their hair and clothes and grimly moved on, picking their way around bits of fallen rock and debris.

"So, what was that?" Sarah gasped as they resumed walking.

"A tremor from an earthquake I think," Tom replied. "There are likely to be more. If it was the main one, there might be smaller after-shocks, or it could be a warning of..." his voice petered out as he suddenly realised what that might mean for them and how knowing about it might not be helpful at all for everyone's nerves. They walked on in silence until Sarah could no longer bear it. It was as if they, and the whole mountain, were waiting, listening, for any sign that might indicate the beginning of another one. She started talking to stop herself from thinking about it.

"How do you know about earthquakes then?"

"There are lots of them in New Zealand. I've only ever felt a little one, once at night when I was asleep – the house shook and everything rattled for maybe thirty seconds. I wondered if I'd imagined it, or if maybe a big truck had gone down the road, but the next day it was on the news that an earthquake had happened out to sea. Auckland hasn't had big ones, but other parts of the country have."

He realised she wanted to talk, but decided it might be safer to change the subject, so instead he asked, "Did you hear any news about New Zealand when you were back in England?"

"Not really. Since you left, you got a woman Prime Minister who's in the news quite a bit. It sounds like she's pretty amazing and lots of countries say they wish they had a leader like her. But not particularly in the last six months. I didn't check out any more about your family, sorry…" she said apologetically.

"That's okay, I was just wondering."

"What about…?" her question was cut off abruptly by Tom.

"Sshhh…" Sarah's heart lurched, thinking he may have heard something that meant another tremor, but then he said "Listen, it's the river, we're nearly there."

Not long after, they stumbled out into the cavern. More rocks littered the floor than before, but it was otherwise the same; an enormous space, their lights barely nibbling at its edges, with the inky black river snaking its way through the middle, splitting the cavern into two.

"What if…" Sarah began, "… the bridge has been damaged?" Tom chimed in, both having the same thought.

"Well you both got across last time without it," said Arthur, "so I guess we could do the same again if necessary."

"Well of course it's still there," said Hermione as if they were all stupid. She'd jumped down from the pack and was prowling over near the river.

"What do you mean Hermione? Can you see it?" demanded Tom.

She flicked her tail. "Of course I can! You keep forgetting I'm not just an ordinary cat!" she said snippily. "Come on, follow me. I can feel Galawand now, and she's ready for us."

They followed Hermione to the bridge, trusting that they didn't need to pace out its location from the remnants of the old bridge. It looked so weird when she turned to jump up and onto the first invisible steps – it was like she'd walked out onto thin air over the river. One by one they found the side rails with their hands and stepped, hearts in their mouths, onto the bridge. Sarah squeezed her eyes shut as she stepped over the water that flowed swiftly, almost silently, dark and deep, through the cavern. They all tried to look straight ahead and trust their feet, as invisible runners carried them safely across to the far side. Feeling a huge sense of relief when they stepped back onto the cavern floor, they took deep breaths before remembering to look for Hermione.

"So, Hermione's got the bit between her teeth now," Arthur remarked, wiping away sweat that had gathered in drips across his brow from the tension. "Look at her, confident again." She was trotting off ahead of them, tail held high, somehow commanding them to get a move on and follow her.

***

They entered the short passage through to Galawand's cavern and arrived a short time later to see Hermione in the middle of the vaulted space, winding herself around Galawand's legs. Their first impressions were a reminder of the beauty of the space Galawand had made her own. Tom had returned each month with Arthur, but for Mary it was her first visit, and she stood there trying to take it in – the atmosphere created by the soft lighting of candles being absorbed in the richly coloured wall-hangings and carpets, and the magical, glowing space that contained the ring of stones. For Sarah, she felt like she was standing there, mouth open in wonder, just as she had the first time she visited. It took a while before she could focus on Galawand moving towards them in greeting, and another person a little behind her. Kayla. The six months since she'd seen her could easily have been a couple of years. What magic had been worked on the thin and anxious young girl that she'd been then? She'd turned into a beautiful swan. Still tall and willowy, but gone was her brittle, emaciated look. Although her flawless skin was pale, so much so it was almost translucent, she was glowing with health, her face dominated by large eyes, framed by her dark hair, looking almost ethereal and very beautiful. There was something more… She no longer looked haunted – she belonged there, with Galawand, and she looked like she'd found a sense of purpose and quiet confidence.

They hugged each other, with Sarah particularly glad to reconnect with Galawand, soaking up her age and experience and wisdom. She felt so grounded somehow. Soon though, a serious note crept in.

"We presume you felt the tremor when you were in the tunnel?" Galawand asked.

"Yes, when we were about half way down from the last fork," Arthur responded.

"Was there much damage?"

"No, it seemed minimal really, but I guess we don't know

159

whether it was a one-off, or whether there will be more. What are you thinking? Are we in danger?"

"Come with us and we'll show you." Galawand led the way over to the circle of stones. They stood together looking at the red glow. After a moment there was a disruption on one side. The red sparked with an overlay of purple, fizzing, then dissolving for a moment, before settling again into its usual smooth pattern. "What you see has been happening regularly over the past couple of days. Something from the south is attacking the barrier. For a moment just before the tremor, it seemed to completely fragment. I think the Mages have found a weak spot that they're projecting their magic through into Greyvyn. It's waking the mountain, which has slumbered for hundreds of years. If they cause further tremors, either we could be trapped inside, or they could force an eruption. Either would be disastrous for us, and for the barrier."

"What could the weak spot be? Do we need to find out and try to stop them?" Tom asked.

"It's not that simple. I have an idea that it's where the river exits the mountain, but we can't get there unless I drop the barrier so that you can go around the outside of the mountain to find it. Yet if I don't, we could die and then the barrier would be dropped anyway…"

"I wonder whether maybe you have an idea about what we need to do?" Mary said. "You summoned us, and I think it's no coincidence that Sarah returned at the same time."

"Yes, you're right. Let's sit down and I'll tell you what I know."

Kayla boiled water for tea while they made themselves comfortable, Hermione finding a soft spot between Tom and Sarah to sit, in her customary sphinx-like pose, all ears while they talked.

"What I'm about to say," Galawand began, "will call for a lot of courage from us all, yet it is part of our destiny, stories of which have been passed down in folklore. The time has come for us to make them happen." Her voice had taken on a resonating quality that forced them to feel the importance of her words, and her power. Sarah shivered and grasped Tom's hand, while Mary and Arthur exchanged concerned looks. "As you know, the prophecies tell us that a time will come when the fate of North Feasgar will be in the hands of two young people. You also know that when Mary and Arthur gazed on the labyrinth pool, they saw that they had a vital role in staying here to support those two special people – Tom and Sarah. You've already played a major role in helping us to secure the ring of stones, and bringing Kayla here to help me in my task. But that was just the beginning..."

They all stared at her mutely. What could be bigger than what they'd already faced, first with Morwyn, and then with Willard when they first entered the mountain? A sense of dread began to settle on Sarah and Tom. Tom's mouth was dry and he took a quick gulp of tea, while Sarah started to feel nauseous, that steady spiral of anxiety uncurling inside her, like a snake waking up and rising to the top of her chest so it felt tight and breathless. Arthur broke the heavy silence.

"Come on then Galawand, tell us what you know so we can make sense of it and get our heads around what we have to do."

In a slightly sing-song voice, Galawand continued her story. "We have long been told that when North Feasgar is close to destruction, the two young people will travel inside the mountain to a great cavern at its heart and there will find symbols of a union that carries enough power to overcome the enemy. I've been given a thought image. Please focus on me and allow me to reveal it to you."

She stood before them and retreated into a trance that seemed to draw out until they began to feel slightly dizzy and mesmerised. She then slowly and gracefully pulled something that looked like a wand from her gown and touched it gently to her forehead. Her lips moved slowly, as if she was chanting something – a prayer maybe, or a spell? Gradually, she withdrew the wand from her forehead, pulling with it a thin, golden thread that pulsed and opened into an oval beside her.

"That's awesome," exclaimed Tom. "It's like an image bubble in a comic book."

"Sshhh…" whispered Sarah. "Look!"

In the oval an image was forming, moving from a vague haze to something more substantial. They could see another large cavern, much bigger than Galawand's. At the floor level, two figures were standing, near the cavern walls that seemed to rise sharply into infinity. In the centre of the cavern gaped an enormous hole, dark and ominous, that the figures were standing well clear of. When they looked more closely they could see that the figures had their heads tilted back, watching something above them almost out of their range of view. Following the direction of their gaze, they could just make out two more figures who seemed to be scaling the almost sheer sides of the cavern, though when they looked more searchingly they seemed to be helping each other up a narrow path carved into, or formed out of the rock. A little above them was a rocky platform that seemed to be their destination. The image shimmered for a moment before fading.

In the silence that followed, Sarah felt as if all the air had been sucked out of her lungs. She gasped. Her two biggest fears – claustrophobia and heights – were like a slap in her face! What had she done to deserve this sort of test? Tom would be okay now that he was settled and secure with the Birches; he was thriving. She was the weakest link. What if she let them down because she couldn't do what was asked of her and the south took them over because of her? She pulled her hand away from Tom's, embarrassed that it was clammy, suddenly feeling inadequate and self-conscious.

Arthur broke the silence, aware that Sarah was likely to be terrified. It would be daunting even for Tom. "But Galawand, they're just two kids – how can North Feasgar's future rest entirely on their shoulders? That's too much of a burden for them!"

"I know it's a lot to ask, but they have far more inside them than they yet know. They're the only ones who can do it. Without them we're lost. And they aren't alone – the two of you will be there. You're their security, their anchor, and they both need you to be strong. They also have another, very special gift – Hermione… I cannot say more, but she's an old soul and will play a vital role in what is about to unfold. Trust her!"

Tom swallowed hard, reaching instinctively to stroke Hermione's head. He felt scared, but mostly about not knowing what to do, or how to make sure Sarah was okay, rather than what it was they might actually need to do. He didn't like to see her frightened and didn't want her to pull away from him, as she just had. They couldn't do what lay in front of them unless they trusted each other and remained together. The prophecy had been clear on that.

"So, what do you know Galawand? What else have you seen? What are we going to need to do?"

"Do you remember the last time you were both here and we talked about two things coming together and allowing the possibility for a third point between them?" They both nodded.

"What I've seen is that the two of you need to go in search of two ancient amulets, in the cavern you saw in my thought image. The stories say that if the two destined people put them on their arms; the female on her left; the male on his right, then something very powerful will emerge between them. If you raise your arms 'together as one', you will unleash that power. If you remember when we came together with the ring of stones, it's the principle of synergy, where your joined power will be greater than the sum of the parts."

"But what do we do with the power? How will we know what to do?" Tom asked.

"I promise you; you'll know instinctively what to do when the time is right. It will be unleashed to combat the black power of the south."

"How do we find the cavern Galawand?" Mary asked.

"Kayla will guide you there. She's been exploring the passageways since the stone circle has been interfered with and has found her way to the cavern. She will need to return to me, but she'll tell you the forks to take so that you can make your way back to us... Just one final thing – when you get to where the amulets are kept, don't pick up anything else! You may see things that are interesting or that you'd like, but don't! If you pick up something that isn't intended for you, you will die..."

Tom and Sarah looked at each other, their faces turning pale and worried. Whatever had they got themselves into? Kayla cleared her throat and they turned to look at her. She'd stayed in the background since they'd arrived and seemed unsure of herself and whether to join the conversation. She seemed so young and unassuming, yet she'd been brave enough to explore under the mountain on her own! Sarah didn't know what to say to her – she'd so misjudged her before, out of a stupid jealousy, but Tom didn't hesitate to call her over to sit with them while Galawand continued talking to Mary and Arthur. As she sank down onto a heavy cushion, Sarah smiled at her, getting one in return that lit up her face.

"I'm guessing you've been searching for any sign of Jonnie while you've been exploring underground?" Tom said.

"Yes, I know it's stupid. If he was still in the mountain, he wouldn't be alive by now. If I found his body I might be able to let him go, but I just can't get rid of the feeling that he's not dead." She looked momentarily lost and they could see how much she cared about him, even though he'd let her down. "I thought I'd draw the route for you from here to the large cavern, then you can retrace your steps to return." She pulled out a sheet of parchment, on which she'd drawn the entrance to Greyvyn and the path to Galawand's cavern, with the two left forks they'd taken to get there highlighted. At the first fork, she pointed to the passage to the right. "That's the one Willard, Jonnie and I took when we came into the mountain. I turned back fairly quickly – it felt wrong, but Willard and Jonnie stayed on it. I'm not sure what they found, but maybe it came to a dead end, because they managed to find their way back and make their way via the left forks to the river. See here, at the next fork, not far from the river, we take the left to Galawand's cavern. If you take the right instead, it leads inwards towards the centre of the mountain. There are three more forks in the passage, and each time you take the right, until you come out in the central cavern. The passages are quite good, though a little rough in places. They don't appear to be as well travelled as the ones to Galawand, but you can mostly walk two-abreast."

"So, returning, we'd go left, left, left, right, to get back here," Sarah said.

"Yes, it's not difficult to remember, but you can take this drawing with you. The scale is probably all wrong, but it'll stop you getting lost. It's really strange walking alone in those spaces – funnily, I wasn't particularly scared, but I needed to draw everywhere I walked to make sure I could return. When I got used to it, it became quite surreal and almost like meditation. The paths feel like they're really ancient."

"Yeah, well, something I'll leave you to enjoy – it's not my idea of fun!" Sarah exclaimed. "You're a strange one, but we're very lucky to have you!"

Kayla's face suffused lightly with pink and she looked really pleased that Sarah had approved of something she'd done. Again, Sarah felt bad about how she'd treated her the last time she'd been in North Feasgar – she was older than Kayla and could have done better!

Suddenly their conversation was interrupted by Hermione flying across the space towards them. The next instant another rumble began from deep in the mountain. It didn't last long, but was intensely scary, a kind of deep grinding, graunching sound that set their teeth on edge. The ground shook and shards of rock dropped down from the high sides and roof of the cavern, enough to make them bend over their knees, arms held protectively around their heads. As the mountain settled again, Hermione emerged from under Tom's knees and washed her whiskers.

"How did you know that was about to happen Hermione?" he asked.

"Just a sense," she replied with an enigmatic look on her face. "If I've got to be under this mountain, I can at least pay attention to what it's telling me!"

"Did you know about the first one?" he asked curiously.

"I just felt unease, but I was still feeling disoriented from being here and didn't pay as much attention as I could have."

"So next time you'll warn us as soon as you can?" Tom asked her.

"Does that mean I have to go to the other cavern with you? I didn't see myself in the thought image…"

Galawand, who had been listening to their conversation, said firmly that Hermione would accompany them, that it was important that she knew her way to and from the central cavern. It crossed Sarah's mind to wonder why, but was distracted by suddenly realising that Galawand, an adult, could understand and talk to Hermione!

"How did you do that?" she asked. "We thought that only kids could tune into her."

"People have to learn to thought-share when they're young, but that doesn't mean they lose that skill as they get older. The two of you could learn how to broaden your ability to other than Hermione and Ryder over the next while if you want to. Kayla has been focusing on different forms of magic while she's been with me, but she may also have the ability if she wants to learn."

They looked at each other in wonder. They'd almost got used to being able to talk to Ryder and Hermione, and had to be reminded by Mary and Arthur that it was a special gift. What if they could 'talk' to each other that way too? Is that what Galawand was referring to? They couldn't ask her right now – she'd already turned away to where Arthur and Mary were lightening their packs to contain just the essentials they may need for their journey to the centre of the mountain. They moved over to them to help, Sarah brushing her hand across Tom's arm, causing him to shiver. He really wished all this was out of the way so they could spend time getting to know each other properly.

When they were ready, they said goodbye to Galawand, a sombre feeling settling on them as they realised that this might be the last time they saw her if anything bad happened on the next part of their journey. They hugged her as she wished them well, then followed Kayla and Hermione silently to the cavern entrance. They didn't look back, their fear of the unknown ahead absorbing all their energy and focus. Galawand watched them as they were swallowed up into the passageway, silently sending out with them a plea for their safety.

Chapter VII

Journey to the Centre

As they left Galawand's cavern, the passage walls closed in around them, with a weighted hush they all felt, but couldn't really put into words. It was about appreciating how small they were inside the vast mountain, fear of what they may encounter, and feeling vulnerable as they experienced the heaviness of responsibility for the future of North Feasgar that settled on their shoulders. It helped that Kayla led the way confidently, first across the river, then through the passages. They tried to keep alert to the turns as they walked further towards the centre of the mountain, the floor beneath them climbing gradually upwards, and becoming narrower and littered with debris. They had to concentrate to make their way without tripping, and were relieved when Kayla eventually turned towards them and said she thought they were almost there.

"Is it my imagination, or is it getting warmer?" asked Arthur. The others had been so busy focusing on watching where they put their feet that they hadn't paid attention to anything else, but when he mentioned it, they noticed beads of perspiration gathering on their foreheads and down the backs of their necks.

"It wasn't this warm last time," Kayla said.

"It's not meant to be an active volcano though," said Tom, puzzled. "Unless maybe the dark magic that's making the tremors is disturbing the mountain's core...?" They looked at each other fearfully.

"Well, it would be far hotter than this if it was thinking about erupting any time soon," said Arthur, putting on a sensible voice to try to calm their fears. Tom and Sarah would have enough to cope with in the cavern without worrying about a possible eruption as well. "We're fortunate to be here now to retrieve the amulets – if we'd waited, it may not have been possible. Let's get a move on and get the next part over with."

When they emerged from the final passage, they stared around them in awe.

"Wow!" gasped Sarah. "That's amazing!"

They were looking at a massive cavern, with a vaulted ceiling that soared high above. Narrow shards of light penetrated down from its apex into the gloom, faintly illuminating a funnelled structure at the top that looked a bit like a short chimney. They really were right in the centre of the mountain.

"It doesn't look like anything I've read about volcanoes," said Tom, "I guess it was the main vent for lava the last time it erupted. The plug in the top must have crumbled since then, letting in the bit of light we can see. Watch out for your feet – the lava on the floor in here will be rough and quite sharp if it's anything like the lava caves on Rangitoto, though it's massively bigger than they are!"

"What's Rangitoto?" Mary asked.

"A volcano in the sea just out from Auckland. It last erupted about two hundred and fifty years ago. I went there a few times on school trips. Can you smell that?" he asked. As they breathed in, they could smell some wafts of sulphur. "That means that there's some activity in the core, way down in that hole in the middle that we saw in Galawand's thought image. I vote we don't go over and try to look unless we want a very long fall with a hot ending!"

The light from their brands scarcely penetrated the surrounding dark. If it wasn't for the dim light cast from above, they wouldn't have been able to see the gaping hole dominating the centre of the cavern. Sarah felt her stomach clench in a knot of fear as she remembered the dream she'd had the first time she was in North Feasgar, and the feeling of absolute terror as she'd fallen down into an abyss. She wanted to be brave, but she couldn't stop herself from starting to shake, suddenly feeling cold and as if her knees were made of jelly. She tried to speak but nothing came out of her mouth. Hermione rubbed herself against Sarah's legs, reminding her that she was with her, and she stopped to pick her up, snuggling into her reassuring presence. Tom reached out to stroke Hermione too, and Mary and Arthur came in close, putting their arms around them all, a small group huddled by the wall in the shadows, partly overwhelmed by the majestic beauty of the cavern and partly by terror. They held each other closely while they gathered the emotional strength to keep going.

Tom took a deep breath and raised his head to look around. "Look across there to our left," he said, pointing to a ridge on the wall. "That looks like the path we saw ourselves climbing in the thought image." They looked in the direction he was pointing. It was hard to make out in the gloom, but he was right. There was a consistent break in the cavern wall, likely to be deliberately made rather than natural, rising on a fairly steep angle from floor level to a dark wedge part-way up the cavern.

"Okay, let's get on with it before my nerves freeze me to the spot," Sarah said, swallowing hard.

"Now that you know where you are, it's time for me to leave," Kayla said. "Stay safe and come back to us soon – we'll be thinking about you all the time! Good luck," she added, giving Tom and Sarah a hug. She waved at Arthur and Mary as she turned away to the cavern entrance, disappearing quickly into the dark.

"We'll walk over to the base of the steps with you," Mary said. "We'll wait there and watch out for you. Hermione, I think you'd be best staying with us since Tom and Sarah can communicate with you and may need to find a way of letting us know if they're in any trouble."

"Hermione just suggested that if we need you to come and find us, she'll start making her way up the steps herself. Otherwise, if you're worried about anything you'll need to ask her the 'Yes or No' questions you're used to with her," Sarah translated for them. Mary and Arthur nodded. They picked up their packs and walked tentatively around the lava clumps on the floor towards the steps, hugging the edge of the cavern, keeping as far away from the central hole as they could.

"Don't you think we should be going with them?" Mary whispered to Arthur from the rear as they made their way single-file around the towering cavern wall.

"Absolutely – everything in me thinks we should. But, if we're to honour the image Galawand showed us, then we're not to do it. Maybe the steps can't support four people... maybe we're too heavy – we have no idea what condition they're in. Or maybe it's important that if something terrible happens, we can go back and report it to Galawand." He squeezed Mary's hand as they both let their minds drift to the possible horror of a disastrous ending for Sarah and Tom.

Reaching the base of the steps, they could see that they were rough-hewn from the rocky wall, clinging to the side of the mountain, rising sharply in clusters of about eight to ten steps. A short stretch of rock separated each cluster, a brief pause where they would be able to gather themselves before the next incline. They turned silently towards each other. Mary and Arthur reached for the packs Tom and Sarah were carrying.

"You won't be needing these for now, and you'll be better climbing as lightly as you can, since you'll have to carry a brand each," Arthur said.

"I just thought, what about the lamps we brought with us just in case we needed more light?" Mary asked. "I wonder whether they'd be better for climbing than the brands? They're smaller and could be set down easily on a step or the floor at the top so Sarah and Tom can use their hands?"

"Good thinking."

They opened each of their packs and took out the small, but sturdy lamps they'd taken the first time they went to Greyvyn, not knowing then that they'd find brands at the entrance. They gave one each to Tom and Sarah, lit them and propped their brands up against the wall, still burning, to fractionally push back the shadows at the base of the steps.

After a final hug, they reluctantly let each other go. Turning away from Mary and Arthur, Tom placed his foot on the first step and Sarah moved in close behind him.

"Sure you don't want to go first?" he asked her.

"No, you're good. I'm happy to follow, then I can grab you if I'm scared."

They began their slow, careful ascent, Tom in the lead, left hands in contact with the rocky wall, lamps in their right. The steps were narrow and uneven, and they took each step cautiously. The lamps cast a pale glow a short distance ahead, but not enough to really see how far they had to go, or what they were heading towards. Sarah was really glad to have Tom's reassuring presence ahead of her, letting her focus on breathing to control her nerves, concentrating on his back rather than thinking about the increasing distance of the drop to their right.

As they reached the end of the first set of steps, Tom paused to make sure she was okay, touching her reassuringly before setting off on the next set. She was really grateful for each pause, breaking up the ascent into manageable bites, with the flat piece representing a moment of safety where she could temporarily draw a breath.

Time passed in a strangely distorted way. They moved slowly and steadily, finding their own rhythm in the quiet of the cavern, the only noise being their footfalls on the rock and the sound of their breathing, becoming more laboured the higher they climbed. They experienced the weirdest feeling of their whole world closing down to consist only of what lay within the little bubble of light surrounding them. Nothing outside it existed or mattered.

"How far now? Can you see anything?" Sarah eventually whispered, reluctantly breaking the silence as they had a brief reprieve on one of the platforms.

"I'm not sure. Here, hold your lamp up by mine – see if that helps." With the strength of two lamps, the shadows immediately around them were pushed back a little further, but it didn't do much to dispel the dark above.

"I might be just imagining it, but I wonder if I can see a darker ledge up there?" Tom pointed upwards.

"Maybe…" It was unclear, and Sarah turned her gaze to the middle of the cavern. The narrow shafts of light were just enough to give a vague indication of the rocky floor, and suddenly she gasped as a wave of vertigo flooded her, making her lean her body back towards the wall, her arm flailing in Tom's direction.

He grasped her firmly.

"No! Don't look down!" He turned her to face him, holding her close. He stroked her hair until her rapid breathing slowed and he felt her body begin to relax. As he looked out into the cavern over her shoulder, he almost stopped breathing as he fought to contain his reaction – what was he looking at? A glow. A long, long way below. It must be down in the core of the mountain, but he could definitely see a dim source of light. The volcano must be activated, as they'd thought. It probably wouldn't pose any immediate threat, but he thought it best not to say anything to Sarah – she had enough of her own demons to deal with.

"What's wrong?" she suddenly asked.

"Nothing. Why do you ask?"

"You went tense."

"Sorry. I was just worrying about you and hoping we don't have far to go." He hated lying, but there really wasn't anything dangerous to worry about right now. He let her go and stepped towards the next set of steps, making sure she was close behind as they ascended once more.

It didn't feel like long before Tom's voice pulled Sarah out of her tight focus on stepping and breathing.

"Look! We were right." He was pointing to a dark line that could be a platform above the next set of steps. By the time they stepped up onto flat rock, they could see it stretching out from the steps, slightly diagonally, to create a large, flat space suspended over the cavern.

"Wow, I wonder how they made this," gasped Tom. "There must have been an outcrop that someone worked on to make a flat ledge. Whatever they've left here has to be important for all that work!"

"We've arrived," Sarah's thought message to Hermione was returned with a reassuring purr, which she could swear wrapped around her like a hug. She smiled in spite of her worry about what they were facing. Hand in hand she and Tom hesitantly moved forward, lamps held high. Within the limits of their light, they could see a mound of objects stretching from the cavern wall, inwards, across a space that looked like the length of maybe two tables placed end to end. They couldn't tell how far back it extended. Advancing slowly, they had to pick their way around debris lying on the ground that became more concentrated as they got closer to the mound. They were so focused on what was ahead of them, that it wasn't until Tom's shoe collided with something hard and he heard it tumble, clattering onto the rock, that he looked down properly, realising with horror that he'd just kicked a pile of bones! He gasped, making Sarah turn her lamp towards the ground. She screamed as she saw a skull's sightless eyes staring vacantly up at her, its mouth gaping in a silent scream.

"Oh my God, people really *have* died!" It was one thing for Galawand to have told them, another to actually see the reality. Sarah felt sick right down to the soles of her feet, and was suddenly overcome by a desperate desire to get out – to flee the cavern, and the mountain and never return. Tom put his hand on her shoulder and steered her away, leading her to the mound.

"Come on, we can do this," he said as reassuringly as he could. Sarah swallowed hard and tried to pull herself together. As they approached it, they saw that rather than being an enormous mound of objects, it was a rock formation, with objects placed on top of it.

"Well thank goodness, there aren't as many things to look through as I imagined," Sarah observed. "We don't want our lamps to run out before we get back down!"

The shapes on the rock were covered in dust and varied in shape.

"We're looking for two amulets... right?" queried Tom, looking down, wondering where to start. "How about you go left towards the wall, while I head around the rock in the opposite direction?" Looking directly in front of him, he could see a large box. "How will we know where the amulets are? I mean, they could be in a box like this..."

"I don't know. I think we have to trust our intuition. Let's just see what happens, and if we can't find them, then we'll have to start looking inside things," Sarah replied.

The box's lid was covered in a thick layer of dust, but he imagined it was wooden. Behind it, he could see some sort of cage. It was eight-sided, with bars that faintly glinted in the light given off by the lamp. Probably a metal then. A gilded cage... The eight upright bars curved together at the top, forming a shape a bit like a circus tent. It looked elegant and was intricately designed. As he reached over to touch it, his arm brushed the box and dislodged little puffs of dust, beneath which he could see a dark timber. Rubbing it lightly with his fingers brought up a deep, glowing patina, with intricate carving. These pieces seemed to be beautifully made, and he wondered why they'd been left there.

A little off to his right, he spied a large, spherical shape that intrigued him. He moved over to look at it more closely, kneeling on the floor to see it better. What was it? The top looked spherical, but other things were in front of it, so if the base was resting on the rock, maybe it was egg-shaped. He ran one finger down the surface. Underneath the dust, it was shiny and very smooth, and was a slightly iridescent gunmetal colour. He shuffled closer on his knees, with the object at eye-height in front of him. It was a little too large to lift with one hand, and it might be heavy, so he reached with both hands over the bowl sitting in front of it…

Meanwhile, Sarah had moved over to three piles of books. The spines were facing her, and in the dim light, she could just pick out shades of blue, red, burgundy and black, with gold lettering. She was attracted to one on top of the second pile. Running her hand lightly over it, she could feel the soft leather under her finger-tips. She blew gently across the cover to reveal a deep blue colour, with a title in gold, written in a language she'd never seen before. Her index finger traced the lettering almost of its own volition, stroking it, and she found herself itching to reach over to pick up the book and open it. She extended her arm, but then a voice in her head said "Stop!" She froze, realising that if she'd lifted it, she too may have ended up a pile of bones. They'd been very clearly told not to take anything not intended for them. She curled her outstretched fingers into a fist and brought it back to her body. She drew in her breath sharply, suddenly realising that the feeling of compulsion was the same sensation as she'd had with the elixir. It was trying to draw her in, to seduce her. Maybe all these things had a spell on them. Suddenly she thought about Tom. *Oh, my goodness, he hasn't experienced this pull before – has he remembered we're not to take anything?* She turned in time to see him touching something several feet away.

"Tom! No! Don't pick it up!" she yelled, just as he reached his arms across to the object. She saw him pause. "Stop, Tom!" she said with so much vehemence in her voice that he moved his hands away and turned to look at her.

"What was that about?" Tom asked, bemused, as Sarah made her way over to him.

"Do you remember Galawand saying to us not to take anything that wasn't meant for us, anything other than the amulets?" Sarah asked.

"Well, yes, but I wasn't going to take anything. I was just looking at it." He felt strangely like a little boy, feeling belligerent and making excuses.

"And it was somehow enticing you to, wasn't it?"

"What do you mean?"

"I think the objects have a spell on them. They feel like the elixir – they draw us to want to pick them up, and anything that has a magical hold on us like that, has to be dangerous. If we want something badly it can change who we are – like, I imagine you were probably quite cross with me for stopping you."

"Yes, I was," Tom said wonderingly. "It felt like you were being unreasonable, stopping me from doing something I really wanted to do, like a little boy wanting a toy."

"Let's keep going – we both need to be very careful," Sarah warned.

For the next half hour or so they slowly looked over the remaining objects, trying to focus on finding the amulets, rather than letting themselves get absorbed in any one piece. They weren't classically valuable pieces, like precious jewels or money; it was more that they were unknown, unusual, interesting, alluring, fascinating, and enticed fingers to touch and explore.

Eventually they'd searched all the obvious places on the rock with no sign of anything that resembled amulets. They felt tired and defeated. Now they'd have to worry about looking inside things that they could be hidden in, and risk disturbing something 'not intended for them'. At what point would the spell deem that they were taking something? If they lifted it, or just if they opened something they shouldn't? How would they know whether to take the risk? Sarah had been confident earlier about

179

her intuition, but now she was full of doubt, and since Tom didn't totally trust himself not to touch something for the wrong reason, they decided to stay together while they kept looking.

"Actually, maybe that's what we always needed to do anyway," Sarah pointed out. "Think about the Anam Cara, what it means, and the prophecy – that two of us, together, have a power that's greater than the two of us separately... Hold on a minute... I'm just thinking about what I read in my book back at Riverstone. It went something like: '*Have courage and stand tall. When the Anam Cara is lined up inside and outside, we'll find our true power*'... I wonder if that means something for us now, whether it's a clue?"

"We've got nothing to lose if we try to figure it out that way. I don't know what else we can do other than risk our lives by opening every box or container on the rock," Tom said despairingly.

"Okay then... The first part about having courage – I think we're proved that in spades coming here. Standing tall?" Sarah looked about her. "We've searched everything down here in front of us. If we were to 'stand tall', what different perspective would that give us? Is there something at head height we could only see by standing up? We've only been looking down at the things on the rock. Is there a ledge or something?"

They gazed around them – the only possibility for something to be at head height would be on the cavern wall. They moved closer so that their lamps could cast light on it. Starting where the steps emerged onto the platform, they explored the wall as it ran back towards the mound, their lamps held high. It was irregular, but didn't have any breaks in the surface until they were just a step away from the mound of objects.

"Look!" Tom exclaimed, his lamp shining on a disturbance

in the wall just beyond them at chest height. They stood together directly in front of it, and it emerged out of the shadows to become a shelf cut into the rock, formed around a natural crevice, but extended by human hands to create a space large enough to hold a rectangular box. They stared at it, suddenly feeling inadequate and scared. What should they do now? Should they open it? Could they move it? Was it intended for them?

"What do we do now?" Sarah whispered, her voice shaking. Tom reached out to touch it – it felt hard and cold, like some sort of metal. He felt around the top of it, finding that it was hinged on the back edge. The top was clearly a lid, but he couldn't find a way into it. There was no key, no springing catch, nothing he could depress or pull.

"It's strong. We won't get into it unless it wants us to, so I guess we need to leave it where it is while we figure out how to get into it."

"What are the indents on the top?" Sarah asked, leaning in a bit closer with her light. They could see a border around the top of the box, and within its frame, there were four separate parts, each with irregular indents cut into the metal. "Is it... is it something like a key?" she wondered aloud. "Well, four keys. It looks like there are four bits to fit into the right position on the top. I wonder if, when they're in place, we'll be able to open it?"

"That's clever," Tom said, admiringly. "So, we need to look for four rectangles as wide as the box, but about a quarter the length." He went to move towards the cluster of objects.

"Wait a minute," Sarah stopped him. "Let's think for a moment... The bit after 'standing tall' must be important too..."

"Say it again?" Tom prompted.

"I don't remember exactly, but something about within and without being the same."

"So, something about the Anam Cara?"

"Yes, I guess we're here, on the outside, searching for the amulets and, according to the legend, we represent the Anam Cara between us. But what could express that on the top of the box to let us get to the amulets 'within'?"

They were silent for a while. Tom felt out of his depth. He was great at the practical things, how they worked, how to make them, but the world of intuition and symbols and stuff was Sarah's and sometimes he felt quite stupid even trying to get his head around it. Sarah seemed to sense his discomfort.

"Tom, you've gone away... Remember, we're in this together. That's what the Anam Cara is about. We both have our parts to play in all this, and it's important that we're different, that we complement each other, because that's how we can be more than the two of us!" He didn't reply, but he squeezed her hand. "Hey, I wonder..." she suddenly said. "What about the Anam Cara symbol? Might that have to fit on the top of the box?" She suddenly felt excited. That feeling that came when her intuition 'clicked' inside her.

"Can you remember what it looks like?" Tom asked. "I haven't ever really looked at it properly, though I remember the top piece for some reason, it's got a flat line crossing the upright near the top, then a few going through it diagonally."

"I kind of remember... Well, enough that if we find four pieces I can probably put them in order. And anyway, the 'key' underneath is different for each piece, so they'll only fit into one set of grooves. Come on, let's look for them."

Tom found the first piece, then soon after saw the second lying close by. The third took more time, until Sarah eventually spotted it, upside down, behind a pile of books. The fourth one though, remained elusive. They searched the objects thoroughly,

182

and still couldn't find it. Sarah was starting to feel anxious. The lamps were getting low on oil – they were less than a quarter full, and Hermione had started sending messages to them to make sure they were okay. Where else could they look? It was so frustrating – they felt so close.

"What about the floor? Maybe it's been knocked onto the ground," Tom suggested. He moved back to the general proximity of where they'd found the other three. An initial sweep with his lamp didn't reveal anything, but when he moved closer to the box, in the corner where the rocky mound met the cavern wall, he found another pile of bones. They must have moved past it without noticing when they first started looking for the keys. He put the lamp on the floor and crouched down. *Ugh!* There was nothing for it, he'd have to look under the bones, even if that was super creepy.

"Eeuwww…" Sarah said, standing beside him, holding the light over the pile. Tom carefully lifted a long bone from on top – an arm, he guessed. Underneath, he could see the rounded edge of a skull, nestling beneath other bones. Sarah gave the pile a nudge with her foot and set off a tumbling avalanche that clacked onto the floor like falling skittles in ten-pin bowling.

"What…?" Tom started to ask, but Sarah just shook her head at him.

"I know we need to be respectful, but we're running out of time. Look…" she pointed at the fourth key, lying amidst the bones. "This person probably picked it up when they shouldn't have, and dropped it when they died."

As they carried the pieces over to the box, Tom suddenly realised that they hadn't given any thought to what might happen to them when they picked them up. In the pressure to find them, they hadn't even thought about it. When he said this out loud to

Sarah, she just said, "So it must have been meant to be – they were meant for us." Tom wished he could be as sure as she was about things that weren't rational, that he could trust himself the way she did. He was much better than he used to be, and trusted people like Mary and Arthur in a way he never could have in the past, but how to be more confident in himself was a 'work in progress', as Arthur reminded him.

Looking closely at the four pieces, they both recognised the first piece, as Tom had described it.

"Let's put them in place together, so it really does represent the Anam Cara on the outside as well," said Tom. "Put your hand on top of mine." He held the piece over the box and, with Sarah's hand resting on his, guided it down so the grooves slotted into the indents on the lid. It slipped into position smoothly, with an almost inaudible click. Between Sarah's memory of the symbol and the indents on the box, they quickly placed the remaining three pieces. As the last one slid into place, they heard a dull clunk.

"Now what?" Sarah asked. Nothing had sprung open; the lid remained to all appearances just as it had previously – closed. Tom ran his hands around the edges, as he had earlier, fingers searching for something new, any small irregularity to press. There was nothing. With a rising sense of urgency, he then slid his hands over the top, checking that all the pieces were properly in place. He suddenly had a thought and leaned hard on the edge opposite the hinges. There must have been a hidden pressure switch, like the ones on the kitchen cupboards back at his mum's place in New Zealand, because as he let it go, the lid clicked upwards and he was able to get a finger underneath and lift it. It swung open to reveal something inside wrapped in a piece of dark brown fabric. Tom lifted the package gingerly, a little afraid of what they might find. Whatever was inside was hard, made of metal maybe, though not terribly heavy. Sarah unwrapped the cloth, and in Tom's hands lay two silver bands, carved with intricate designs that looked ancient. They were both the same size, and were larger than either of their wrists.

"The amulets..." Sarah breathed. "What if they're too big for us?"

"Let's just see what happens. Which arm do I put mine on?" Tom asked.

"Mine goes on my left; yours on your right," Sarah replied.

They slid them over their hands and onto their wrists. Then they gasped in astonishment, as, remarkably, the amulets adjusted themselves to fit onto their arms perfectly, like a glove. There wasn't even a seam between the amulets and their skin. It was as if they'd become a permanent part of them, forever. Sarah looked at Tom in shock.

"What have we done? How do we get rid of them?"

"I guess we don't – I think they're meant to be part of us now."

They didn't feel like they were wearing metal, but when they ran their fingers across the silver surface of the amulet and onto their skin, their sense of touch could pick up the coolness and different texture of the metal compared to their arms.

"I don't even know what to feel any more," Sarah finally managed to say. "This is all too weird. How come you're so calm?"

"I guess it's so far out of my experience that all I can do is be practical about it. Like, all I'm thinking now is that we've got to get out of here, and we'll sort out how we feel about it later," Tom replied.

"I wonder what would happen though if we clasp hands,"

Sarah's curiosity was getting the better of her terror. "I'm just thinking about the principle of something being greater than the two of us. I'm guessing that we have the amulets on opposite wrists so we can join them together somehow. Can we just try it before we go?" She extended her left hand to Tom, which he clasped in his right. Nothing happened immediately, but then they noticed a warmth growing between their palms, and a sense of energy. They looked at each other.

"What if we point our hands towards something?" Tom suggested. They positioned their clasped hands towards the cavern wall and suddenly a stream of golden light surged from their hands and ricocheted off the wall, bouncing off an earthenware vase on the mound, shattering it into hundreds of pieces. They jumped in fright, breaking their handhold.

"Oh my goodness," Sarah exclaimed, "what just happened?"

"Wow!" was all Tom could say for a while. "Can we try again, but this time aim upwards to we don't hit anything?"

"I think you were right before – it's time we got out of here. Look how low the lamp oil is. And, if we wait until we see Galawand, she'll be able to help us learn how to use them."

With a strange mix of reluctance and eagerness, they moved over to the stairs, leaving the objects behind for someone else to find in the future. Tom went first, his hand on the cavern wall for balance as he started to descend the steps. Sarah felt too disoriented to go down upright, worrying about being hit by an attack of vertigo. She turned and backed down, feet first, with her hands on the steps above. It was a bit clumsy, as she had to manoeuvre her lamp from step to step to take it with her. She sent Hermione a message, letting her know they were beginning their return.

They made good progress – in their minds it seemed much

easier than it had when they were going up the stairs.

"Probably because we were so afraid, heading into the unknown, or a bit like going anywhere for the first time – it always seems longer," Tom said when Sarah commented about it.

Now that the unknown part of their journey into the mountain was over, they both experienced a sense of relief so profound that they felt a surge of light-heartedness. They chatted about North Feasgar and what they wanted to do in the future, avoiding their deeper worries about what they may need to do next. It was like they were creating a little island drenched in sunlight, while not far away the mainland was being enveloped in a dark storm they were choosing not to look towards.

They were laughing about a story of Tom's, where Ryder carried a still-alive rat and dropped it at Mary's feet as a gift, when suddenly a growling, guttural sound came from deep in the earth below them. It jolted them out of their complacency, immediately plunging them back into their earlier terror. It was like the mountain was waking up, hungry, and any minute could send out a fiery tongue in search of food to capture and devour them. Tom yelled as the steps bucked momentarily beneath their feet. He lunged to grab Sarah's arm, but in the process was thrown backwards down the steps, falling heavily onto the flat area below. He heard a clanging sound and realised he'd dropped his lamp. It clattered off the rock – then there was a brief silence, followed by a crashing sound as it hit the cavern floor below. Sarah's light inched down towards him.

"Are you okay?" she asked, shakily grabbing hold of him as they huddled together on the narrow platform. They clung together, shaking and breathless until their nerves calmed down.

"That was close. I've just got a bruised bum I think. I thought

I was going to keep tumbling down. Thank goodness you're okay."

"I was just lucky a bit of rock was jutting out near my hand that I could grab," Sarah said. "Backing down in my paranoid style made me more stable too, I think."

"Thank goodness you've still got your lamp. Shall I carry it?" Tom asked. "If we keep close together, with it between us, we should be all right…"

"So, I need to go first then if I'm going to carry on backwards. Then the light will be on my face and hands, but close enough to your feet if you're going to continue upright the way you were."

"I think I'll copy your crawling style, but that means I'll go down first so I can hold the light near your feet!" he gave a half laugh as he manoeuvred himself into position ready to back down the narrow steps into the endless gloom below.

They were subdued as they continued their descent. All their light-hearted humour had evaporated along with the loss of their lamp. It was as if it signalled the approaching darkness of a re-emerging unknown. The last sets of steps seemed endless. Sarah started talking to Hermione for reassurance, with her calm presence accompanying them down the last stretch. It was just as their lamp showed them that they were almost back to ground level that they felt another tremor. It was sudden, longer than the one before and very intense. Tom managed to hold firm, huddled up against the wall, but Sarah was caught unawares this time and tumbled past him down the last steps onto the rocky floor.

"Sarah!" Tom yelled. He'd tried to grab her as she fell past, but it happened too quickly. He rushed down the steps and arrived at her crumpled form at the same time as Hermione, closely followed by Mary and Arthur. Sarah stirred.

"I'm okay… I'm okay," she managed to say, struggling to sit up. "Ow!" she exclaimed as she put her hands to the ground to lever herself up, "my wrist hurts!"

They helped her to her feet and walked her over to where they'd been waiting a little back from the steps. She felt shocked and shaky, her legs sagging as if her bones had been turned to liquid.

"Let's have a look," said Arthur.

"Oh, my word," exclaimed Mary, "what's this you're wearing?" They were looking at her amulet, glowing dully in the light of a brand. Tom held his wrist out too, showing them the matching pair. "The amulets," Mary breathed in awe. "You got them!" She gave them both a hug.

"Your wrist, Sarah," Arthur pulled them back to practicalities. "It might be broken just below the amulet."

"Should we use the elixir to see if we can heal it?" Hermione asked.

"No!" Sarah said firmly. "We might have more need for it yet. I don't want to use it for this, when we might need to save someone's life later."

"Okay, then we'll need to bind your wrist so you don't move it. Mary, could you get the bandages from the pack?"

Mary wrapped Sarah's wrist tightly. It hurt, but Sarah tried to put it out of her mind, determined to get away from the cavern and back to Galawand as quickly as possible. As they prepared to pick up their belongings, she noticed herself wiping her forehead. Was it her imagination, or was it substantially warmer than when they'd arrived? Kayla had said it was warmer this time than when she'd last been here, but she was sure it had changed even further in the relatively short time they'd been looking for the amulets. Maybe it was just stress and reaction to her fall? She then noticed that Tom was sweating too.

"Is it getting warmer?" she eventually blurted out, not wanting to worry anyone.

"Yes," Hermione confirmed. "With each tremor the heat has increased. The core of the volcano is warming up. It doesn't mean it will erupt, but it's a serious problem, especially for Galawand and the barrier."

Sarah passed on what Hermione was saying to Mary and Arthur.

"I wonder whether the Mages are doing that deliberately, or whether it's just a side-effect of them trying to disturb the barrier?" Arthur wondered.

"Come on, let's get out of here!" Mary said. They put on their packs and moved across to the cavern entrance, with Hermione and Sarah leading the way. Sarah had Kayla's piece of paper, but she'd also memorised the directions to take at each fork, and Hermione just knew – her sense of direction didn't need a map!

***

Their return was uneventful. It didn't seem long at all before they stepped out of the final passage to the river crossing. Once again, Hermione led them across the invisible bridge and they hurried to Galawand's cavern, entering it to see Galawand and Kayla standing by the stone circle, intently studying the red field.

"Galawand, Kayla," Tom called out. They turned towards them and crossed the cavern chamber, arms extended in welcome.

"Oh, my goodness, you're back! What happened? How did it go?" Kayla exclaimed excitedly.

They met and embraced, the relief palpable between them. Tom and Sarah extended their wrists, revealing the amulets gleaming softly against their skin.

Galawand gasped. "You did it then. Oh, well done! But what's this, Sarah? What have you done to your wrist?" she asked, concern in her voice.

"I fell. It might just be a sprain, but it's pretty sore."

"Let me have a look. Kayla, go and get the healing balm, and a cup of my nectar." Sarah extended her wrist, which Galawand took gently in her hands. She undid the bandaging and felt the bones with her eyes closed. "I sense there's a break, through the bone that goes from your elbow and down to your thumb, just here, at the bottom of your wrist. It's called your radius."

"We thought a drop of the elixir might help to heal it, but Sarah wants to save it in case we need it for more serious injuries if things go wrong with the barrier," Mary said.

"Thank you for being so thoughtful, Sarah," Galawand said as she started putting a thick layer of balm on her wrist. "I really hope we don't need it for a crisis, but we just don't know!... My own nectar should help, along with the balm. It has arnica in it to limit the swelling, as well as turmeric and ginger for pain. We'll splint it too." She took the bandage that Kayla was handing to her and tightly wrapped it once again. Kayla had also brought from the cupboard some small wooden splints latticed together with a heavy thread, and tied the bundle securely under her wrist on top of the bandage to brace it. Sarah drank the nectar from the cup Kayla handed her, remembering the first time she'd had it when she met Galawand – *was that really just six months ago?* Like last time, it had a magical quality and immediately soothed her weariness, also dulling the ache in her arm.

"Now, we need to talk about what happens next," Galawand

said, leading them to the cushions to sit. "Kayla and I are very concerned about the barrier. Those last tremors followed stronger assaults on it – we could see serious disruptions in the field. I'm also concerned that the tremors are becoming more frequent, and stronger. They could damage the passages through the mountain and make it too dangerous for us to stay, which will obviously mean that we can't maintain the barrier. Whether or not that's what they intend, we just don't know. With their intent to harm the barrier, they may not realise that their magic is also causing internal damage."

"The core of the volcano is heating up too," Tom added. "It'll take a while to get anywhere near erupting, but it seems to be being activated either by the magic or the tremors."

"What do we do?" Sarah sounded panicky.

"I'm not sure… I have an idea of what needs to unfold, but not how the next stage will begin. We have time yet to plan."

"What are you thinking though?" Arthur asked.

"Well, for a very long time we've existed in the north in harmony, because we've been isolated from the south. But they're growing stronger, and we're using more and more of the energy and magic available to us trying to hold them off. I'm thinking that the arrival of Sarah and Tom signals that it's time to change the existing order; time to face the dark of the south, to overcome the evil Mages and forge a new world with the good people who must be living in the south." Galawand saw the expressions of horror on their faces and said, more softly, "I know that must feel like so much responsibility, but if the time is right, you have been chosen because you're capable of this. And you won't be alone. Mary and Arthur are essential in supporting you, Kayla and I have our own roles, and all the good people of North Feasgar are rallying while we're together here, creating

192

backup either for a fight, or for organising a new order – we don't quite know what that will be yet."

"Don't forget Hermione and Ryder," Sarah reminded her, stroking Hermione, to which she responded by arching her back to encourage her to rub it vigorously.

"Yes, you'll not find better friends than Hermione and Ryder – you only know half their capabilities yet. The Mages aren't going to have it all their own way!"

Silence hung in the air for a while as they absorbed all Galawand had said. She decided it was time to help them to think practically again so they didn't get lost in their fear.

"Have you tried out what you can do with your amulets yet?" Galawand asked.

"A bit, but we decided to wait for you in case we accidentally destroyed something. Our first attempt was a bit random," Tom said sheepishly.

"Okay, we'll start with that then. Come and stand together facing me." She moved to the centre of the cavern and stood them both in front of her. She slowly led them into a similar form of the meditative state that she'd taught them for holding the energy of the stone circle, focusing initially on their breathing; deep breaths in, using their diaphragms, then out, repetitively. When they were calm she talked them through to a feeling of being centred and whole, and to feeling connected to each other. She then invited them to hold their hands, Sarah's left connected to Tom's right, amulet to amulet. The feeling between them intensified, so strong now that they both found tears leaking from the corners of their eyes – they'd never experienced anything like it before. She then guided them to raise their joined arms up into the air. A pale beam of golden light streamed from their hands up towards the vaulted peak of the cavern. As they maintained their position it grew stronger and lighter.

"Okay, that's enough for the first time," Galawand said after a short time. "Sarah, how is your wrist?"

"It's okay. It throbs a bit, but I can manage it."

"Now we're going to try to intensify the effect with the support of Mary and Arthur. Mary, come and stand to the right of Sarah, your left hand on her right shoulder; Arthur, stand on Tom's left with your right hand on his left shoulder." She led them all through the exercise again. This time the effect was much more powerful. The beam of energy, now almost white in its intensity, streamed up above Tom and Sarah. Where it reached the dome of the cavern, bits of rock started crumbling off the surface of the rock, dropping down to hit the floor near where they were standing, so Galawand stopped them. *Just in time*, Sarah thought. She grabbed her wrist, which was now aching with a deep throb, not sure whether to massage it, or whether that would aggravate it further.

"Enough for now. Sarah, you need to rest your wrist. Kayla, could you please get her some more of the nectar..." Galawand continued, a very serious tone in her voice, "When you need to really harness and unleash your power, use those principles but focus on what it is you want to effect, wrap your collective energy around the energy from the amulets and concentrate it on whatever you're aiming for."

"But what if it's a person? Would it kill them?" Tom asked, afraid of what the answer might be.

"You'll know what you need to do at the right time," she responded, without giving him a direct answer. "I don't know what's going to happen, but I trust that the four of you will do what's right. None of you are cold-hearted killers, but you may need to make some hard decisions for the good of the land and the people who live in it… Now, it's time you all had some dinner and a rest, and in the morning we'll consider what we need to do next."

***

A few hours later, Tom and Sarah were lying on cushions on the floor, talking quietly, unable to switch off and go to sleep, despite being bone-weary.

"Tom, how come you don't get scared like I do? I feel so stupid sometimes because I feel so small beside all the things happening that are outside my control – the vastness of the mountain, the tremors, the magic of the south. How can two of us make any difference to that? I kind of become even smaller when I'm scared. But you… somehow you stay strong and don't lose it the way I do."

Tom didn't say anything for a while. "Well, I guess I've spent most of my life feeling small, feeling totally useless and humiliated because of the way Gerald treated me. I felt so small because of one person who had power over me – he was the source of *my* feeling of having no control. And now he's not in my life, not even in this world, so somehow natural events just kind of… are… They're here and happening but they're not personal to me. They're not picking on me, they don't have a personal vendetta to bring me down, and as well as that, we're all in it together. I've never had a together before. Does that make sense?" Sarah reached out to hold his hand in the dark. He was quiet again while he thought about how much to reveal to her. "When I was, like, really little, not long after my mum met Gerald, I remember when she went out and he was meant to be looking after us, he used to make me stand behind the door in the kitchen, in the crack between the open door and the wall. I had to stand there, sometimes for hours, with nothing to eat or drink. I wasn't allowed to move, not even to sit on the floor when my legs started to shake. If I needed to go to the toilet and peed myself, I had to clean it up and he'd tell my mum I'd been a baby. I learned then that the only way to survive was to split a little piece of myself off so I could leave my body behind and be with the best part of myself somewhere else where I didn't need to live like that."

"What? Why would he do that?" Sarah said, shocked that anyone could be so mean.

"To make himself powerful? To make me seem small and weak so he could feel strong?"

"Oh, Tom, that's awful." She squeezed his hand. "I suppose he had to have control over something smaller than him to make himself feel better. He must have had something horrible happen to him when he was little. Maybe he wanted you to suffer like he had. Maybe he got confused and you became a little part of him in the dark parts of his mind... Did you ever refuse to stand there?"

"Yes, but I got hit!"

"Did you tell your mum? Didn't she notice what was happening?" Sarah asked, feeling horrified.

"Uh-huh. I asked her to take me with her when she went out, but when I told her why, she believed him, not me, when he said I'd misbehaved and couldn't take what I had coming. She said I was just being a baby." Sarah wriggled over closer to him and he put his arm around her. He thought it was funny how he could talk about this now. In the past he wouldn't have been able to get past the lump in his throat.

"Hey, I just had a thought," Sarah said, "maybe coming here,

196

through the rift, is a bit like splitting yourself off for real. You've managed to leave that world permanently to be with people who love you! And you didn't have to leave your body behind like I did the other times."

"Just as well, I probably would have died..." he said flatly.

Arms around each other, it wasn't long before they fell asleep, completely unaware that Kayla had been close enough to hear their quiet conversation. She felt really affected by what Tom had said. On the one hand it brought up memories of her own about her mad mother, but it also let her see that they all had crazy stuff to deal with and it was possible for things to get better. She loved Galawand, she loved being in this world where she had a real purpose, and an idea about what she could do in the future. Tom and Sarah, and the Birches, were good people too. In fact, everything would be good if only she knew what had happened to Jonnie!

**

They all had broken sleep that night, despite Galawand's nectar and its calming effect. With too much on their minds, they were also disturbed by multiple, small tremors that set their nerves jangling. Each time Sarah and Tom woke up they saw either Galawand or Kayla keeping vigil over the stone circle. In the morning, after about six hours of trying to sleep, Kayla woke them with tea, telling them that it was daybreak. "How does she know?" Sarah whispered to Tom. Time seemed to have little meaning so deep within the mountain – it could have been midnight or midday for all either of them could tell.

There hadn't been any disturbances to the barrier through the night. On the one hand this seemed positive, but it was also

197

worrying because it meant that the tremors were now being generated by the mountain rather than from the Mages' magic. Sarah's wrist was aching. The effects of yesterday had caught up with her, and she was finding it hard to rouse herself, appreciating the sentiment of one of her mother's sayings – that she felt like she'd been run over by a steamroller. Tom went to get breakfast for the two of them, flatbread from a hotplate suspended over the fire, with jam and butter. It smelt delicious, and he was returning, one plate in each hand, when a strong and sustained tremor hit. The ground shuddered, groaned and shifted beneath his feet. As he lurched, trying to keep his balance, he dropped a plate, which shattered as it hit the stone floor. Straightening up again, he was caught off-balance by Hermione launching herself at him, hitting him full in the chest like a cannon ball of fur, pushing him backwards to fall on his bottom, where he landed hard, jarring right up his spine. "Hermione, what the…?" Then they heard a creaking noise that turned into the sound of something splitting and cracking. A large piece of rock broke off a crevice high up the cavern wall, falling and landing with a crash on the floor where Tom had been standing just moments before. A billow of dust and rock fragments was released into the air, sending them into fits of coughing that left them feeling like they would choke.

They huddled together, holding each other for comfort, Sarah and Tom making a fuss of Hermione – she'd saved Tom's life. When the dust cleared, they could see that there had been numerous, smaller rockfalls. One of Galawand's wall hangings was on fire, from candles that had been knocked out of their stony crevices onto the fabric below. A cabinet that stored food was completely destroyed, lying beneath a large lump of rock. The stone circle was somehow still intact, but rocks were littered around it. It seemed that it was now only a matter of time before the cavern would be destroyed and it was evident that they needed to get out while they could.

They looked at each other. No one wanted to speak first, and the silence was eerie, only punctuated by a groaning sound from somewhere deep within the mountain, and a few small cracks as fragments of rock continued to drop to the ground and shatter.

"You must leave," Galawand suddenly announced.

"What? We're not leaving you, Galawand!" Kayla and Tom cried simultaneously.

"Yes, you must. It is my calling to protect the stone circle, and if I cannot, then I will give up my life trying."

"I'll stay with you, Galawand – you need me to hold the circle with you," pleaded Kayla.

"No Kayla," Galawand responded gently, "You have more life yet to live, more causes to fight for – you must go with the others... Now sit down all of you and listen to me..."

They sat together in a circle on the dusty cushions, Hermione curled up on Sarah's knee. Galawand reminded them that it was inevitable that the barrier would come down, so it was better that they timed it to work in their favour than to wait for the Mages to destroy it and have them reactively trying to contain the dark magic. She'd been thinking overnight and had decided that they would plan a time for her to drop the barrier, allowing them to pass into the south and move around the base of Greyvyn to where the Mages were trying to access the mountain. She thought that they would be aiming their magic at the opening where the River Dearth exited the mountain.

"But what do we do once we get there, Galawand?" Arthur asked. "How can the five of us, sorry, six, Hermione, fight against the might of the Mages' magic?"

"That's where you need to trust that Tom and Sarah will know what's required of them when the time comes. Trust your instincts and act immediately, all of you together. It's early in the morning now – you'll be out of the mountain and at the barrier in a few hours. When the sun is directly overhead I'll drop the barrier – you'll then have ten minutes to cross to the south before I attempt to restore it again. I may not be successful, because I may not have the strength, but get across there quickly to limit the chances of the Mages finding a way to enter the mountain before you get there. Hermione, it's not clear to me what your role in this is going to be, but carry that elixir safely. And Kayla...," she smiled at her, "thank you so much for the time we've had together – you're very special to me and whatever your role is going be in this, stay true to yourself."

In silence they gathered their belongings, helping Kayla to pack up the few things she'd accumulated over the past six months. Still in silence, they one by one embraced Galawand, wondering whether they'd ever see her again. Kayla went last, lingering over her hug, not wanting to let her go. She'd been more than a mother to her – she was the most positive influence she'd ever had in her life.

"Go! Now!" Galawand then commanded, her voice swelling and filling the chamber. As they hurried to leave, she called out after them, "Don't look back, and don't stop, whatever happens, until you're outside Greyvyn and down the steps! Stay safe!"

Chapter VIII

The Shard

The months since Linden became an Affiliate had passed quickly. The break he spent with his family had seemed much too short and he'd left Jonnie behind with conflicting feelings of envy and regret at having to leave, along with anticipation and excitement at starting the new phase of his training. The Affiliate level required less study, but long clinical hours with intense one-on-one supervision with three supervisors. While he'd kept working with Sarraphin, he'd also picked up another two supervisors, Jonas and Finola, the idea being that he needed to experience different styles of practice.

Outside his long hours of work, a groundswell of dissatisfaction with the power structures enforced by the Mage and Guardian Orders was seeping through to his friends and colleagues. With Sarraphin becoming actively involved with the group of people – Artisans, Healers and increasing numbers of the uninitiated – leading a call for change, Linden had offered his support. To begin with, he'd just attended meetings, but they'd been completely eye-opening. How come he hadn't seen what was happening before the arrival of Jonnie? Maybe because he'd been so focused on his study and didn't see much of the world, but maybe also because he hadn't really wanted to. He thought that a lot of other people were probably the same – keeping their heads down and getting on with their own lives so long as the problems others were having were kept from their awareness. Now that he'd met Jonnie though, and knew first-hand the lies they'd been told about their land and the north, it seemed incredible that he'd been so blind.

They were very careful each time they met. Different venues were used, and invitations were made person to person, never in writing. According to the Artisans and the uninitiated, who were freer to move about the city without being noticed, the level of unrest and support was growing rapidly. At first their concerns had been about the level of control the Mages had over decisions made about the land, but increasingly they were worried at the way they were being manipulated to believe the Mages' stories, which seemed to exist to keep them in power. People who spoke out, or did anything they weren't supposed to just disappeared, or were harmed, like the man who'd helped Jonnie when he'd first arrived in South Feasgar.

Over time, their group had enlisted a wide range of people who had access to the Mage and Guardian headquarters, Darthmore, the black building that dominated the Scathach landscape. The locals called it 'The Shard', although strictly speaking that was just the building's tallest spire that the Mages' magic streamed out from. Cleaners, cooks, people who were involved in the up-keep of lighting, construction, decorating, the gardens – they now had people everywhere. None of them knew who was asking them to keep watch for interesting or unusual activity; they only knew the one person who had enlisted them. There was no incentive offered to recruit, like money or position, as that could too easily lead to betrayal by a higher bidder. Instead, they were invited on the basis of being known for their good principles.

Recently Linden had been assigned to a small group of

people who sifted through details sent to them by their informers. They were mostly of little value, but random observations that had Linden's intuition standing to attention were starting to appear in a steady trickle. Combined, they showed a pattern of increasing activity – more comings and goings; an increased number of patrolling Guardians; and what looked like preparations being made for travel.

One interesting snippet came in from a cleaner, who reported a cluster of stones kept on a silver tray in the high tower, near the locked turret that the purple light emanated from. He noted the curious way the stones were moved each day, almost as if they formed patterns that had meaning. He was never allowed to linger; a Guardian kept an eye on his every move and hurried him to clean the room and move on. When Linden read this note, he felt a stab of excitement. It sounded like a form of scrying, which was one of the magical arts described in his book about divination, and he'd always wanted to try it. Why would they need to contact anyone that way, rather than by more conventional means? It wasn't a precise art, but it was useful for communicating over distance or barriers. Barriers…? What if they used it to communicate with someone in the north? What if the recent escalation in activity had something to do with that? It probably wasn't a coincidence that something different was happening so soon after Willard had been discharged from the hospital into Argin's care…

When he shared what he was thinking with Sarraphin, she added other things she'd been made aware of. Like the fact that a number of additional Guardians had moved into the barracks near the Shard. There had been reports of groups of Guardians being seen training in combat and weaponry. As they grew more concerned, Sarraphin decided that it was time to get Jonnie back to Scathach.

"If they're going to make a move on the barrier, they'll use Willard's local knowledge to help them to launch an attack on the north. We could use Jonnie here with us – even though he doesn't know North Feasgar well, he's the only one of us who's been there, who knows some of the people and a bit about the geography on the other side of the barrier," Sarraphin said.

"Okay… but how do we keep him safe? If the Mages see him they'll immediately try to dispose of him," Linden found himself feeling protective of Jonnie.

"Do you know Cowan? The man in our group who's the Master builder for the Mages. I thought that rather than being disguised as a Healer, Jonnie would be able to get about the city more easily, and hopefully into the Shard if we need backup, if he becomes one of Cowan's apprentices."

"Good thinking! Where would he stay though – an Artisan could hardly get in or out of our hostel without being noticed?"

"I'll get Cowan to sort something out for him closer to the centre of the city. How about you arrange to get a message to him, set up a time for someone to meet him, and I'll talk to Cowan?" Sarraphin suggested.

Linden sent a message and clothing for an Artisan Apprentice via the vegetable seller from his village, asking Jonnie to return to Scathach the same day in a week's time with the stall-holder. He would arrange for someone to collect him from there and take him to where he'd be staying.

***

The week passed quickly, between working with his patients and meeting with the group to sift through reports. One of the cooks had told them that they'd been asked to prepare dried meats, dehydrated fruit and vegetables, and grains for packaging. This seemed to indicate that preparation was being made for a journey. By the time the week was up, Linden was feeling edgy, wondering whether Jonnie would turn up. He didn't quite know why he was worried. He could trust the villager to pass the message on and to provide Jonnie with transport to the city, but part of him had the idea that Jonnie may like life on the farm and be reluctant to return.

The day he was due to arrive, Linden walked into the city, strolling casually between stalls, chatting to people, examining goods, all the while heading in the direction of the vegetable stall. When it was within his vision, he casually leaned against a cart and watched the stall. The stall-holder was busy bagging vegetables and talking to customers. An Artisan was sitting nearby on a folding chair, whittling at a piece of wood with a sharp-looking knife. Jonnie? He kept watching and about twenty minutes later another Artisan, an Affiliate, arrived at the stall, striking up a conversation that resulted in the two of them going off together towards a street on the far side of the marketplace. Linden waited a moment before following them, having checked first that no one else was. They took several turns that ended up in a maze of small lanes, densely packed with old, three-storied, terraced houses, sitting unevenly together, a bit wonky as if they'd been built randomly and stuck together for fun. Eventually they stopped outside a dark blue door, and the Affiliate walked up the steps and rapped on it sharply. The door opened and Linden could see the dark shape of a person inviting them inside. They entered and it was closed firmly behind them.

Linden hoped that he'd remember how to get back there. He had another hour to wait before Sarraphin joined him in the market and he couldn't loiter here, where a Healer wouldn't be a common sight. He retraced his steps, making a better mental map of where the house was – it was easier in this direction because he could follow the noises from the market.

When he stepped back into the city square, he caught his breath. He hadn't approached it from this angle before, and his view was dominated by Darthmore, towering over the city from behind. It reeked of authority and power. No, more than that, it felt somehow malign, with its severe planes of black glass giving nothing away of what was inside – something black and evil, presenting to the outside like a stark, reflective void. Maybe it was just the change of lens he was looking at it with, now that he knew things were going on that he hadn't previously been aware of. A building couldn't be evil, but the people occupying it could be…? Then again, maybe it was all in his imagination…

***

Linden and Sarraphin felt conspicuous walking through the lanes to the house, which turned out to be Cowan's. With his new-found suspicion, Linden wondered whether wearing a krill was in fact about what they'd been taught – to change their focus to inner sight and aid concentration – or whether it was more about disguise for some, or identification for others, depending on who had control.

"Do you realise, Sarraphin," Linden said as they walked, "that the Mages have ultimate control by concealing their identities when they carry out their shady business; meanwhile we stick out like sore thumbs in our white clothes – two healers in an unusual area, far from the hostel and hospital. They could set Guardians on us at any time to find out what we're up to.

We're open targets on the grounds of our clothing. How come we've never questioned the way things are before?"

"Because that's what we've always known," Sarraphin replied. "It serves the people in power to create a hierarchy. Remember too that we're far higher up in the order of things than the uninitiated. They're not even given the choice of being able to educate themselves, and that's how they're kept in their place."

"And we're all so busy being of service that we don't have time to question…"

"Once we gain awareness of what's happening there's no going back. I wonder if they're aware that there's an uprising afoot? Maybe that's what's pushing them on with whatever they're mobilising right now."

Arriving at the house, they knocked and were let in by a woman, Cowan's wife Amitra, who showed them through to the living room. Jonnie was sitting at the table with a hot drink in front of him. When he saw them, he stood up, walking across the room to embrace Linden, clapping him on the back.

"So, look at you – an Affiliate now," he said, looking at his new braid. Linden pulled off his krill and grinned at him.

"Good to see you! I'm glad you got here safely."

Behind them, the front door opened and closed again, and another Artisan called Vagan came into the room. They all sat around the table, Cowan and Amitra at each end, he and Jonnie sitting together on one side, and Vagan, and Sarraphin facing them. Sarraphin removed her krill and Jonnie drew in his breath sharply. She'd revealed thick, silver-white hair cut short to frame and accentuate a strikingly angular face, with high cheek bones and steel grey eyes. He hoped she hadn't heard him – his reaction had been to the long, wavelike scar, maybe a burn, that ran from her chin, undulating up over her left cheek, bending in to reach her ear. She turned to him and he flushed.

"Don't worry, Jonnie, it happened a very long time ago. It's the main reason I wanted to become a healer."

He felt awful, as if he'd been caught out, stealing something from a kid. He supposed she was used to people's reactions, but then again, how many people ever saw her face-to-face without her krill? He noticed Linden smiling reassuringly at him across the table and he made himself stop thinking about his discomfort to concentrate on the conversation.

"Thanks for coming, Jonnie," Sarraphin began, formally, as if she was addressing a meeting, making Jonnie suddenly realise how serious this was for them. "It was risky for you to come back, but we think the situation here is escalating, and we need you. Let me fill you in with what we think is happening. You can trust everyone here."

She proceeded to summarise the growing unrest in the city and how their group thought that the Mages and Guardians were preparing for some form of action. She told him about the intelligence gathering that supported their view.

"So where do I come in?" Jonnie asked.

"Argin has taken Willard into his care. That can only mean that he needs him – we assume for his knowledge of the north. If they're making a move towards the barrier, we'd like to follow them and keep a watch on what they're up to. And stop them if we can, of course! You're the only person we know who has any knowledge of the region around the mountain and north of the barrier. We think there has been communication between them and someone on the other side."

"The strangers?" Jonnie asked. "That wouldn't surprise me. They weren't from the north – no one knew them, and they were, well, strange! They have some sort of magic that stops the locals from seeing them clearly. Willard said that's why they needed us to do things for them. Anyway, they were getting Willard and I to spy for them." He flushed, remembering how easily he'd got sucked in by trying to impress Willard.

"Could you see them?" Cowan asked.

"Well yes, kind of. Those of us who come from my world can, I don't know why, but the people of North Feasgar can't unless the strangers choose to show themselves to them. The locals said that when the barrier was made, their magic was taken away. Something about needing it to hold the barrier, and it seems that that stops them from seeing them. It's even deadened what the strangers can do there, other than letting them conceal themselves."

"What would they be communicating with the Mages about? Given their increased activity, do you think they're planning a trip to the barrier to meet up with the strangers?" Sarraphin asked of the group.

"Well, there's one way we might be able to find out," Cowan said. "Can anyone read the symbols they use in scrying? If we can find someone who can, we could try to find a way to the tower to see what they've communicated. That would give us a heads-up to their plans."

"Scrying?" Jonnie said, "You mean like what's in Linden's book? Wow that would be cool! Linden, you know a bit about it, don't you? You talked to me about it one night."

"I haven't done it, but I understand the principles of it, and I think maybe if I centred myself like I do when I'm healing, then I might be able to get a general impression of what it means..." Linden replied hesitantly. "But how would we ever get into that building to check it out? It's fiercely guarded."

Vagan entered the conversation. He'd been sitting, listening quietly, percolating an idea.

"I've been making a locking wooden chest that the Mages have demanded that I complete in haste... I don't know what it's for, but it's big, and they obviously have something important they want to secure inside it. They want it permanently fixed to the floor or the wall, and they've been arguing with the Guardians over whether it should be located in the tower, or in the Guardians' security room in the basement. The Mages want it close to their centre of power; the Guardians want to be able to safeguard it by having it near at hand. Cowan, maybe you could take Jonnie, as your apprentice, to measure up both locations and see what you can find out. According to the cleaner who tipped us off about the scrying tray, it's located in the small room off the main tower room. You'd need to find a way to distract the guard to get in to look at it, but I'm sure we could think of a way. The main thing is to get access to that part of the building. The guard is there mainly to keep watch on the door from the tower room to the actual spike, the Shard, that the purple magic emanates from. I imagine there will be spells on that door too, to protect it, so there's a chance that the guard will have moments of being complacent and dropping his attention."

"If I remember correctly, when the lift exits into the tower room, the door to the Shard is to the right, so the smaller room with the scrying table will be on the left?" Cowan clarified.

"Yes. I haven't been there for a while, but that's what I remember," Vagan replied.

"But if I go with you Cowan, even if we can get into the scrying room, how would we know what the stones mean? Wouldn't you be better to send Linden disguised as an Apprentice?" Jonnie asked.

"I can't do that though," Linden broke in, "I can't get away from the hospital during the day for the next three days, and I think it's important to find out what we can before then – the way the Mages seem to be escalating their movements, they're planning to do something sooner rather than later so we can't delay!" There was a pause for a long moment. "Though... how good is your memory, Jonnie?"

"*Ummm*, okay I guess...?"

"I wonder, if you were to get into the scrying room and have a good look at the arrangement of the stones on the scrying tray, and memorise them, I wonder if I could 'see' them as an image if I scan your emotional body... Though of course, it may not work because it's not an emotional memory," Linden was double-thinking himself.

"Could Jonnie create an emotional memory somehow by attaching the image of the scrying stones to a feeling about someone or something?" Amitra wondered.

"I could do that! I could think about my sister Kayla and how sorry I am that she's on the other side of the barrier – something about not being able to communicate with her even though the stones are connecting to where she is. I can think about something like that and genuinely feel upset!"

"What do you think, Linden?" Cowan asked.

"It's worth a try," Sarraphin said. "And if it doesn't work the first time, I guess you can try again when you go back to install the chest, assuming that you can show that the tower is the best place for it."

Amitra brought some refreshments to the table and they spent a short time quietly eating and chatting. Linden was quiet. Eventually he interrupted the conversation.

"If the guard is standing by the door for several hours a day, presumably he'll take a break at some point, but I bet he makes you leave the room if that happens. He'll get totally bored during his shift though, especially if the Shard is secured by magic anyway... What if the two of you take flasks of drink containing one of our relaxing elixirs? You could sip on it while you work and then eventually offer him some. It'll make him feel really good. The next time you offer it to him you could slip into it a draft that makes him desperate for the toilet – you can pretend to drink it yourselves. If he has to rush away, you may have a short time to get into the scrying room to check it out."

"Hah, that sounds like something we can work with," Cowan said. "Linden, do you think you could get the potions ready for us by tomorrow? I think the sooner we try the better, in case we have to invent a reason to go back. I like the idea of fitting the chest, but they may decide they don't want it in the tower, so I'm not sure what we'll do then to give us enough time to get him to take the spiked elixir? I guess we'll just have to think on our feet."

"Yes, I can get them to you by tomorrow," Linden agreed. "I'll organise it tonight and I can drop them off when I come back for our group meeting."

A bit later when the others were talking amongst themselves, Jonnie and Linden sat out on a small terraced area at the back of the house to talk. Linden wanted to know about his family and how he'd got on with them since he left. Jonnie had brought messages from them that Linden put in his pocket to read later when he was on his own.

"Linden, I'm kind of thinking that if ever I ended up here for good, I'd actually like to be Cowan's Apprentice. Of all the things I've seen since I've been here, working with wood feels like the most natural thing for me to do."

"I wondered about that – you said something of the kind

212

when you were in hospital. And Cowan is a really good man – he's solid, honest, and you couldn't have a better teacher," Linden replied.

"But what puzzles me is, if they're in an Order, doesn't that mean they have some sort of magic? What sort of magic would a carpenter have, because I don't know anything about magic?"

"You can't say that yet... look at how you can see the strangers. You might not know what magic is where you come from, but in our land you're different somehow. And you're here for a reason, I'm sure. The magic of working with wood is about being able to feel with your hands the 'life' inherent in timber. A good carpenter can handle a piece of timber and feel its life, its grain and what it wants you to do with it. You'll know where to cut it, where to join it and how to orientate the grain so it thrives, so it has lustre and aliveness. You could say, soul. A really good craftsperson can divide or join wood with their hands – that's where their respect for the wood becomes magic!"

"Wow, that's amazing. If I could do something like that it would mean I could do something useful. Where I came from I couldn't see how I could ever be anything other than something ordinary – going to work, going home, unending nothingness! There didn't seem to be any point. I think that's why I latched onto Willard – at least he offered me something different, even though I knew he wasn't a good man."

***

As they approached the Artisan's side entrance to the massive building the following day, across a forecourt paved with grey stone, Jonnie looked up and felt stunned by the stark black façade rising sharply above them, blotting out the sky, powerful and menacing. He could see a reflection of the purple magic from the Shard tower flickering across the black mirrored surface, creating a strange feeling in his gut, part electrifying, part terrifying. Power and magic together as a physical presence reminding the population who was in control.

Cowan led the way through the entrance. Inside wasn't what Jonnie expected. Where he'd imagined impressive archways and vaulted ceilings, instead it was ordinary. A corridor led towards the centre, with doors off either side.

"This is just the trades entrance," Cowan responded, when he commented about it. "They save the grand bits for important visitors and the Mages, who enter at the front of the building. We only get to see the functional parts, which are just like any old building, though you'll get to see some of the more impressive bits when we go to the tower."

Cowan took him first to a workroom on the ground floor where a large wooden box was sitting on a trolley ready for transporting. The Master Artisan working in the room said he'd been told that if it would fit in the tower room it was to be installed there, if not, the Guardians would have their way and it was to go to their quarters in the basement.

"Any idea what it's been made for?" Cowan asked.

"No, but the locks are to have spells on them, so it's intended to house something important," the man replied.

Cowan and Jonnie measured up the chest's finished dimensions, noting them down on a piece of paper. It crossed Jonnie's mind that it may be useful later to jot down the layout of the scrying stones to help his memory, so he stuck it, with the pencil, in the pocket of his tunic. The other pocket carried the small vial of liquid to add to the flask that was looped through Cowan's belt.

"We'll check out the Guardians' quarters first," Cowan said. "It'll be good to have a genuine reason to see in there. Keep your eyes open for any information we can pass on."

They walked down a gloomy set of stone stairs to the basement, lit only by irregular lights set too high up to have much impact on the shadowy interior of the stairwell. At the bottom of the stairs a door opened out into a corridor. It was painted grey, and was austere and functional, with nothing other than plain lighting to break the bleak walls and ceiling. As they walked along the corridor, a door opened and a Guardian stepped out.

"What are you doing here?" he demanded.

"We're looking for the security room. We have to measure up for a chest we've been making – it will end up down here if it doesn't fit in the tower room," Cowan said, trying to sound business-like and a little deferential.

"And you are?" the man asked.

"Cowan, Master Artisan, and this is my Apprentice," he responded.

"This way," he said abruptly, leading them to a door further down the corridor, which opened into a large room where two Guardians were standing at attention between racks of weapons and boxes that were stacked against the walls.

"If it comes down here, where will it go?" Cowan asked.

"To the side of that weapon rack," the man replied, pointing to the other side of the room.

"Right, well there's plenty of room, so we don't need to measure," Cowan said briskly. "I'll just check the wall to see how it can be bolted. We've been told it has to be permanently secured." He walked over to the space the man had indicated, trying to notice as much as he could on the way. The boxes all seemed to be identified by a letter and a number, but there was no indication of what their contents were. He examined the wall until he found a place for a bolt and called Jonnie to him. "Pencil lad," he said, taking it from Jonnie and marking the wall with a cross. "That's all we need. We'll go to the tower now. Do we need an escort?" he said to the man.

Another Guardian was arranged to escort them to the tower, taking them through a confusing maze of underground corridors. Jonnie lost his sense of direction completely, before they emerged into a vestibule of sorts that contained another stairwell and a structure made of black metal struts that created an open-topped shaft. The Guardian pushed a button and they waited until a teardrop-shaped pod made of glass, supported by a black metal cage, dropped soundlessly into the enclosure. It was a lift, but not like one he'd ever seen before! Where were the pulleys and weights? How did it move up and down the shaft? Doors opened silently.

"You'll be met at the top," the Guardian said, stepping back and indicating that they were to enter.

The ascent was rapid. As the cage rose above the basement, Jonnie had a brief glimpse of the main entrance to the tower before they rose into its higher structure. The entrance vestibule was tall and imposing, with internal walls also crafted from obsidian into sharp planes. Masses of silver lights reflected off the dark glass to create a vast, silvery grotto, very beautiful in a cold, hard and formidable way.

The lift shaft was a sleeve between the outer obsidian façade and the inner workings of the tower. As they got higher, the view of Scathach and the surrounding countryside was incredible, though filtered as if through dark glasses. Jonnie wondered how come they could see out but no one could see in – it was a bit like a one-way mirror.

"Shit this is high!" he exclaimed. "You wouldn't want to be up here with vertigo! Hey, isn't that the barrier over there in the distance; and Mt Greyvyn beyond it?" pointing to a pink shimmer in the distance through which there was the vague impression of a mountain peak.

"Greyvyn?"

"The mountain we were talking about yesterday, the one we think they're going to be heading for, where the barrier is in place."

"I've not ever heard it named. We don't talk about anything in the north for fear of reprisal. We've grown up with a fear of being watched and listened to, even though I don't believe they actually do. We don't know the extent of the Mages' magic – they keep it to themselves, other than what they show us to keep us in awe and under control. It's used as a threat, so better to create an unknown dimension to it I guess."

"Well, I've seen it in action," said Jonnie. "It was used to mute a man who had helped me and it was brutal! I don't know how we stand up to that – I guess that's how they keep everyone cowed."

"Yes," Cowan replied, "I think we have to use our wits and work behind them so they're not expecting us, rather than confronting them head on. I don't know how we're going to defeat them, but I hope we have a few tricks up our sleeve that they don't know about!... Ah, I think we're there."

The doors of the pod slid open smoothly into the tower room. They were so high up it was as if they were in an eagle's eyrie, and stepping into the room, Jonnie experienced a sense of wonder at the same time as a wave of vertigo. He'd only ever been this high once before when he went up the Skytower at home in Auckland. He remembered there too the wave of dizziness he felt

217

as he stepped onto the glass floor and could see the cityscape extending out beneath him. Now he was looking down on South Feasgar stretching below like a tapestry of colours stitched around him as far as he could see. Surrounded by glass, the only direction completely blocked from his view was to his left, where a room bit into a corner of the main tower room – the room he had to get access to.

He became aware of voices interrupting his distraction and looked across in the other direction to see Cowan talking to a Guardian standing in front of a door, beyond which he assumed was the stairway to the Shard. He was demanding to know who they were and why they were there.

"We're here to check whether the Mages' new chest will fit in this room," Cowan replied. "We're going to measure up now, and if it'll work, we'll be back soon to install it." The Guardian just grunted, shuffling from foot to foot to keep the circulation going in his legs. "How long have you been on shift?" Cowan asked. "It must be hard standing still for hours on end!"

"Four hours," the Guardian grumbled.

"We were up most of the night getting the chest ready, weren't we, lad? Must be for something important." Jonnie just nodded. They'd decided it would be better for him to speak as little as possible, given his unusual accent.

Cowan gave Jonnie the tape measure. "Here you go. Show me what you've learned. Where's the best place for the chest, and will it fit?" Jonnie made a show of walking around the walls of the room, now and then putting the tape measure against a vacant stretch of wall to see if it was long enough. Eventually he indicated a stretch of glass on the side looking out to the North. "Lad, I know you're tired," Cowan said, patiently, "but think! There's space there right enough, but why won't it work?" Jonnie just shrugged. "Apprentices aren't like they used to be, are they?" Cowan said to the Guardian, who laughed. Turning back to Jonnie he spoke slowly, as if to a half-wit: "It won't work because we can't attach the chest to glass, or at least, not without a lot of bother! Come over here for a bit and have a swig of my nectar; it'll wake you up." He held out his drinking bottle to Jonnie. They both took a couple of sips and made a point of becoming more animated. And it *was* good! It spread through his body, melting away his body aches, some still lingering from his broken leg, and the weariness in his muscles and his brain – it felt blissful!

"Want a bit?" Cowan asked the Guardian.

"No… thanks."

"Fair enough, but you don't know what you're missing."

They worked together measuring up a space on the solid wall backing onto the second room. When they were finished, they took another swig of nectar and, again, Cowan asked the Guardian if he was sure he didn't want any, telling him that a Healer had made it for him and it was rejuvenating. In the end the Guardian accepted it with a brusque 'thanks.' He obviously liked it, asking for another mouthful when they told him they were leaving and would return shortly with the chest.

They didn't have an escort on their way back down, as they only needed to make their way to the carpentry room rather than the basement. They got out of the pod on the ground floor, finding themselves in the atrium they'd passed on their way up. They walked through it quickly, making their way to the corridor leading to the trades entrance, but what he saw looking towards the front of the building was breath-taking. He could make out, even from a distance, grand, vaulted ceilings and staircases, all in the same stark black and silver. It felt like they really were making a statement about the Mages' position in the land.

"What's in the upper part of the tower, Cowan? I mean, I know that's where the magic flows from, but who controls it? Does anything else go on in there?"

"There are three Mages who control the magic, and who control us all. They call themselves the Elders. They live in the tower – no one other than Mages has ever been there. They get their Apprentices to be their lackeys, taking care of their food and cleaning and anything else they need. I guess that's where they hatch their plots, but it's so well locked up we'd never have a chance of getting in there, and I suspect if we tried we'd be instantly killed!"

"What if we passed ourselves off as Apprentice Mages, like the way I'm pretending to be an Artisan now? I mean, if the Shard is the source of magic, if it was stopped somehow, the Mages would lose their power over the land wouldn't they?"

"Look Jonnie. They're in a different league. They're dangerous. Anyone trying to get in there would be found out very quickly – I'm sure they'll have spells on everything, not to mention that they'll teach their Apprentices what to do and say that you wouldn't have any idea about. Please don't try to be a hero – don't do anything without all of us knowing. You don't have anything to prove!"

Oh, but I do, Jonnie thought to himself. He'd done plenty to make up for...

It didn't take them long to return with the chest on the trolley, which they manoeuvred quite easily between them. Cowan tipped the vial of liquid into his flask and they went over their plan again as they ascended to the tower room, and knew it was as good as they could make it. If anything went wrong they'd just have to think on their feet.

"Hey, give us a hand please," Cowan called across to the

guard when the pod opened to the tower room. The Guardian helped them get the chest off the trolley and into its place against the wall. It was heavy and awkward, and it was a natural gesture afterwards for Cowan to pull out his flask and offer it to the other two. Jonnie pretended to take a hefty gulp, and the Guardian greedily took two before going back to his position by the door to the Shard. Jonnie and Cowan set about securing the chest using heavy bolts screwed into the wall behind it.

Jonnie started getting anxious as they drew near to finishing their task. What if the liquid in the vial didn't work? What would they do? The door to the other room was shut, but didn't appear to have a lock on it. His mind raced, trying to think about how Cowan could distract the Guardian if necessary so he could get in. He then heard a gurgling and looked towards the guard, who was bent over, holding his stomach.

"What's up? Are you all right?" Cowan asked, moving over towards him.

"Oh God, I feel awful!" He farted and a sulphurous smell permeated the room, making them almost gag.

"Have you eaten something bad?" Cowan asked, full of concern.

"I don't know. Ohhh…" he groaned in agony, as more noises of turbulence and bottled-up air ripped through him. "I've got to go to the bathroom. Quick, get the pod!" Cowan helped him to the pod and saw the doors close behind him before striding over to the closed door to the second room. He pulled the door open and went to step inside, but suddenly looked as if he'd been hit full-on in the face and body. He went rigid and gasped, and was thrown back into the tower room.

"What happened?" Jonnie asked.

"I don't know," Cowan managed to wheeze out of his

221

constricted chest. "It felt like something hit me with a sledge hammer! They must have a spell on the room to stop anyone getting in. I don't know what we do now," he gulped, rubbing his face and neck.

Jonnie walked over to him and looked through the now open door. He could see the table used for scrying, but couldn't see the layout of the stones that lay on it. He could also see a map on the wall, but couldn't make out its details. How frustrating! Without even thinking, he moved towards the room, wondering vaguely whether the same thing would happen to him.

"No, don't!" Cowan called in warning, but Jonnie kept going. He entered the room… and nothing happened… Walking forward, he went over to the scrying table and noted the pattern of stones, remembering to think about Kayla and make an emotional connection to them. He also took out his pencil and paper and briefly noted the position of each stone, though he was no artist and it was only a rough sketch. He noticed then that he was starting to feel nauseous. His gut was tightening and he could feel something rising – almost like anxiety, but actually he felt dizzy and thought he might throw up. He had to hold on a little longer, so he took a deep breath and turning, he looked over to the map on the wall. Now that was interesting! He could see Darthmore marked on the map, within the city, and a line drawn from it across to a mountain peak – Greywyn! The barrier was drawn across the map at the base of Greywyn and an oval marked a spot not far from where the barrier intersected with the mountain, with 'base camp' written over it. Jonnie quickly sketched what he could see, but was interrupted by Cowan.

"Jonnie," Cowan hissed, "someone's coming!"

He wheeled around and moved over to hide at the side of the open door, breathing heavily to try to stop the feeling that he was going to vomit.

"What are you doing here?" an unknown male's voice demanded.

"I'm installing a chest, as you can see," Cowan replied.

"Where's the guard?"

"He's gone off to the bathroom. I think he was unwell."

"That's very irregular – he should have called one of us."

As they were talking, Jonnie risked snatching a look around the door frame. The Guardian was standing near Cowan, side-on to Jonnie. When Cowan saw Jonnie watching, he moved so that the Guardian had to change position, with his back to Jonnie, to keep looking at Cowan directly. What should he do? Surely it would only be a moment before the Guardian thought about the door being open? He had nothing he could hit him with, and their tools were lying too far away. Could he do that anyway? Did he have it in him to hurt another human being? He guessed he could if their lives depended on it. Suddenly a thought came to mind. He remembered when he was about twelve the way he and his friends used to fool around and trick the boys they didn't like. One thing that really wound them up was if one of his gang got into a conversation with someone they didn't like and another of them crept up and crouched down behind him on hands and knees. Then the one having the conversation would push him so he tripped backwards, falling over the boy behind and winding himself as his back hit the ground. Maybe… Anything would be better than being discovered in the room and the two of them being marched off to goodness only knows where.

He silently stole out of the room while they were talking about the chest. He mimed to Cowan the action of pushing the Guardian and quickly knelt down directly behind him. The Guardian must have sensed him at that moment, because he started to turn just as Cowan gave him a hefty shove that sent him sprawling across Jonnie and onto the floor, which he hit at an angle with a sickening whack on his head. Cowan and Jonnie looked at each other for a moment in silence – the Guardian seemed to have been knocked out, but for how long? Cowan quickly leapt into action, dragging his inert body across to the chest. Jonnie pulled himself out of his shock and helped with his legs. They shoved him into it, his legs doubled up to fit them inside, and quickly shut and locked the lid.

"We need to get out of here quickly. Did you get everything you needed?" Cowan asked him.

"I think so. I felt really horrible in there – I don't know what was going on, or why I could get in there and you couldn't…"

"We'll talk about that later. Let's go! Hold on a minute – to give us some more time…" Cowan crouched down in front of the chest and placed his hands on the timber. He looked as if he was praying or something. He then drew his hands gently around the four sides of the lid, over the join. When he stepped back, there was no sign of the lid at all. The top of the chest had resolved back into a solid piece of wood and the Guardian was sealed inside. Jonnie looked on in amazement, not really understanding what had just happened. He'd been told that the Artisans had their own form of magic, which he'd just witnessed, and he felt blown away.

"I hope he can breathe," Jonnie whispered, concerned.

"Should be okay," replied Cowan, sounding grim. Then he relaxed a bit and smiled under his krill. "He'll be fine, there are ventilation holes in the back of the chest. He'll just have a bad headache when they get him out."

He then got Jonnie to help him load up their tools onto the trolley. They called for the pod and exited the tower room as fast as they could.

***

Later that evening they met up again with Linden, Vagan and Sarraphin at Cowan's house. As they described the events that had happened in the tower, Jonnie felt a lingering sense of unreality about it all. He'd never experienced magic before coming to this land; in fact, he imagined he'd have taken the piss out of anyone who'd told him the kind of story they were telling right now, but this lot took it in their stride. Linden asked if he could have a look at the sketch he'd made of the scrying stones, then asked his permission to access his thought images, coaxing him to first relax and find a quiet place internally where he felt centred, as he'd taught him previously. The others were quiet, hardly breathing so they didn't disturb his thoughts. At first, when he pictured the stones, Linden couldn't get anything from him, and prompted him to think about Kayla instead. An image of Kayla staring in horror as he fell into the river in Greyvyn came to mind – the last time he'd seen her. Then Linden guided him to think about Kayla, to bring his feelings for her to the scrying image, as he had when he was in the room in the tower. An image came up of the stones, with an overlay of love and concern for Kayla. And something else…

"Are you okay Jonnie?" Linden asked.

"Yes, why?"

"It was like you were really ill when you were up in that room. What was happening for you?"

"Well when Cowan tried, he couldn't go into the room and we guessed they'd put a spell onto it, but somehow it didn't stop me. I went in, but I felt really nauseous and unwell the whole time I was in there," Jonnie replied.

"That would have been their magic. Isn't it interesting that

225

you, and from what you said before, the others from your world, could see the strangers in the north, and that the spell they put on the room didn't stop you?"

"And I'm pretty sure that Tom and Sarah, the other two I knew in North Feasgar, had some sort of weird relationship with a cat!"

"There are people here who can communicate with animals, and share thoughts with each other," Sarraphin contributed. "It sounds as if those of you from another world can still experience the old magic from Feasgar that has been lost completely in the north, and divided up into Orders here in the south so that none of us, other than the Mages, can use it effectively. I suppose that's another way they control us... So, can you make out what the scrying message is saying Linden?"

Linden was quiet for a while, feeling his way into the image in his mind and flicking a glance at Jonnie's sketch to check. "It's a date. Three days from now."

"The date they're going to mobilise and leave Scathach maybe?" suggested Cowan.

"Or the date they're going to meet somewhere?" Amitra added.

"Oh, I forgot to say," Jonnie added, "they had a map in the room. Look, I scribbled the main parts of it on the back of the drawing of the stones. See, here is Scathach, with a line drawn between Darthmore and a point just across the barrier from North Feasgar, which would be Greyvyn, the mountain. And here," he pointed to the oval drawn just south of the barrier, "might be where they're meeting up – it had 'Base Camp' written on it."

"Okay, so it's likely that they're preparing to move to their base camp just south of the barrier in three days. The question is, do we follow them, or do we attempt to get there first and hide out? That would mean moving really quickly in two days' time," Cowan asked, after they'd had a minute to digest what Jonnie and Cowan had told them.

"I think we need to get there first and keep one step ahead," offered Sarraphin. The others agreed. "But we need to get word out to the other supporters quickly to make sure they're with us. I think we should plan what we think needs to happen, share it with the other groups, and if they give the go-ahead, prepare to move the day after tomorrow."

The supporters of their movement against the Mages were organised into five groups, with only the leaders knowing each other. In this way, if one group was compromised, even if they were tortured by the Mages or Guardians, they wouldn't have any information to give up about the other groups. After much discussion, they decided that four people from each group would be selected to go to the barrier, plus Sarraphin and Linden as Healers. They had no idea how many Mages and Guardians would be there, but their information about the supplies being gathered suggested a limited number. And they could always send for more supporters if needed. Cowan and Amitra volunteered to stay and co-ordinate operations in Scathach, to pass on messages, to get word out to people in the city, and to drum up additional support in case they ended up fighting. Amitra was tasked with contacting leaders from each group and arranging for them to be at their place the following evening, so that if they agreed, they'd have twenty-four hours to choose and prepare the four who were going to go with them the following day.

"I'll go from our group," said Vagan.

"Me too," Jonnie added. "I presume I count as one of your group now?" He felt sorry that Cowan wasn't going – he trusted him and had thought he'd make a really good leader for their journey, but then again, he and Amitra would have a big job on their hands staying in Scathach. And Vagan was a bit younger and seemed really strong and reliable.

"Of course you do! I'll co-ordinate packing the supplies and weapons we need," Vagan offered. "It's fortunate we began putting things together when we realised that the Mages were preparing for a journey!"

"And I'll arrange for two small mopas, with supporters as drivers, able to take twenty-two people between them," Cowan added.

They left the meeting feeling solemn – they'd put something into action that could completely change their lives, and maybe South Feasgar forever, but what the outcome would be they just didn't know. It felt to Linden like the eve of something, a stepping off point. He struggled to express it to himself – it held excitement and fear; a potential opening out of their lives, or alternatively their doom! Talking to Jonnie before he left, he tried to express something of how he was feeling.

"Yeah, I know. I mean, I'm not even from here, but it feels huge, what's happening," Jonnie replied. "I hope I get the chance to get to know all these people properly. I really like Cowan – it would be great to actually be his apprentice."

"Yes, he's a good man; steady and practical. And people like him. He'll be really good leading things from this end. And Amitra – she's clever and knows how to motivate people to get things done."

"It doesn't seem like women have much authority in South Feasgar," Jonnie remarked. "I mean, I haven't heard anyone talk of women in the Mage or Guardian Orders."

"I think there are a few who are Mages, but you're right,

they're kept behind the scenes. I feel bad that I've never wondered why. And I don't think they're ever selected for the Guardians. Is that different in the north?"

"I wasn't there for long, but at the community meetings I went to, women had equal say to the men. And Arthur and Mary, who I stayed with when I first arrived, were both engineers, and both shared the running of the house, so it seemed more equal than here."

"That's something else that needs to change. Maybe we have the possibility of over-turning the whole order of things as we know it. It'll take wisdom and firmness from people like Cowan, Sarraphin and Vagan to keep it from descending into chaos, if we ever get that chance."

Chapter IX

Journey to the Barrier

Late in the morning, two days later, they gathered in an empty school yard in the outskirts of Scathach, with everything so far having gone according to plan. Cowan and Amitra were there to see them off, solemnly wishing them a safe journey. They gave Vagan, Jonnie and Linden a hug goodbye as they clambered onto one of the mopases.

"We'll see you soon. Keep safe," Amitra said as she embraced Sarraphin.

"You too," Sarraphin responded, waving as she followed the others onto the mopas and shut the door behind her.

Although their destination was supposed to be less than an hour away, it took longer due to the roads deteriorating as they travelled further from the city. They bumped along a rutted, unsealed road, musing between themselves about how it didn't seem to be important for the Guardians to maintain the roads that they and the Mages would have no normal reason to use, even though the uninitiated, who lived away from the city, were the ones who provided food and services for them. They'd decided to discard their headgear for the journey, and somehow it made them freer to talk about things they wouldn't have expressed outside their own Orders before. Linden and Sarraphin had also changed into more hardy tunics – the idea of pristine white where they were going seemed a bit crazy.

"Isn't it interesting," Vagan said, "that we're all Artisans and uninitiated, other than you two of course. I wonder, if it came to a war, what would happen. The power and might of the Mages and Guardians against our greater numbers."

"Don't discount the Healers either Vagan. Some would be reluctant to be involved in anything they thought that may cause harm to others, but just as many, like the two of us, can see that more harm may be done by doing nothing!" Sarraphin asserted.

"And don't forget that the uninitiated have had to learn to be cunning to survive, and have had years of being treated as uneducated servants who don't count for anything to put right. Their anger will give them energy that will be a force to be reckoned with," Linden chipped in. "As I see it, they, and the Artisans, also have a practical wisdom the others don't have in the same way."

"Imagine if people had more choice about who got into Orders and who didn't," Jonnie said a little later. "I mean, why does it need to be controlled? Why can't people who have the right talents have the right to train?"

"Are you thinking about Anika?" Linden asked.

"Well yes, and people like her – they shouldn't have to live a life that doesn't let them use their abilities."

"Maintaining a hierarchy keeps the population under control," Sarraphin said. "From what Linden's said, Anika is clever and deserves the chance to do more than stay at the farm."

"Jonnie, you never said how you got on with my family. What was it like being there?" asked Linden.

"It was great. You've got a really good family and I loved helping them out on the farm," Jonnie said, his face flushing a little. "Your dad and brother took me out on the farm with them, and in the evenings, Anika taught me how to play chess." Linden

231

noticed that his flush deepened when he spoke of Anika. He didn't say anything, but smiled inwardly as he caught one of Jonnie's thought images of the two of them, heads together, looking at a book.

As they drew closer to the barrier, the road travelled alongside a river, which Jonnie imagined must be the River Dearth, though it didn't go by that name in South Feasgar. This would be the river he was found in, so they must be somewhere near the home of the man who found him. The countryside was much less populated now, with farms and small-holdings spread out in a landscape that was becoming more sparse, other than pockets of denser growth close to the river. The barrier cast a red glow as a constant reminder of the strangeness that lay ahead – it couldn't be far now to the Mages' base, so they started looking around for cover for their own campsite.

"Should we find a place first, then look for theirs, or do the opposite?" Sarraphin asked.

"If we look for theirs first, we might be seen by their advance party, but if we find a place then go on foot, we can be more careful to make sure we're not noticed," Vagan answered.

Just then, the driver from the other mopas tooted at them from behind, so they drew over to the side of the road and one of the Artisans came on board to talk to them.

"Hi Vintra, what's up?" Vagan said, addressing a man who looked to be in his thirties, wearing a serious expression behind his deep-set brown eyes, though Jonnie thought that was possibly just because his eyebrows were so dark and thick that they almost met in the middle of his nose.

"Hi, we're coming up to the last village before the barrier." His voice was gravelly, somehow matching his eyebrows. "My uncle and his family live there, so I thought it might be a good idea to stop and find out what they know about the Mages. Follow us and when we get there everyone can have a quick leg stretch while I talk to them."

Five minutes later they drew in behind the other mopas outside a house on the outskirts of a village, which consisted of a cluster of shops and services either side of the road as it curved in a lazy S, with the river, around a rocky outcrop. A modest number of houses were arranged around the village centre. They clambered out and wandered over to the river. Ten minutes later Vintra re-joined them where they sat on the grassy bank to talk. He told them that a couple of Mages had passed through the village the previous week. They had commandeered a farmhouse close to the barrier, ejecting the owners. Two villagers had been offered good money to cook and do jobs for the Mages at the farm and had reported back that while there were two Mages and about half a dozen Guardians staying there now, they'd been told to prepare for a larger group. The farmhouse had been readied to accommodate six Mages, and five tents were being erected in the yard for the Guardians, which could comfortably house between twenty to thirty people. The farmer and his family were staying with relatives in the village and were very angry at being thrown out of their home. They, and the other villagers wanted to help however they could. One of them was going to ride with them now, with an idea about where they might find cover for their vehicles a bit closer to the barrier. As they moved back to the mopases, a tall, dark-haired woman strode out of the house towards them.

"Hello, I'm Thylane, a friend of Vintra's family. My uncle lives north of here on a small land-holding. He has every reason to want to help you and I think his property has enough cover for you to be able to hide your mopases. You'll have to camp outside

– his place is small, but I imagine you brought tents with you?"

"Yes, we have," Vagan replied. "Thanks. We're really grateful for your help!"

Thylane got into the mopas with them and directed them to continue north on the main road. The road's surface was full of pot-holes that they had to carefully navigate, slowing their journey to what felt like a crawl. She explained to them that it was no longer serviced by the local works authority even though they paid taxes for its upkeep. They didn't have grading equipment in the village to do it themselves, and had to make do with repairing ruts and holes manually. They nodded to themselves as she confirmed their earlier thinking.

"So why does your uncle have a particular reason to help us?" Sarraphin asked her.

"Several months he ago, he did his duty in reporting someone washing up in the river who wasn't from these parts, and they repaid him by muting him!" Thylane replied angrily. Jonnie felt sick. That must have been him! He'd always felt bad about what had happened to the man who was so kind to him.

"Th-that was me!" he stuttered, feeling anxious about what she'd think of him. "He rescued me and was good to me and the Mage just flicked his finger and did that, as if he didn't even matter! I've not been able to forget it."

"Well, at least you're alive – I'm sure you'll have a story to tell my uncle. He won't blame you for what happened!"

Shortly after, Thylane pointed out to them a farm set back from the road, down a long drive-way lined with trees.

"That's where they've set up their base," she said. Two large, black tents were already up and others were being erected in a cluster to the side of the farmhouse. Thylane directed their driver to continue along the road until they came to a small house about five minutes' drive closer to the barrier. They could now see the barrier clearly.

"How close is the barrier?" Vagan asked. "It's hard to tell because it stretches across the whole horizon."

"About ten minutes in a vehicle; maybe thirty minutes on foot?" Thylane replied. "We don't have much cause to go near it, but of course, as kids, we all had to explore it just so we could brag that we had!"

"What happens if you touch it?" Jonnie asked curiously.

"It just fizzes and feels kind of warm. It doesn't hurt you, but you can't get through it."

As they drew up to the house, a man came out the front door and Thylane jumped down from the mopas to talk to him. They saw him smile and nod his head, and when she got back on board he directed them to a track that led along the side of the house to the buildings behind. They were in good order – it looked like he grew a variety of crops, and had a packing shed and another building for his equipment. A tractor was parked outside and they could see a plough housed inside it.

"Karim, my uncle, farms several crops in rotation and sells them in Scathach," Thylane explained. "He lives simply and he's a really hard worker. His business gives jobs to young people from the village. He didn't deserve how he was treated, but he just gets on with it, though he has to take someone with him to the market now that he can't communicate with his voice."

They drove their mopas past the sheds, then along a rougher track used by the tractor to access the fields that lay behind them. A stand of trees stretched along the fields as a wind-break, and it was in their shelter that they parked and climbed out.

As they gathered together around Thylane and Karim, Jonnie saw his eyes widen in surprise when he saw Jonnie and registered who he was. He felt incredibly awkward and uncertain about what to do, and forced himself to go over to him and shake his hand and thank him for saving his life. He surprised himself when his eyes filled with tears and his voice came out huskily. When he blurted out that he was sorry the Mage had treated him so badly, Karim just patted him on his shoulder and smiled.

They were all assigned jobs for the day. Most of them were tasked with putting up the tents and making their camp as organised and comfortable as possible, checking their provisions and weapons. Four of them were to walk to the barrier, with Thylane guiding them, to scout out whether the Mages had already started any activity there. Jonnie quickly volunteered to go with Vagan and two others he didn't know. Linden and Sarraphin exchanged a glance and said they had something they needed to do and excused themselves.

***

When the others were occupied with their tasks, Sarraphin and Linden walked together back to the house and knocked on the open front door, calling out to Karim. He came to the door smiling, and gestured that they were welcome inside, holding open the door for them to enter ahead of him. They found themselves in a small, but tidy living area. He indicated that they should take two of the chairs at the table and pulled out another one for himself and sat down.

"Karim," Sarraphin began, "my name is Sarraphin, and I'm a Master Healer, and this is Linden, an Affiliate Healer who works with me."

Karim nodded in acknowledgement.

Sarraphin continued, "We'd like to see whether we can do

anything to reverse the spell that the Mage put on your vocal cords. We may not be able to, but we'll give it our best shot – with both of us together, we may be able to overcome his power."

Karim looked at them, a sceptical look on his face. Or maybe he was just anxious, Linden thought, which he'd have every reason to be since they were strangers to him.

"How about we explain to you what we do," he suggested quietly. "You don't know us, and I'm sure you'll be concerned about whether we might make it worse for you." Karim nodded. "We both have the gift of healing, but it's different for all of us. Sarraphin's gift is centred on touch – she puts her hands on a person and can sense where their illness is and uses her power to change the unwell cells and purify them. My gift is one of the mind, so I 'feel' my way into a person and can sense where they're unwell and build a healing lattice around that place. If you would allow us to, all you'd need to do would be to lie down and relax and let us find out what the spell they've put on you is like, and try to break it up. You won't feel any pain... Would you like us to try?"

Karim thought for a moment – a mixture of emotions passed over his face, from hope and anticipation, to fear. Then, slowly, he nodded. Sarraphin suggested that he move over to lie on the couch and try to relax. He stretched himself out, a cushion behind his head, and breathed deeply as they pulled their chairs over beside him.

"Who should start?" Linden asked.

"You try first, then I'll come in when you have a good sense of what the spell has done to him," Sarraphin replied.

Linden looked down at Karim, lying calmly in front of him, trusting that the two of them would do their best to help him. He slowed his breathing until it matched Karim's, breathing in and out with his diaphragm, reaching to mingle their energy fields together. Slowly and gently probing with his gift, he sent it towards the bundle of nerves and vessels supplying the muscles of the vocal cords, and the associated focal point of energy their teachings called the throat chakra. As he moved through Karim, he sensed his strength and goodness, until his own blue energy began to perceive a foreign, malignant darkness beginning to push back against him. It felt knotted and dense and unyielding, resisting him and trying to turn him back. He drew on another line of his energy, sending it alongside the first, aligned with it to double his strength. He jabbed at the blackness, and it was as if he'd poked a ferocious black dog that snarled and bared its teeth at him, bristling and daring him to try again. Droplets of sweat broke out on his brow as he concentrated his power against the black.

He slowly, painstakingly, called his gift to create criss-crossing lines to surround and contain the throat area, leaving the blackness with nowhere to go. When Sarraphin gently placed her hands on Karim's throat and joined her gift with his, her strands of red sought out and twined around his blue, creating a powerful magical field. From all directions it reached into the blackness, probing and insinuating their interwoven strands anywhere they could find a way in. As the blackness tried to attack back, sending out its own penetrating tentacles, the lines of red and blue surrounded them and pulled in tightly, choking them off. Slowly the energy changed. Instead of the blackness attacking, it was focused on trying to hold its ground, then gradually moved into a slow retreat as their unrelenting push encroached further and further into its snarling evil. They reached its vortex and in one final push, they focused all their energy into breaking through and exploding the remaining knotted mass of toxic black. Karim coughed, and sat up, a look of astonishment on his face. He cleared his throat a few times, marvelling that he could make a noise.

"Thank you," he whispered, tentative after months of not being able to speak. A large smile spread over his face, and at the same time tears of joy ran down his cheeks.

***

Thylane led her small group across the road and headed north through the fields, not wanting to run the risk of coming across the Mages as they travelled to or from their base to the barrier. Karim's small-holding was one of the most northerly in the area, closest to the barrier, and on leaving it, the landscape rapidly changed, becoming increasingly barren and rocky. Thylane chatted as they walked, about her family thinking Karim was mad when he bought his property. It had been in poor condition, but it was all he could afford for a size large enough to grow the crops he had in mind. After a lot of hard work and irrigation from the plentiful water supply of the river, he'd turned the land around into a profitable business.

Further north, the land stretched as far the eye could see without apparent boundaries. There was little shelter, other than trees planted near waterholes, and scrubby bushes and hard-wearing grasses that had survived the rocky ground, around which a scattering of cattle and sheep clustered. The bushes looked to Jonnie remarkably like gorse and thistles; *weeds the same across worlds*, he mused. They had a good view of the road in the distance and kept vigilant, looking out for any signs of movement. With so little shelter, the most they could do if a vehicle drove past would be to flatten themselves to the ground.

They were far enough from the road to possibly get away with it.

As they drew close to the barrier, Thylane asked whether they had any idea where the Mages would approach it.

"We think they'll try where the river comes out of the mountain. That's where Willard and I got through the barrier, and even though it may be easier exiting in this direction than going against the magic back the other way, it's probably the weakest point."

"Right then, we'll move across to the river and follow it up to the barrier. At least there's a little cover by the river, but we'll need to move quietly now."

"What's their magic like?" Jonnie asked. "I mean, are they likely to sense us somehow?"

"No one really knows," one of the others, a woman called Jaelin responded. "They can cast spells to control people, like they did with Karim, so we don't want them to see us. And they can thought-share, but only people in their Order know the full extent of what they can do. They can't do what the other Orders can do, but they're more powerful than us, and use their power for their own gain."

"So, it's because of the barrier that they have to scry to communicate with their mates in the north, otherwise they could just thought-share?" Jonnie asked.

"I imagine so," Jaelin said.

"Shh… no more talking," Thylane interrupted. "We're getting too close. Keep low and we'll stop and hide out as best we can once we can see them… if they're even there at the moment."

When they reached the river, Thylane led the way, followed by the others in single file, Vagan immediately behind Thylane so he could help her to scout for the Mages and avoid being seen in return. He caught sight of them first. Reaching out to tap her on the shoulder and get her attention, he gestured ahead and slightly to their right, where the river curved after exiting the mountain. He could just make out some small moving specks. As they inched forward, the specks resolved into small figures, two dressed in black. They risked moving a little closer, then dropped themselves down into the scrubby bushes at the river's edge. They were close enough now to see the small stick-figures reaching towards the barrier and sending out purple shafts of magic to hit the barrier above their heads. The barrier sparked and rippled. The figures repeated their assault over and over, each time the barrier's reaction becoming more sustained, with the ripples spreading further in either direction.

Lying there, wondering what they would do now, Jonnie could swear that he felt the ground shake slightly under his stretched-out body and looked around to see if any of the others had noticed. In doing so, he caught a movement out of the corner of his eye and twisted over onto his back in a half-sitting position just in time to see four Guardians behind them. He only just had time to register *'how on earth did they get there without us sensing them?'* before they slammed at them with some sort of spell. The other four were immediately immobilised and he had the presence of mind to copy them, letting himself drop back to the ground, limbs drooping at his side. He caught sight of the panic in Jaelin's eyes as she tried to move, but was completely arrested in a position front-down, with her head turned towards him. *What just happened?* he thought. And why wasn't he affected by their spell? He supposed it was like the one in the tower room – he must have some sort of immunity to it. He mustn't let the Guardians know if he was to have any chance of helping them to escape whatever happened next.

241

Judging by their voices, the Guardians were all men. The largest one bundled Thylane and Jaelin up together, while the other three grabbed one of them each, throwing them roughly over their shoulders and walking off with them towards the Mages.

"They'll be happy with us for finding this lot," one of them commented. "They won't want anything getting in the way tomorrow."

Jonnie felt jostled like a sack of potatoes as the men made short work of the distance to the Mages. When they arrived, they were dumped on the ground. The air was knocked out of Jonnie and it was all he could do not to yell when his newly healed leg hit the ground. The Mages walked over to them from where they'd been casting their magic at the barrier.

"What do we have here?" one of them asked.

"Five people caught spying on you," one of the Guardians replied, his voice brusque. For Jonnie, his tone brought to mind someone wanting approval – that would have been him in the past, sucking up to Willard to be noticed. The Mages looked them over. Jonnie hoped neither of them was Argin – it would be better if he wasn't recognised right now. He needed time to think about what he would do next.

"Get them back to the farmhouse. We're finished here for today."

They were bundled into a mopas that was parked a short distance away. They hadn't noticed it as they made their way up the river, being focused on the intersection of the river and the barrier. Thrown onto the floor between the seats, he tried to catch Vagan's eye. All he could think to do was give him a wink, but because he couldn't respond, Jonnie couldn't tell whether he could actually register what was going on around him. He was left hoping that Vagan understood that he hadn't been affected by the spell and would do everything he could to rescue them.

A short, but uncomfortable fifteen minutes later, they reached the farmhouse. Jonnie had had to let his body remain inert, which meant being thrown around on the floor of the mopas between the seats. Each time his leg hit one of the metal bars supporting a chair he wanted to scream, but bit it back, trying also to control his facial expression in case he was being watched. Arriving was a short-lived relief. They were taken from the mopas and dumped on a hard floor in a shed that stank of sheep droppings. Flies buzzed around their bodies as they lay on the ground where they'd fallen, and they couldn't adjust their limbs to make themselves more comfortable, or brush away the flies that congregated around their eyes and mouths. Jonnie was desperate for the Guardians to leave so he could at least twitch some of them away – it was agonising knowing he could move but not being able to! It seemed, though, that the Guardians had been told to wait for the Mages to give them their next orders. Eventually one arrived, looked them over and told the Guardians they could take turns to keep an eye on them – it was obvious they weren't going anywhere, and they just had to make sure that no one turned up to look for them before the rest of their group arrived tomorrow.

The rest of the day passed in a blur. Only one Guardian was left with them at a time, but it was still agony only being able to make tiny movements to ease the cramping of his limbs each time the man looked the other way. The thing the most difficult to tolerate was keeping absolutely still when flies were crawling around his mouth! He wanted to spit and scream, and couldn't. He wondered what it was like for the other four. They had no choice; they couldn't move, but at the same time maybe that meant it wasn't so hard for them? He was hungry, and SO thirsty and time just ticked slowly by. No one was even going to notice they were missing until nightfall, and even then, they may not think they should try to rescue them just a day before the rest of the Mage group were arriving for a major assault on the barrier. It might jeopardise their whole mission, so really, it was down to him!

As the night started to draw in around them, he could hear scurrying sounds somewhere behind him. *Oh my god, rats?* He'd always hated them, and imagined their beady eyes looking at him, thinking about the tender meal he would make. Someone had told him once that their teeth were as strong as steel and that was why they could bite through wood and other hard materials. He swallowed and willed his attention away from the sounds... The hard floor was getting colder and the dark was creeping its shadowy fingers from the corners of the room towards them. Jonnie began to pay more attention to the movements of the Guardian. If he was going to get away to get help it would need to be under the cover of the night, when the Guardian was tired, fed up and probably not concentrating. He was seeing signs that the one on watch currently was getting a little blasé – he'd been with them for more than three hours now, and what was there for him to do just watching over five inert bodies, obviously not going anywhere...? His eyes were drooping and his head was starting to do that lolling thing, where it dropped back, rolled to one side, mouth open, then suddenly jerked back upright with a moment of being half-awake before settling into the same pattern over again. It meant he was mostly asleep, but not quite. When should he make his move?

He waited until it was completely dark and the Guardian was more reliably asleep before slowly drawing himself into a foetal position on his side. His muscles screamed at him, punishing him for not moving for the past several hours, but he forced himself to take it slowly, one small movement at a time, constantly checking the Guardian for any signs of waking. He got a fright when the Guardian jerked his head forward and snorted, but he then settled back into his slumber again. Once Jonnie got onto his side, it wasn't so hard to push himself to a sitting position. He couldn't risk whispering anything to Vagan, lying beside him, so he touched him on the arm and gave him a thumbs-up sign, hoping he could see him in the dark. He tensed his leg muscles to wake them up and eased himself to his feet, silently creeping from where he'd been lying to the door. Once outside, it was relatively easy to reach the trees, slipping into their deep shadows, with only a hint of moon to light the driveway alongside them as he made his way to the road.

***

"Where have you been?" Sarraphin called out. "Where are the others?" She was standing outside the house in a manner that looked like she was taking a turn at being on watch for them.

"We got caught!" he gasped. He'd been running up the road, partly to put distance between him and the farmhouse as quickly as he could, but also because it felt so good to be moving his cramped muscles again after his enforced stillness. He had his breath back by the time he got inside, where the leaders of their group were sitting with Karim around the table and on the couch. They looked puzzled and worried when they saw he was alone. Linden went over to greet him, asking if he was okay and for a while he could only shake his head. When he managed to tell them what had happened, they sat looking stunned. They knew

245

they would have to face the power of the Mages and that people were likely to get hurt, but they hadn't been ready for it yet. It was too soon, and suddenly what they were trying to do was too real!

"Well, we have to go and rescue them," Linden said.

"But it's likely that the Guardian has woken up by now and has seen that I've gone," Jonnie said. "He'll have raised the alarm and they'll surely have extra people on guard."

"Yes, and we don't want to compromise what we may have to do tomorrow by getting caught ourselves. Think about the greater good – rescuing the four of them, or trying to do our best for South Feasgar," one of the leaders from the other mopas said.

"I guess there's a small chance that the Guardian hasn't noticed though?" Jonnie added, not wanting to sacrifice their friends.

"Thylane?" The word was whispered. Karim was still struggling with his voice, having not used it for almost six months. It felt like he'd had terrible laryngitis and was just getting his voice back.

"What?" Jonnie said in astonishment. "You spoke!"

Karim nodded at Sarraphin and Linden, smiling his thanks again.

"We can't just leave them there," said Sarraphin brusquely. "We'll take a small group and scout out the farmhouse carefully before we do anything. If we have to leave them until we know what's happening tomorrow, then at least we'll know we've tried." Everyone nodded in agreement, some reluctantly. "There are four, probably inert bodies to carry, so I suggest eight of us. I'm volunteering to go, because we may need a healer, but I want you to stay here Linden. Our cause can't afford to lose both of us."

"I'm going," said Jonnie, "I know where they are and can save us time."

"Okay… so six more. Vintra, do you want to choose four of the strongest from your mopas and we'll ask for two more volunteers from ours? Quickly now, meet back here in ten minutes."

"I want to go," Karim whispered to Sarraphin. She frowned. He'd already been treated badly by the Mages and she didn't want him to have to put himself in danger, but then she thought about how harmful it might be to him if he didn't have the chance to do something to help Thylane. And he was strong and resourceful… She nodded at him and he clapped her on her back before setting off to find some tools they could use as weapons.

When the eight of them were gathered, they briefly talked about who would go first to check out the shed, agreeing on Vintra and Jonnie. If they had to overpower Guardians, they had an array of weapons from hammers and chisels to knives. But if the two Mages were involved, they may have to back off. One of the people Vintra had chosen surprised Jonnie. Alora was a slight woman, carrying no apparent weapon. Vintra must have noticed him looking at her, reminding him that Artisans had their own form of magic, and that while a hammer in his hand was a force to be reckoned with, Alora made tapestries and her needles were lethal. When she inserted them into a fabric, her magic caused the fabric to relax and flatten, allowing her to create beautiful designs. The same needle pushed into flesh had a sedative effect that would knock out a horse!

They said farewell to their friends and set off silently down the road. When they approached the farmhouse, they crossed into the field immediately before the driveway, silently sliding through the dark two by two, until they reached the farmhouse and its yards. With Jonnie and Vintra in the lead, they found cover behind trees that had a view of the shed. The doorway was dark – they couldn't see anything or anyone moving either inside or out. Maybe the Guardian was still asleep, but that seemed too good to be true. If they'd realised that Jonnie had gone, surely, they'd have someone on lookout. Cautiously Vintra and Jonnie moved from the trees across a small paved area and flattened themselves against the shed wall, holding their breaths. Nothing happened... Vintra slid around the corner and stretched his neck to see through the doorway. He could see shadows that looked like motionless bodies on the ground. With his eyes used to the dark, he thought he could make out five... Five? He moved his body to insinuate it through the door, but he was thrown violently backwards. It was as if he'd hit a huge electric force. He lay on his back on the ground, feeling winded.

"Are you okay?" Jonnie whispered. "What happened?"

"I think they've got a spell on the door. We'll have to leave them."

"Hold on a minute, let me try," Jonnie replied.

As Vintra got to his feet and moved back to the side of the shed, Jonnie slid around to the door and, holding his breath, stepped inside. Nothing happened. Just like in Darthmore! Inside, his four friends were still in the same positions he'd left them in. The fifth body was the Guardian. He'd either been stunned, or he was dead! He moved over to Vagan, managed to roll him onto his back and started trying to haul him over to the door, fighting against the same nausea he'd experienced in the tower. Vagan was a dead weight and it took all the strength he had to move him just a short distance. He whispered to Vintra to get two of their group to come and get him, as he dragged him through the doorway, dumping him outside and going back for Thylane. By the time he'd managed to get all four through the door, he was exhausted. He and Vintra carried the last one, Jaelin, between them across to the trees, then through the field and from there back to Karim's house. It took much longer than it had taken to get there. Carrying their friends was like carrying sacks of potatoes and they were exhausted by the time they arrived. Once they'd laid them gently inside on the floor, Linden and Sarraphin asked everyone to give them some space while they tried to reverse the spells on them. It took less time than it had with the more complex spell placed on Karim's throat, and eventually all four were awake, though feeling extremely thirsty, hungry and bruised. Sarraphin gave them a healing nectar to soothe and revitalise them until eventually they were ready to talk.

"Could you tell what was going on around you," Jonnie asked, "or were you unconscious? Your eyes were open."

"It was awful. We could see and hear everything but we were totally paralysed," Jaelin said.

"A while after you left, a Guardian brought some food to the one guarding us, and he raised the alarm. It was incredible... One of the Mages came racing out and was so furious with the Guardian for falling asleep he couldn't control himself. He yelled at him that he was an idiot, that anyone should be able to guard a bunch of immobile scum and then he just kind of pointed at him. He immediately fell over – I imagine he's dead! The Mage ranted at the other Guardian saying that his magic was more effective than a bunch of useless guards and that he was going to spell the door to stop the person who had obviously found and taken one of us from returning for the others," Vagan reported. "He was so sure of himself that he couldn't even consider the idea that Jonnie might have got himself out. How did you, by the way? Why didn't their magic work on you?"

"I don't know... Same way I could get through the spell on the door and Vintra couldn't. And in the Shard, I could get into the spelled room with the scrying stones when Cowan couldn't. We thought it was probably because I come from another world." He wasn't used to being thought of as special. It felt strange, bringing with it a confusing mixture of pride and embarrassment. Linden had his arm around his shoulders and he experienced an unfamiliar sense of being accepted and liked that warmed him from the inside out.

They were all exhausted, and shortly after eating a meal prepared by the others who'd stayed behind earlier, they went to bed, needing to get as much rest as possible before facing the unknown challenges of tomorrow.

***

Vintra and Sarraphin roused them from their tents early in the morning. They, and Vagan, had been up much of the night talking and planning. They were worried. The events of the day had brought home to them how dangerous their situation was, and how helpless they felt against the power of the Mages. Responsibility for the people they'd brought with them weighed heavily on them, and in reality, they had no idea what they were going to do, what they *could* do, other than keep an eye on what the Mages were up to. Should they be risking people's lives to do that? But if they didn't at least try to do something, they'd just be perpetuating the corrupt society that had had its way for so long. The Mages functioned because they kept the population afraid and compliant.

By morning, when they were all gathered to talk about what they were going to do, they didn't feel they'd progressed far, and their sombre mood pervaded the group. They were subdued, communicating very little as they ate their breakfast. Jonnie had a sick feeling in his stomach. He supposed it was anticipation, and maybe even some sort of premonition that the day was going to be really important to their future.

"Vintra, Sarraphin and I want you all to know, before we do anything today, that no one will think badly of you if you don't want to go with us to the barrier," Vagan said to start the conversation. "It's a lot to ask of you, particularly those of you involved in the situation at the farmhouse yesterday, when we still don't really know what, if anything, we can do to stop the Mages if they break through the barrier."

They all looked at each other, feeling despondent.

"We think our best plan is to get the drivers to drop us off at the barrier this morning and find a place west of the river to wait, before the Mages and Guardians arrive from Scathach," Vintra continued. "They may try to get into the mountain via the river, the way Jonnie and Willard came out, but that will be difficult. We think they're more likely to try to weaken the barrier sufficiently to be able to get through further around the base of the mountain, entering it from the north where Jonnie and Willard did. We're not sure why they even want to get into it, but their map suggests that's their first destination in the north. If we can find cover close to where they try to go through the barrier, we may be able to pick them off as they pass us. We certainly won't have the means to overcome their magic if we face them head-on."

"We realise you're probably wondering what the point is of trying to stop something so much more powerful than us," Sarraphin added, "but remember, this isn't just about us; we may be part of leading a change for the whole of our land. Imagine being free to train and do whatever we're drawn to, to be who we

251

want, to be able to speak freely without being controlled..."

"Makes me realise how fortunate I was in my world, but I couldn't appreciate it before! I'll do anything you need me to," Jonnie said.

"Yes, let's get on with it," Jaelin said. "If they turn up at the farmhouse say, late morning, they may get to the barrier early afternoon. It would be good to have time to do our own search of the area first and find a place out of sight. I'm not keen for a repeat of what happened yesterday – they must have sent out Guardians to patrol their periphery, and we didn't have any cover to speak of."

They all agreed – no one wanted to stay behind, and they left shortly after, with Karim and Thylane joining them as well. By mopas the trip was short. They were dropped off where the road petered out, a little west of the river. Exploring where the river exited the mountain didn't reveal anything – the Mages hadn't left anything behind. Trying to direct their magic beneath the barrier through the water wouldn't be easy, as there was a small waterfall at the exit. They would have to clamber over rocks to position themselves to the side of the waterfall and aim upwards, or climb to the level where it came out of Greyvyn. When he saw the drop that he must have fallen down into the rocky pool below, Jonnie realised how fortunate he was to have only injured his leg.

Walking west along the barrier, there was little vegetation that could offer them anything to hide behind until they were a fair way from the river, just after they'd stepped across something that looked like an old path coming through from beyond the barrier. They sent Vintra back to the river to check whether they could see him well enough from that distance, which they could, so they dug down into the ground behind some low bushes to make sure they were well covered, and hunkered down to wait.

Chapter X

Beyond the Barrier

They could see light up ahead and started walking faster, with Hermione running off ahead of them. Suddenly still being inside the mountain was just too much – the tension from continual tremors, watching out for falling debris, being careful where they stepped, and the dust, was getting to them, and anxiety tinged with a panicky edge pushed them forward. Seeing the growing pinprick of light, they knew now that they'd get out safely, but they were over it and it couldn't come soon enough! Tom had his dream at the back of his mind and was feeling increasingly desperate to reach daylight. Their breath was laboured by the time they exited the tunnel to see Hermione on the rocky platform scanning the sky for sight of Ryder, who they'd called to meet them. They all heaved sighs of relief and threw themselves down on the rock beside her. After a moment, Hermione's tail flicked across Sarah's face.

"Aw, Hermione, what was that for?" Sarah demanded, sitting up. "Oh, it's Ryder!" she exclaimed, as he sank gracefully down beside them on the platform. He sidled up between Tom and Sarah, nudging them gently with his beak, pleased to see them safely returned from inside the mountain.

"Ryder, I think Hermione's rubbing off on you. You're behaving remarkably like a cat, showing us that you like us!" Sarah said with a smile. He jumped backwards with a squawk, and Hermione bristled, the fur on her back standing up on end and her tail swishing.

"Oh, go on," Sarah scolded, "stop pretending you're not friends. We all know you like each other! What news do you bring us?" Ryder shook out his wings in a bit of a huff before settling on the rocky plateau.

"Flying over Hunterdale there are signs of humans gathering each evening from different parts of the town in the town hall with your friends."

"You mean Corrin and Gwynn?" Sarah asked.

"Yes. In Greyvyn village the same thing is happening, but today the strangers are making their way from where they were staying on the outskirts of the village towards the mountain, probably on their way around here to the barrier. I have a message for you from the village." He extended his leg and Tom untied the piece of paper attached to it.

"*If you're reading this,*" Tom read, "*you must have survived your journey into the mountain. We hope it was successful. We've done as we discussed and both the village and Hunterdale are armed and prepared should the south breach the barrier. Go well – our love goes with you.*"

Arthur and Mary were asking for a translation of what Ryder had said to Tom and Sarah, and while Sarah told them, Tom's mind was racing.

"If the strangers left this morning for the barrier, we need to head there right now ourselves so we don't run into them. We'll need to find a place we can wait without being seen so we can slip through to the south as soon as Galawand drops it, and hopefully they won't be close enough to follow us," he said.

"Unless they're going to head into the mountain," Arthur said. "Maybe that's their plan – to somehow connect to the south from inside Greyvyn if the Mages manage to force a breach through the barrier. I mean, they're from the south, so why would they need to go back there until they've done what they came here to do?"

"That means Galawand is in even more danger than we thought!" Kayla said, panic in her voice.

"Come on, let's not spend our good energy worrying – we need to hold ourselves together a bit longer yet. I know it feels big, but maybe we're heading towards the end, hopefully without too much of an altercation with either the strangers or people from the south," Arthur said, getting to his feet. Sarah looked at Tom. She didn't share Arthur's optimism – she could sense something really scary approaching, more of a conflagration than an altercation! Or some other big word like that! Tom caught her eye and squeezed her hand. He wished they'd had time to learn to thought-share before they'd got to this point. He pulled her to her feet and helped her and Kayla with their packs. Then the five of them, Hermione in the lead, made their way down the steps to the base of the mountain.

It felt so good to have their feet on flat ground again, outdoors, where they had no fear of either falling, or being entombed! The air still had a hint of morning crispness, but the sun was well up and they had no need for any layers of clothing over their T-shirts. They picked up the trail that continued on around the mountain, away from the direction of the village. It was rougher going, being less travelled than the first section of track from where they'd left the truck, to the mountain steps. They wondered why anyone would even come this way when the barrier had been in place for around one hundred years. Maybe for hunting? At some point, it must have led directly into the south, so there was probably a village or something equivalent to

Greyvyn Village on the other side…

Hermione was scouting ahead, and when they approached the barrier they could see her pacing up and down, then sitting, sniffing the air, then pacing again.

"What is it, Hermione?" Sarah called out to her in her thoughts.

"I'm sensing humans on the other side, not far from the barrier. I don't get a sense of menace, but there's a fair number of them."

When they caught up with her, they had a quiet conversation. They couldn't hear anything from the other side, so they supposed their voices wouldn't travel, but they felt the need to be secretive, a bit like whispering a secret to a friend even when there was no one else around, Sarah thought.

"I think we should head downhill a bit, west, and find cover, so that when the barrier lifts, which won't be long now, we don't find ourselves face-to-face with the Mages!" Arthur suggested. With the others in agreement, they picked their way, now off the trail, around rocks and scrubby vegetation until they found a spot where they could hide themselves right by the barrier, but a clear distance from where the trail intersected with it.

Ryder swooped down to join them and, while they were idling time away waiting for midday, they told him what had happened inside the mountain and about Galawand dropping the barrier so they could go through to the south. He said he'd fly through with them and scout out what the land was like.

"Thanks Ryder," Tom said, "if we have some knowledge about South Feasgar we might feel more prepared for what's coming."

It was intense, sitting and waiting, keeping one eye out for any sight of the strangers and another eye on the barrier.

Hermione moved between them demanding attention, but Sarah knew it was really for them, that she was trying to distract them from getting anxious while they waited. It seemed just too hard keeping up a superficial conversation when they all knew they were avoiding the immensity of what might happen next – the scariness of the unknown. They found themselves sinking into their own inner worlds. After a while though, Tom became aware of a caught breath, a bit like a sob beside him and turned to see Kayla, head buried in her knees, fighting back tears.

"Are you okay?" he asked quietly, shuffling over closer so he could put his arm around her. She just shook her head but didn't reply. "Is it Galawand?" he suggested. She took a long breath, as if she couldn't trust herself to speak.

"Maybe... Yes. It's just... well, you all have someone. You and Sarah, Mary and Arthur. I only have Galawand, and she might not survive. She's a frail old woman, alone inside a mountain that might collapse around her. She might be buried alive. I can't bear thinking about that. And then there's Jonnie..."

He didn't know what to say. How could he make it better for her?

"I'm so sorry that it's so hard for you, Kayla," Mary's reassuring voice cut into the conversation. "You've had a rough time, and meeting Galawand has been the most decent thing that's happened for you. We can only say that we hope it will work out all right, that we'll do everything we can to make that happen, and of course that you're not alone – you'll always have the four of us!"

"It just feels like everything could collapse around us!" Kayla said, feeling panicky.

"Kayla, I don't know if it helps – you weren't with us when I read out what my tarot card said, when it kind of made itself known to me, but I think it's important…" Sarah said, pulling the card out of her backpack. She'd slipped it in there thinking she might want to remember it on their journey. "Look at this." She handed her card showing The Tower.

"What does it mean," Kayla asked, looking at it carefully.

"Loosely, it's about us needing to break down the existing order, that when it's time for this to happen, there's nothing we can do to stop it; if we go with it, with an open mind, there might be something really positive in it for us, like a new beginning, but if we fight against the change, it could be really difficult for us. Or that's what I took from it anyway! I wonder what it is that needs to fall? I'm imagining the barrier, and something about what we're going to find in the south. Hopefully it's not to do with the mountain."

"Sshhh…" Tom whispered, "look!" They looked up in time to see the barrier changing. From its usual reddish glow, it paled through shades of pink, to white, then lifted, like an evaporating mist, so that suddenly they could see the land beyond. They didn't stop to check it out. This is what they'd been waiting for. In an instant they were up on their feet with their belongings, and moved forward, quickly crossing to the other side from where the barrier had been before stopping to check their surroundings. Sarah gasped. Not far from where they were there was a group of people huddled behind some bushes. They were staring in amazement at where the barrier had been, and two of them were looking down the hill straight at them, signalling at them to get down. They dropped to their knees, not sure what they were hiding from, but noting the urgency behind the warning. They couldn't see beyond the bushes, but when they were beckoned, they instinctively knew that they didn't pose a danger and slowly started to crawl towards them. By the time they reached their hideout, following gestures to keep down, Tom managed to sneak a look through gaps in the scrubby cover and could see another party of people further away in the distance, looking towards where the barrier had been. They were excitedly picking things up – were they weapons? – and were starting to move down the hill in their direction. *What now?* Tom thought. They didn't have anything to fight with, and the second group looked scary. They were dressed in strange clothing; head to toe in either black or dark blue so that their features were completely covered. They felt menacing, and they were moving towards them! One of the men in the group whispered to him that the strange looking people were moving towards where the barrier had been and didn't know they were there, so they needed to keep still and quiet.

Suddenly though, their movement stopped. Tom looked up to see a shimmer return to the space the barrier had occupied. *Yes!* Galawand was managing to restore it. Its presence ebbed and flowed for a minute, then darkened to a dusky pink, rippling slightly in a way it hadn't before. The group of black and blue figures turned back to where they'd been previously and seemed to regroup at a place that Tom realised must be where the river exited Greyvyn. He turned to look at Sarah, now at his side, then beyond her to their companions crouched behind the bushes. They seemed to be a bunch of ordinary looking men and women, looking earnest and determined. Some were well-built men holding hammers and other implements as weapons, a few looked like farmers, there was a small number of women, one particularly striking with white hair and a scar on her face, and… Jonnie!

"Jonnie?" Tom whispered. Kayla's head whipped around from where she'd been looking ahead towards the river, an incredulous look on her face as she scanned across the strangers' faces until it fixed on Jonnie's, his mouth open in shock as dawning recognition flooded his awareness.

"Kayla?" They saw his head move a little to either side of her, registering the rest of them. His face flushed with emotion, mirroring Kayla's, as he scrabbled to move towards them while keeping low to the ground. When he reached her they clung to each other, tears streaming down their faces.

"I thought you were dead," Kayla gulped.

"And I thought I didn't deserve to ever see you again!" Jonnie said eventually, pushing her away a little to look at her properly. "Whatever's happened to you? You look incredibly well, but so pale!"

"Later," she said. "What's happening here – what have we walked into?"

"I'm not entirely sure. We're here to see what this lot are up to," he replied, nodding towards the dark-clad figures, "but they're too powerful for us, and I'm not sure what we can do to stop them if they manage to get through the barrier and head into North Feasgar. The ones in black are Mages, the ones in blue are the Guardians, who carry out the Mages' dirty work. We're hiding out here in the hope that we can pick them off from behind if they do cross over, because head-on they'll just stun or kill us! Their magic is strong! I guess we've been hoping for some sort of miracle!"

"Well, it seems quite miraculous to me that you've all turned up, through the barrier, just when we wondered what to do next." Linden had crawled over to Jonnie's side and was looking at them with great interest.

"Oh," Jonnie said, "this is my friend Linden. He and Sarraphin, the lady with the white hair over there, are the Healers who looked after me when I was in hospital. The man beside her, Karim, is the man who saved me when I got spat out of the river with a broken leg. Linden, this is Kayla, my sister, Tom and Sarah, and Arthur and Mary. They all come from the same world as me."

They acknowledged each other with smiles, but Vagan pulled their attention back, quietly indicating that the Mages had resumed their assault on the barrier, two at a time, with renewed intensity. Streams of purple magic were hammering at the barrier at its weak spot where the river exited the mountain, and they could see it shimmering in response, as if its strength was beginning to waver at the onslaught. Jonnie thought he could feel the earth tremor again beneath him and asked the others if they'd felt it.

"Yes, it's been doing that for the last few days," Tom answered. "They're getting worse, and the core of the mountain is heating up – it's like the magic has woken it up and it's starting to rumble now of its own accord! That's why we're so worried about Galawand, our friend we left behind. She and Kayla have been holding the barrier in place from inside the mountain, but she's there on her own now and she's an old woman who's getting tired." Jonnie looked at Kayla in astonishment. She'd been doing what? He was used to thinking of her just as his little sister, but it looked like he hadn't really seen her properly, or what she could do. That was the whole problem – he'd been so wrapped up in himself that he'd had to nearly die to be able to see things around him more clearly.

Their attention was diverted by the shrill cry of a large bird – Ryder was calling to them as he flew in great arcs that took him higher and higher, before heading towards the south.

"Is that the hawk that…?" started Jonnie.

"Yes, it's Ryder. He came with us and he's on his way to check out the land. And Hermione came with us too, of course. Hermione?" Sarah looked around, puzzled. "Where's she got to?"

"Has anyone actually seen her since we came through the barrier?" Mary asked. "Now that I'm thinking about it, I haven't." They looked around, and at each other, Sarah in particular, feeling panicky.

"Why wouldn't she have come with us?" she said eventually, feeling strangely hurt.

"Maybe there was something she had to stay for, but she didn't want to tell us in case we wouldn't go through without her," Mary suggested.

"I bet I know," said Tom. "I bet she's gone back to make sure Galawand's okay. She wouldn't want us to worry, or to try to go with her."

"Well, I *am* worried anyway," Sarah said, suddenly feeling like crying. Something scary was going to happen while they were here, she just knew it, and she needed all her special friends with her if it was right that she and Tom were supposed to somehow save this crazy world they were in. Tom put his arm around her.

"She'll be okay," he reassured her. "You know Hermione, she has lots of lives left yet!"

"Have you tried talking to her through the barrier?" Linden unexpectedly asked.

"How do you know we can talk to her?" Sarah looked from him to Jonnie.

"Jonnie mentioned that you seemed to have a special relationship with a cat, but actually, I can pick up people's emotional images, and I saw a really clear one of you

262

communicating with a beautiful grey cat when you were thinking about her just now."

"Wow, that's amazing!" Kayla gasped. "Can all Healers do that?"

"No, we mostly have different talents that we're taught how to use for healing."

"Can anyone learn to become a Healer?" Sarah asked. She and Kayla were both fascinated by the idea.

"Until now, we've been chosen when we're at school, and not many of us get to train. One of the reasons we're here is because the Mages control us and decide what we can and can't do – they limit our choices and a lot of people have had enough."

"In answer to your question," Sarah said, "I don't seem to be able to get through the barrier, or she's not responding anyway. We've been told that the barrier was put in place to stop the magic of the south, so I guess it must kind of blank it out, though Hermione could sense that there were people on this side."

The others in the group had been looking at them curiously. Half-hearing their quiet conversation, they'd gathered that Kayla was related to Jonnie, but Vagan obviously decided it was time for them to focus on the activity at the barrier, which was showing signs of being worn down. He warned them to keep low and quiet, and to save their conversation for later. Linden manoeuvred himself over to tell him and Sarraphin who they were and their information about Galawand and the state of the mountain.

The barrier was getting paler, with its flickering quality more pronounced. They saw the Mages grouping together to make what turned out to be a final attack. They concentrated all their combined power and thrust it aggressively at the barrier. Everything seemed to stall for a moment as they held their breaths watching, then as if in slow motion, the veil dropped. It was a bit, Sarah thought, like the water features in Singapore that tracked droplets of water down wires so fine they couldn't be seen. One moment a curtain of glistening water, then the next minute they collapsed downwards into nothing. For a moment no one moved... It was like a giant sigh was released, then the Mages could be seen barking orders at the Guardians, gathering them together to mobilise them to cross into the north. They left two Mages and a handful of Guardians behind; the rest gathered in a loose double-file and started walking west directly towards their hiding place. One person walked with the Mages towards the front of the group, his different clothing and shambling gait setting him apart. He was quite tall, yet a little stooped. *Willard!* thought Jonnie. They flattened themselves closer to the ground, sucking in their breaths and keeping themselves as still as possible. But the troop stuck to the track and veered off before they got to the bushes they were using for cover, turning north to cross to the other side.

"What do we do now?" someone whispered to Vagan.

"Some of us will stay, some will follow them," he said. "I'll lead the team that goes. Who will volunteer to go with me? Say, ten of you? Sarraphin and Linden, you can work out one of you to go, one to stay; Vintra will remain with the rest of you." Several of the group, including Sarraphin, scrambled to their knees in preparation to go with him. Tom and Sarah looked at each other, then at Mary and Arthur.

"I think we need to stay – it seems the right thing to do, or why would we have ended up being here?" Tom said.

"I think you're right," Mary agreed. "Are we all okay with that?" The others nodded.

The team going north moved off quietly so they didn't attract the attention of the remaining Mages and Guardians, and just as they crossed over and moved out of sight around the first curve of the mountain, Jonnie stood up.

"Sorry, Kayla, I have to go! They'll need a guide in the north. I'll see you again soon, I promise. I love you!" he said. Without stopping to listen to her indrawn breath or plea to stay, he dashed after the others, running swiftly to catch up to them.

Kayla looked stricken. Her eyes pooled with tears as she looked in the direction he'd just disappeared. Linden put his arm around her.

"Kayla, he has to go. I think he feels like he has a lot of making up to do for how he was when he arrived in North Feasgar. He's always felt bad about how he left you in the mountain, and this is one way he can try to deal with his guilt. Hopefully he'll stick with the others and won't do anything daft. I've seen some dark memories driving him, from before you even got here from your world."

"But I only just found him again," she gasped. Mary moved over to her other side and sat beside her, talking soothingly to distract her from her distress. The others sat in a huddle to talk through what they thought might happen now.

***

Galawand came back to consciousness sprawled on her back, arms spread out either side of her from where she'd tried to save herself from falling, and with one leg twisted at a crazy angle underneath her. She moaned. Her whole body felt black and blue; one long scream of pain, from her leg that felt ripped in two, to her back and pelvis, which were in agony. It was dark. All the candles had been snuffed out by falling debris and the dust that had been sucked into the vacuum after the tremor. She couldn't hear any sounds, other than the sporadic ping of small pieces of rock as they hit the cavern floor. The last Mage attack had broken through her hold on the stone circle, and the massive tremor that followed had dropped a huge slab of stone, split off from the cavern ceiling, right on top of it. One hundred years of work destroyed! And what about her as its guardian? As she drifted in and out of consciousness, she began to accept that maybe her time had come. She so would have liked to have a little time feeling the sun on her body and the fresh air on her face before she died, but if her time was over, she could only accept it and try to die peacefully. She gathered all her remaining strength into herself, trying to be calm and centred as she drifted towards being reunited with the One.

It slowly came to her awareness that her neck and head were feeling warm, as if she was enveloped in a soft, downy wrap. She tried to focus on the sensation of being softly held and cushioned. There seemed to be some wonderful aspects to this dying process, if only she could handle the pain! A quiet rumble reached through her semi-conscious state, and she hoped that if there was about to be another tremor, something would take her out quickly. She couldn't bear the thought of dying slowly, in agony, because she couldn't get out of the cavern. But as consciousness pulled her back, she realised the sound was much too close. It was somehow wrapped around her head.

"Galawand, wake up," a voice came insistently into her head as a thought. Was she dreaming? "Galawand! You have to wake up, now! Open your eyes."

She opened her eyes to small slits, blinking away the dust that still seemed to be drifting through the cavern. Something was near her, but she couldn't focus... She blinked again and slowly, as her eyes adjusted to the dark, the shadow near her face resolved into Hermione. Oh, that was what the softness had been – Hermione draped around her neck. She licked her dry lips and tried to croak Hermione's name, but nothing came out.

"Sshhh… don't try to talk. I need you to move your arms – can you do that?" Hermione asked. Galawand concentrated her brain on the task of curling the fingers of her right hand. It worked. They slowly curled into her palm. She then managed to move her arm until her hand was in front of her face. She wiped some of the dust away from her eyes and nose and mouth.

"Good. Now, move your hand to my back and take the elixir out of the pouch harnessed to me." Very laboriously, she managed to make her fingers work to extract the container of elixir and bring it up to her face. "Open it," Hermione continued. "Dip your finger in the liquid and lick it off. That's right. Again… Now make sure it's securely closed."

Galawand could feel the elixir spreading a soft glow through her body, gradually unfurling the deathlike grasp of the knotted fingers of pain and tension. It was as if her whole body heaved a sigh and started to relax, to heal, whispering to her that she would be okay, that she still had time to spend in this world. She closed her eyes, letting herself drift towards some longed-for sleep, but Hermione wouldn't let her. She gently patted her on her face with her paw.

"You must get up now, Galawand. I know your body needs to heal, but you must get away from here. There could be another tremor at any time and your cavern is no longer safe. It's time to leave the mountain."

She struggled into a sitting position, no longer feeling any pain, but her bones felt like they'd turned to liquid, which was so odd that she didn't know whether she could trust them to hold her up.

"On our way out, be wary. The strangers from Hunterdale arrived some time ago and have made their way to the central cavern of the mountain. There they await the Mages from South Feasgar, who've entered the mountain while you've been unconscious. They've probably passed the fork to the river already, but we'll need to take care in case they've left a sentry at the entrance."

"But, Hermione, shouldn't I stay here to find out what they're doing and try to stop them?" Galawand asked.

"No, you know that's not your job. Others will come to do that, and Tom and Sarah have their role to play on the outside. It's best that you're safe out there to help with anything they may need from you later. I can pick up their thoughts now that the barrier is down, and things seem to be unfurling in a way that will bring everything to a crisis point very soon."

***

Jonnie quickly caught up with Vagan and the others, who seemed grateful that he'd joined them.

"I'm sure the Mages will be heading for the western entrance into Greyvyn, since that's probably where the strangers have gone," he said to Vagan. "They were on the heels of Kayla and the others earlier, but seemed to stop before they got to the barrier. It's not far to the steps that go up to the tunnel."

"Do you know where they might be heading inside the mountain?" Vagan asked.

"I'm not sure... it would help if we knew what they're looking for. When Willard and I were there we didn't find much, other than Sarah and Tom and the Birches. I didn't think to ask them anything more before we left, though they did talk about an old woman, Galawand, who they're worried about. She's the one who's been holding up the barrier, so maybe they're looking for her?"

Jonnie and Vagan led the way along the path. Jonnie hadn't walked this end of it before, but he recognised the steps when they got there, with a lurch in his stomach as he thought about the last time he was here and how badly he'd tried to impress Willard and ignore Kayla, pretending that she didn't mean anything to him.

"I'll go first," Vagan said, "in case they've left a sentry at the entrance to the mountain." They moved up the steps in silence, trying to keep any sounds of their arrival to a minimum. When they approached the top, Vagan signalled to Jonnie, next in line, to stop, as he slowly raised his eyes above the level of the platform at the top.

"What the...?" he breathed, raising his head and turning to look at Jonnie in puzzlement. He moved onto the platform so Jonnie could join him, whereupon he saw an old woman with very long, white hair, her skin so pale it was almost translucent, sitting cross-legged on the rocky platform, her face raised to the sun with her eyes closed as if she was meditating. In front of her there was a grey cat, sitting regally like a sphinx, watching them intently.

"That'll be the woman Kayla talked about, the one who made the barrier," Jonnie said, "and that's Tom and Sarah's cat – I can't remember her name." As he walked over towards them, he suddenly said, "Hermione – it's Hermione. How did I suddenly remember that?" Hermione stood up and stretched, arching her back, which had something strapped to it, then stretched out her front legs, as if basking in the sun halfway up a mountain was as usual as being in her garden at Riverstone. Jonnie looked from her to the old woman, who still had her eyes closed, trance-like.

"Jonnie." He jumped in fright; just that one word. How did she know? Her eyes weren't even open. She slowly opened her eyes and looked at him. His eyes met hers and it was like he was looking into a deep, deep pool that was bottomless, and he was mesmerised. He'd never felt anything like it – he was pulled into a depth and calm that could go on forever. It was like he was connecting to something ancient. His attention was reluctantly pulled away as the rest of his group arrived on the platform, gathering around to look at the unexpected spectacle.

"My name is Galawand. I'm the keeper of the barrier and the last of the holders of magic in North Feasgar." Her voice was formal and clear. "I'm very happy to meet you all. I was once a Mage, before they turned to the dark ways and we had to remove them from this part of Feasgar. Today is the first day anyone from the south has openly walked across the barrier in one hundred years, although some of your Mages crossed secretly some time back when my energy was waning. They've lived here without their powers, waiting for today. Jonnie, I thank you for your sister Kayla's contribution to strengthening the barrier and putting off this moment until we were more prepared."

Jonnie just looked at her with his mouth partly open. Since he'd looked into her eyes, he'd felt awe from his experience connecting with her, and a deep sense of acceptance. He suddenly felt different. Like, he felt… good… worthy? His view of himself as not good enough, always getting it wrong, seemed to have fallen away. He weirdly experienced himself as standing a little taller in front of them all.

"I'm Vagan, a Master Artisan from Scathach in South

270

Feasgar," said Vagan in reply. "We're here to do what we can to stop the Mage and Guardian Orders of South Feasgar from trying to take over and control your land. Many of us are rising against their control of us, but they're powerful, and we don't yet know what we'll have to do to stop them. We wonder whether you have any wisdom to help guide us." He too, seemed to be experiencing a sense of awe in her presence. Jonnie could imagine them all bowing to her with the feelings she evoked. Feelings so opposite to the Mages of the south; it was like good/bad, white/black. Where the black Mages forced people to obey them by fear and the use of their power, he could imagine people wanting to please Galawand because of who she was and the wisdom she held.

"The prophesies said that this day would come. I don't know what lies ahead of you inside the mountain. The strangers arrived earlier today, and your Mages followed a short while ago. They are headed for the central cavern of the mountain, the one that connects both to the core and its apex. I don't know what they'll do there or what is required of you. But I do know that Tom and Sarah were brought to this land to be instrumental in uniting the north and south. They are far more than what they seem, and Jonnie and Kayla have been brought here for a purpose too, so guard them all well."

"Can you tell us how to get to the cavern?" Vagan asked.

"Yes, Kayla mapped it for us when she was living there with me."

"I've been inside before," Jonnie said, "with Willard, but we didn't find either you or the cavern."

"Here... I can draw the forks in the passages for you. And the strangers have left markers for the Mages to follow," Galawand said, sketching on the dusty rock with a shard of sharp rock. "Hermione tells me that Willard is with them as well. He

271

seeks recognition and riches, but I fear his time is drawing to an end. He's outlived his usefulness to them, especially as it was based on his own sense of importance, not reality."

"So, Hermione can talk?" Jonnie asked. "I always thought Sarah had a funny connection with her."

"She can share her thoughts with Tom and Sarah, and myself. You're young enough, and also come from their world, so you may be able to understand her too, if she chooses to let you. How do you think you 'remembered' her name before? She put it into your mind." Jonnie looked stunned. "Now, I think you need to continue your journey. Time is pressing, and this is like the calm before a storm. You'll find brands inside to light your way. Jonnie knows where they are. May you all keep safe and have courage. The mountain has been activated and its tremors are becoming more frequent and stronger." She closed her eyes again and they felt dismissed.

Jonnie had been copying the rough sketch of the passages Galawand had made on the platform. Thank goodness he'd kept the pencil and paper he'd had in the Shard. If he got scared inside Greyvyn, he'd never remember her drawing by memory alone. They moved together into the tunnel entrance and found and lit the brands. Setting off down the first passageway, the sudden change in the quality of the air, the hush, and the feeling of being so small inside the vastness of the mountain flooded him in a way it hadn't the first time he'd been there. Then he'd been so busy trying to impress Willard that he hadn't really thought about it, whereas now, with Kayla and Linden, the people he most cared for, outside, the enormity of being surrounded by masses of rock pressed in on him and was almost overwhelming. It wasn't that he was claustrophobic, but he felt completely inconsequential, heading off into the unknown.

They experienced their first tremor only a short distance into the mountain, shaking the ground beneath their feet so that they lurched, hands to walls, while small bits of rock broke off and danced around them, sending puffs of dust into the air, up their noses and into their mouths. They coughed and tried to pull their clothing over their faces. While it was short-lived, it drove a feeling of dread into Jonnie, draping like a cloak over his shoulders, tucking itself around him more tightly with every step he took deeper into the dark.

Jonnie walked in the front with Vagan, checking his sketch when they came to forks in the passages, passing the point where he'd turned off with Willard and plunging instead, first more deeply, then rising again as they turned towards the centre. The strangers had left markings on the rock walls at each fork, with something that glowed slightly in the dark, a violet colour, so they knew they were headed in the right direction.

Eventually the passage ahead opened out into a cavern that glowed with an amber colour. Vagan signalled for them to stop.

"I think we've arrived," he said. "We need to put out the brands and make our way forward quietly."

"Why is it so hot?" one of them asked. They were all sweating profusely. At first Jonnie had thought it was just from the tension they were all experiencing, but then realised that the closer they got to the centre, the hotter it was, so he hadn't been surprised to see the glow reflecting down the passageway.

"We're at the core of the mountain. Galawand told us that the magic had activated it. We're lucky there weren't many tremors on our way."

Quietly they extinguished their brands and made their way cautiously, single file into the cavern, hugging the edges so that they could remain lost in the shadows. The scene that appeared before them looked apocalyptic. In front of them was a yawning chasm, glowing red and amber from down in its depths, ringed by the dark rock of the remaining cavern floor. It cast an eerie glow, its blushing fingers reaching into the cavern to diffuse and soften the rocky borders and dark shadows. From above, narrow beams of light penetrated from the apex of the cavern in shafts that picked out dust motes still hanging in the air from the previous tremors, but further down towards the cavern floor, their ghostly illumination was obliterated by a light source more powerful by far, coming from a platform about half way up the cavern walls.

The platform extended across from one wall towards the middle of the cavern, and on it three intense beams of light were focused on a mechanism that was in the process of construction. Small figures could be seen moving around it, but it wasn't possible to tell the Mages and Guardians apart from such a distance. When they looked closely they could see a jagged line, probably steps, extending from the floor level up to the platform.

"What're they making?" Jonnie whispered to Vagan.

"I don't know... It looks a bit like a lightning rod," he replied. The figures were assembling long, tubular pieces together that reflected the light as a dull metal would.

"Or a giant magic wand?" Jonnie said, thinking of Harry Potter, the only reference he could think of to anything magical. They couldn't tell from a distance how it was attached to the platform, or what stabilised it, but it looked solid and unmoving. "So, what do we do, Vagan? How do we stop them?"

Vagan considered for a moment, then signalled to the others to come closer, though still keeping to the shadows.

"I want to ask for four volunteers to come with me over to the base of the steps. We'll wait there until we think we can safely get up to the platform without being seen. I don't know how we'll manage to pull down or destroy the rod, so I don't ask for volunteers lightly, but I think that if it's central to their plan, we have to try. The rest of you are to stay here unless you can genuinely do something to help, or if it's clear that you need to get out in a hurry. If you do, don't look back and don't feel guilty about leaving us. It feels important that what's happening in here is witnessed, and important that whatever that is, it's communicated to our friends outside."

"I'll go with you," Jonnie said immediately.

"Look, lad, you don't need to prove anything here. You're not from this land, it's not your fight."

"But I need to do it for me," he replied, "It's important. And I have unfinished business with Willard."

"I'll go too," Sarraphin offered.

"No, we need you to stay here. If any of us are injured we'll need you, so we can't risk you putting your own life in danger," Vagan said firmly. Vagan accepted three more volunteers who Jonnie didn't know.

As they were about to move off, Sarraphin put her arm around Jonnie. "Take care Jonnie. You've changed a lot since we've known you and you have plenty more to live for yet! And friends to come back for."

"Thanks, Sarraphin. If things go wrong, please tell Kayla and Linden that I've put things right for myself, and that I love them both." He felt emotional and turned away quickly towards the others so she wouldn't see his eyes starting to fill with tears. They slipped silently through the gloom cast by the walls until they found a spot close to the base of the steps that was partly hidden by a lump of lava and was in deep shadow. There they stopped to wait for a cue to ascend to the platform.

275

Time passed slowly. They moved their weight from foot to foot to keep their circulation flowing, each privately wondering how on earth they'd know when it was the 'right' time to move. Jonnie felt helpless just at a time when he knew he needed to be on edge and ready to act. Suddenly he felt Vagan nudging him with his elbow. He was pointing at the platform above, where the activity seemed to have changed. The figures were no longer moving backwards and forwards across the platform. They now stood still looking up, and they heard a faint cheer that seemed to indicate that something was complete.

"What are they doing?" Jonnie asked quietly. Most of the figures moved back from the base of the rod, leaving four, who looked like they were arranging themselves around the rod, at ninety degrees to each other. Although the figures were small, they could be seen clearly in the sharp light trained on the platform. They each extended their right arm up, parallel to the rod. They were too far away to hear anything, but their stances were so purposeful that Jonnie imagined they were making some sort of incantation.

"They're the four Mages," he breathed into Vagan's ear. "Look!" He could see small flurries of purple starting to puff out from the tip of the rod, very unfocused and dispersing quickly into the air. It was as if the mountain inhaled, the core glowing more brightly (it reminded Jonnie of the glow on the end of a cigarette when he sucked in), then exhaled with each burst of purple. He wondered whether they were drawing on the energy of the core, harnessing it to enhance their power. The Mages stopped, moved to their right through ninety degrees and repeated the process. This time the purple was a more focused ripple. Another quarter turn and it became a thin band of a deeper colour. Several more turns and it became a steady stream of deep violet flowing out of the rod, advancing higher and higher towards the apex of the cavern. The Mages' voices had been getting louder and they could now pick up a chant that made their skin prickle. One of them raised both arms and slowly brought them down together, the signal to stop. A hush fell, all the figures suspended and still and silent.

"Wait for it," Vagan whispered, "something's about to happen!"

The four Mages moved in closer to the base of the rod as if they were going to embrace it. Now the distance between them was small; they formed a tight circle surrounding it. Raising their right arms again together, someone called an instruction, and suddenly the cavern was plunged into darkness as the lighting was extinguished. They could still see shadowy forms as their eyes adjusted to the light provided by the background glow from the core and the narrow shafts coming down from above. There was no time to think about what it might mean.

"Quick," commanded Vagan, "up the stairs while it's dark. Feel your way against the wall."

They made their way as quickly as they could from their hiding place to the base of the steps, Vagan in the lead, carefully feeling with his foot for the bottom step. The others close behind, they started ascending, one hand on the wall, the other touching the person in front to keep oriented in the gloomy surroundings. Vagan proceeded carefully, bent over so he could place a hand on the steps above his feet when he needed to for balance. They had just reached a small platform, a break between sets of steps, when a deep purple colour suffused the air around them.

Stopping to look up, they could see a broad shaft of violet streaming straight up through the apex of the cavern. It hovered, seeming to hesitate – *was it seeking something?* Jonnie thought – before turning at right angles and streaking off somewhere out of sight.

'Oh shit," Jonnie whispered to Vagan, "that'll be the line on the map connecting the mountain with Darthmore!"

"Keep moving," Vagan encouraged them with urgency, setting off again up the steps. The violet glow cast sufficient light that they could make faster progress. When they reached the top set of steps, they stopped again to check what was happening before venturing onto the platform. The stream of light, or magical power, as they imagined it to be, was now steady. Everyone was watching, enthralled, as the Mages moved together to link left hands with the raised arm of the Mage next to them, completing their circle, then raising their voices in the chant they'd vaguely heard earlier. The hairs on Jonnie's arms stood up as goose-bumps overtook him. It was totally eerie, and he shivered. As the chant gained in momentum, Vagan nudged them forward onto the platform and they slid along the left hand wall to where a rocky looking mound stretched out from the wall towards the Mages. They hunkered down against the wall, hoping the bright light would stay extinguished. The Guardians were mostly clustered behind the rod, a few with their backs to them, between them and the Mages. Jonnie caught his breath... Willard... his scruffy frame was unmistakeable amongst the Guardians dressed in their robes and krills. Though he couldn't see him in detail, he could imagine him standing, mouth open, slack-jawed in astonishment, staring at the spectacle playing out in front of him. As Galawand had said, now they'd achieved what they came for, he would have outlived his limited purpose. Even as he thought this, he wondered what was happening outside; what the actual purpose of the magical link to the Shard was.

Suddenly above them, there was a disruption in the violet. *What's happening?* Jonnie stared in amazement as a fiery white light streaked along the violet stream in the opposite direction, from outside, creating mayhem in its path. It sparked and fizzed with raw energy, seeming to devour the Mages' magic. It raced down towards them at such a speed they could only watch in wonder. One Mage barked out an order, but no one had a chance to do anything before the white blaze pelted into the end of the rod, creating a massive explosion that shook the whole cavern. Anyone standing was thrown to the floor, the noise of the blast ringing in their ears, their vision dancing with sparks. Just as Jonnie was pulling himself into a crouched position, a massive tremor generated by the explosion threw him to the ground again, where he lay shaking until he heard Vagan asking whether they were okay. He managed to get himself into a sitting position and look out at a scene of destruction. The ground was littered with debris from falling pieces of rock. Some had fallen on the mound beside them and he could see now that the lumpiness of its surface consisted of various objects, many of which were now lying smashed on the ground around them. Across the platform, the rod no longer existed. Two of the Mages were lying inert on the ground; a third was sitting propped against the remains of the base of the rod. Only the fourth, the one who seemed to be the leader, had pulled himself to his feet. He was standing hunched over, with one shoulder cradled in his opposite hand, an injured arm dangling limply at his side. He barked another order to the stunned Guardians, a few of whom were now standing. This time Jonnie recognised the voice as being Argin's. Jonnie fixed on him – Argin was his to deal with!

279

The order must have been to turn the lighting back on, as suddenly two of the three lights streamed out, illuminating the destruction strewn around them on the platform. The Guardians were standing transfixed; Argin was barking orders at them that were being ignored. *The worm has turned,* Jonnie thought. One of them stirred and walked slowly over to the mound of objects. Jonnie and his group watched, puzzled, as he picked up something that looked like a pottery urn. No sooner had he lifted it and brought it close to his body, than he seemed to freeze. One minute he was upright, the next he'd collapsed on the ground. Another went across to him, but not to help him; he too picked up an object, freezing and dropping in the same way his fellow Guardian had a moment ago.

"It's like they have a pact. They can see it's over and they're killing themselves maybe?" Vagan said wonderingly, as another followed suit. They looked around them and now that there was more light, they could see piles of bones in various places near the mound where people must have died before.

Argin was yelling again, standing upright now, but clearly still in pain. Jonnie stood up. Suddenly he knew what he had to do.

"He's mine!" he yelled, pushing himself off to run across the platform towards him. He sensed indrawn breaths from his friends as he launched himself and wondered if they would follow. In that moment, Argin turned and saw him. Though Jonnie couldn't see the expression on his face, he just knew it would be a mixture of surprise and anger. Argin threw his good arm out wide, sending a stunning spell through the space. It thumped into Jonnie, making him gasp, and he could see everyone near him on the platform, including Willard and the Guardians, frozen, arrested in whatever movement they'd been making. And... Jonnie ran on... the spell didn't stop him. He flew towards Argin and threw himself at him in a rugby tackle, his arms catching him around his legs, sending him flying backwards, his momentum carrying him along with him. Too late he realised his mistake, as Argin's feet caught the edge of the platform and suddenly the two of them were falling, over the edge.

Oh god, here we go again, went through his mind, before all he knew was falling, falling forever into the abyss.

***

From below, Sarraphin watched in horror as the two small figures plunged over the edge. She could tell that one was a Mage and the other one, she guessed, would be one of their group. Because of the angle she was watching from, she couldn't tell whether they'd plunged into the core, or had hit the cavern floor. Whichever, it wasn't as if either of them would survive. There was nothing she could do. She sighed and acknowledged her feeling of being helpless and sad about the loss of one of their own. Looking up at the platform, the stunning spell she'd seen the Mage cast had lifted and the figures were picking themselves up. Two of their group moved over to where the rod had been and lifted a Mage to the edge of the platform and dumped him over the side. She could see him turning over and over as he plunged downwards to his death. Two more were dragged to the side, though they were limp and probably dead already, dumped unceremoniously after the first. For some reason there seemed to be very few Guardians left. Some walked to the side of the platform and disappeared from her view, a few others were rounded up by the remaining four of their team and walked to the steps ahead of them.

"Time for us to get out of here," she said to her companions. "We need to get back to the others and tell them what's happened. Vagan will bring his prisoners back – we can move much more quickly without them." They entered the tunnel and began their journey back to the outside, feeling sombre and exhausted, coping with another strong tremor on the way back without even really feeling it. As if they were in a grey stupor, they didn't even stop to protect themselves. They walked on, subdued and stony-faced, feeling like they'd been to the end of the world and back.

Chapter XI

The Final Confrontation

"I remember the first time I saw you," Tom said. They were sitting on the ground talking quietly in the sun following the departure of Vagan's group, wondering what would happen next. "My head was sore and I was trying to open my eyes. They were all blurry, but I could make out the face of this girl with fair hair and blue eyes looking at me as if she was really worried about me. I think I thought you were gorgeous even then! Even if I did give you a hard time for a while... I was in such a bad mood from my sore head, and then later from Morwyn's poison!"

Sarah had a lump in her throat. She felt choked up with emotion, thinking about Tom, and her huge fear that something might go wrong now, just when they had the chance for something really good. Not being able to talk, she just squeezed his hand. Tom, noticing the glassy look in her eyes, pulled her closer and hugged her.

"We'll be good," he said, trying hard to believe his own words. "Stay strong with me. Everyone says to trust our instincts, or intuition... whatever. And if anyone has good intuition it's you!"

"But what about the tarot card?" she managed to blurt out. "What if it means everything good is going to collapse around us?"

"I think that's just the scariness of what's happening talking.

That's not what the book said. It said something about accepting that sometimes our old ways of being need to give way for something new and it talked about having an attitude of acceptance. If anything needs to fall right now, it's the corrupt structure here in the south that's controlled Linden and the others for so long and is threatening the north."

"All this waiting doesn't help, does it?" she responded. She looked over to where Linden was talking to Kayla – they looked relaxed – it must have been so good for Kayla to find out that Jonnie was alive.

"You know, you look a bit like my sister Anika. Her hair isn't as dark as yours and she's not as fair-skinned, but there's a definite likeness," Linden was saying.

"I'd like to meet her sometime. What's she like?"

"She's very clever. Spends as much of the day as she can with her head buried in a book. But she's also sad and frustrated because she's not allowed to study."

"Why?" Kayla said in astonishment. "Won't your parents let her?"

"It's not them, it's the ruling power. The Mages limit how many of us can study certain things and she missed out on being chosen because she was unwell during the time the teachers from school recommended them."

"Oh no! That's not fair! I'm not especially clever. I much prefer getting lost in a novel to serious books, and my teachers always said I was too dreamy. But Galawand sees me differently. She says I have a well of stillness inside me that I can use to do great things, though goodness only knows what that means. She says she noticed my depths when we joined our energies to maintain the barrier. And I seem to be able to sense things with my hands, like this…" She laid her hand lightly above Linden's, not quite touching. "I can feel something like your warmth and your goodness and I can kind of imagine your blood flowing... Oh, I don't know, maybe I'm just making it up... Galawand loved me giving her massages too when she was tired. I'd started trying it with different herbs mixed with massage oil..."

"It sounds like in our way of organising the world, you'd be in the Healing order, like me."

"It's funny," Kayla continued, "I always thought there was something wrong with me because I was different to my friends. I thought that when I dropped into what I've always thought of as 'my space', it was a bad place because I lost contact with the world. I learned how to do it to protect myself from the horrible things that happened with my mum. In there no one could hurt me. It was a bit different for Jonnie. He escaped by doing crazy things on the outside, like taking risks."

"Well maybe you both learned those things as a defence, but it doesn't need to stay that way. Maybe here you won't have to have a place like 'your space' to escape to, rather a place you can use to help other people? My sense of you is that you have a lot to offer to others."

Vintra slid over just then to Tom and Sarah.

"The two Mages left behind seem to be waiting for something. They're sitting about with the Guardians. Do you think the others would have had time to get into the mountain by now?"

"It's been about... what, an hour since they left?" Tom suggested. "So, they shouldn't be far off the central cavern if that's where they're headed."

"All right, we'll wait another thirty minutes to see if anything happens, then we'll try to move closer. It would help if we knew what we're waiting for!"

Their conversation tailed off as the sun did its magic on them, relaxing their fears, giving them a sense that things would be okay. Other than the three on watch, they were all feeling sleepy and unfocused, when suddenly they were jerked abruptly out of their reverie by a cry from one of the lookouts.

"Look!" he said, as loudly as he dared, pointing directly upwards at the mountain, which loomed intimidatingly close without the barrier in place.

From the top of the mountain a shaft of purple light had appeared, hovering for a moment above the mountain peak, before turning through ninety degrees and streaking off towards the south.

"Wow, it's like a heat-seeking missile!" Tom gasped. "What *is* it?"

"And where's it heading to?" Sarah added.

A cheer from the Mages and Guardians up the hill broke out. They could see them excitedly patting each other on the back.

"It's the direction of Scathach," said Linden. "Oh, of course! The tower on Darthmore – it's the same magic – they're going to join up!"

"What will that mean?" asked Tom.

"It'll mean no more barrier, ever. And dark magic will be free to dominate the whole of Feasgar, north and south!" Linden replied. They looked at each other in horror.

"What do we do now?" Arthur asked. "Seems like now's our chance to do something, while they're congratulating themselves, but I'm afraid I'm lost for ideas. I can't remember the last time I felt so helpless."

"When we were stuck in Willard's basement?" Mary threw in. "And Sarah came and saved us. She and Tom will think of something."

"I know what we have to do," Sarah said quietly. A moment passed and no one acknowledged her, so she said it again, more loudly. They all turned to look at her. "Tom, we need to get closer, directly under the purple beam."

"What? What do you mean?" he demanded, hoping his voice didn't come out too squeaky with his sudden fear.

"It's our time. This is what we were brought to this land for. Trust me," she said looking directly at him, her hand on his arm. She then turned to the others from South Feasgar who were waiting with them. "What can you do to help us to get close, in line with the beam? It doesn't need to be where the Mages and Guardians are, it could be further south if that's easier."

"Then we need to head back towards my farm," Karim said. "There's not much cover getting away from here, so I suggest we go now, in twos, while they're preoccupied."

"Okay, you and Thylane take the lead, followed after a gap by Tom and Sarah, then Mary and Arthur. I'll bring up the rear with Linden and Kayla," Vintra decided. "Jaelin, are you okay to stay with the others to keep an eye on what's happening here?"

"And to watch for anyone returning from the mountain," Linden added.

"Yes, I can do that. Go safely," Jaelin said, with her hand held across her heart in a gesture of respect for their courage.

"Come on, follow me. We'll keep to what little cover there is, so that means we'll have to go down the slope a way, then across to that tree line there... see?" Karim was pointing the direction out to them. "Then up again towards the road, and the purple line. Thylane and I will go first. Give us a short time and then follow in your pairs, keeping low. I can't see why they'll even be looking out for anything now they've got what they set out for, but be careful none-the-less."

Karim and Thylane set off in a low crouch. There was no sign of any change from the Mage group, so after a minute, hearts pounding, Sarah and Tom followed.

The ground was uneven in a way they hadn't noticed earlier in the day, when they were walking upright and without hurrying. Where they were headed now was on a slight slope downwards, and underfoot was mostly rocky, with bits of stringy tussock and the type of scrawny bushes that could tolerate growing in thin patches of earth stretched over rock. They soon learned to keep their feet close to the tussock where they could, to stop their feet from slipping on loose pieces of rock, though as they headed further away from Greyvyn it became easier. The land levelled off and the vegetation became denser and more varied. After walking hunched over for what seemed like ages, they were relieved to stand upright when they reached Karim and Thylane, who were standing waiting for them in the trees. And even more so when they looked out to see Mary and Arthur not far behind them. They all felt like they could breathe again, and it seemed to take no time at all to get back up to the road, walking behind the trees.

When they arrived, Karim guided them across the road and a short distance into the field on the other side until they were standing beneath the purple beam.

"Here is as good as we can get I think. No Mages in sight and a direct line to the magic."

"I don't know what you're going to do, but we'll do anything we can to help you," Vintra added, "Just be quick please. It gives me a bad feeling being so close to the magic, and the longer it's there, I suspect the harder it will be to get rid of it."

And indeed, when they focused on the energy above them, they had a sick feeling, not just in their stomachs from anxiety, but somehow also in their heads. Linden shook his, as if trying to clear it.

"There's a blackness coming out of it. It feels bad, sick somehow, and invasive. I wonder if that's how they plan to control us all. Maybe having control from two points across the land allows them to take over our minds...?"

Tom and Sarah looked at each other, Tom with a questioning look in his eyes.

"You know what we have to do," Sarah said. "Galawand prepared us. We need to centre ourselves first. Come on." She took his hand and led him a short distance from the others, calling Mary and Arthur to join them. They stood, Sarah's left hand grasping Tom's right; Mary contacting her right shoulder, Arthur to Tom's left, as Galawand had taught them.

"How's your wrist," Kayla called out to Sarah.

"Okay enough I hope," Sarah replied.

Kayla murmured to Linden that he might need to help her with her injured wrist after what she thought might happen next.

"Breathe deeply," Sarah prompted, trying to talk them through the centring process the way Galawand had. It was hard though, talking and trying to combat her own nerves at the same time. After a while, she asked Kayla if she could help. She looked dubious but made to move towards them, until Linden put his hand on her arm and said he could do it. He joined them and used his gift to smooth their anxieties, sending calming energy through them until they were breathing deeply, inhaling and exhaling in tandem with each other, focused on the still point inside themselves. Linden sensed a ripple of disturbance behind him, but didn't allow himself to be distracted, using his magic to keep the four of them in harmony with each other. He watched as Sarah and Tom raised their clasped arms, noticing the amulets on their wrists gleaming dully in the sun.

Behind him there was a shout. Two Guardians had stumbled on them and were fighting with the rest of their group. They hadn't noticed them in time to cast a stunning spell, but they were strong, and it was all Vintra and the others could do to keep them at bay while Linden maintained the calm environment Sarah and Tom needed to call up their energy.

With Linden's healing vision he could see a white aura starting to form around them. It coalesced into a point of focus, then suddenly a sheath of pure white energy streaked upwards from Tom and Sarah's clasped hands, tearing a path through the air, ever upward until it reached the Mages' magical field. For a moment it seemed to hover, suspended, or maybe it was just an impression because they were holding their breaths, then it ripped through the forcefield. An ear-splitting explosion pierced the air. The purple band turned darker, shuddered, then split apart with an angry sounding shriek that penetrated through to the core of their beings. Their legs turned to jelly and they both dropped to the ground. Sarah's wrist was in agony; her stomach heaved and she found herself on her hands and knees vomiting. Tom grabbed her arm and shakily pointed up at the severed ends of the band. Their white energy was penetrating into the band at both ends, making it quiver before it gave way. They could then see the white starting to gain momentum, moving along the core of the purple band in both directions, until it moved so fast it was a blur. They looked at each other, wondering what was on earth would happen next – it felt momentous. They didn't need to wait long – minutes later, a booming sound came from the direction of Greyvyn, followed after a short delay by a dull noise, much more drawn out, coming from the direction of Scathach. Everything went quiet.

It was as if they were all stunned. Shock, Tom supposed, as eventually they managed to summon the energy to look at each other. The Guardians had gone, scarpered, Vintra said. Linden was tending to Sarah; the pain in her wrist was already dulling and she managed to pull herself to her feet, where Tom joined her and held her in his arms.

"We did it," he whispered. She turned her face to him and they kissed, joining their mixture of fear, excitement and hopes for the future in such fierce passion that it left them gasping. After leaving them for a time out of respect, the others joined them, clapping them on their backs and hugging them, until they all collapsed, laughing, onto the ground.

"I guess we should make our way back to the others," Thylane said eventually. But before they could move, they heard the noise of people approaching and then saw the rest of their group walking down the road towards them.

"What did you do?" Jaelin called out to them when they saw them in the field. "The magic has gone and the Mages and Guardians have fled."

As the two groups embraced, Sarah heard something in the distance. She went still, putting her hand on Tom's arm to get his attention. There it was again, a screeching noise from the sky. Ryder! They both scanned the sky around them, and there he was, a small black dot, rapidly approaching, that resolved into a recognisable hawk gliding towards them. He sank down to the ground gracefully a short distance away. Sarah and Tom raced over to him to hear his news.

"The black tower has fallen," he rasped, his voice croaking

from his rapid flight and excitement. "It collapsed in on itself, shards of glass screaming and breaking; the whole building is shattered! People are dancing in the streets and teams of people have moved in to catch any Mages or Guardians who were outside the building and survived. They're running for their lives."

"The card, Tom! The tower has fallen..." Sarah said. She translated for the others, their excitement building as they started to let themselves believe their terror could be over.

"Cowan will be leading them," Linden said. "He's a good man – he'll do well until the people of Scathach regroup and choose someone to lead us all forward, hopefully with a united Feasgar."

"And before I saw you," Ryder continued, "I circled Greyvyn and saw a small trail of people leaving the mountain. The ones at the back were supporting Galawand. I think they're on their way towards you."

"Hermione? Was she with them?" Sarah asked.

"I didn't see her, but something tells me she's all right. After all, she's a cat!"

"What about Jonnie?" Tom asked.

"I didn't see him."

While Kayla couldn't understand Ryder, she picked up on Tom's question and was looking expectantly for an answer. Tom shook his head and told her Ryder hadn't seen him, reminding her that that didn't mean anything; he could still be inside.

"We're going to go back to meet the others coming out of the mountain," Vintra announced. If you don't want to come, Karim is going back to his farm to prepare for our return with food and drink! Feel free to join him. You've all done more than enough today."

"I have to go with you," Kayla said.

"Of course, we'll come too," Tom and Sarah both said at the same time. While a few from the group went back with Karim, most decided to return to the mountain, wanting to complete the events of the day.

They walked in a straggling group, feeling both elated and exhausted. Before they reached where the barrier used to be, they saw a trail of people walking towards them.

"That's Sarraphin in the front," said Linden, with relief in his voice.

Kayla's eyes scanned the group. No Jonnie... Tears welled up in her eyes and she felt ill, knowing this would just be the beginning of her pain if something had happened to him. But... there was Galawand towards the rear. When she saw them, Galawand raised a hand in greeting, then put her hand to her heart, raising it again to the sky as a mark of respect for their courage and all they'd achieved. The others around her all stopped and joined her, dropping to their knees, hands crossed over their hearts, then raised to the sky. Kayla broke off from her group and ran forward to meet Galawand, throwing herself into her waiting arms.

"Oh Galawand, I'm so glad to see you! I wondered whether you'd get buried alive inside the cavern, especially after the explosion."

"I was already out by then, but I had been injured. Hermione saved me; she gave me some of the elixir."

"Hermione! Where is she now?" Sarah had caught up with Kayla. "I can't thought-share with her, so she must still be deep in the mountain."

"I don't know. She got out with me, but she must have gone back in to see if she could help. She'll be all right," she said, seeing the look on Sarah's face. "She's got quite a few lives left yet I think, and the tunnels are still clear enough to get through."

"And Jonnie?" asked Kayla in a small voice, part of her not really wanting to know.

"Sarraphin, could you please tell Kayla what you saw," Galawand asked, holding Kayla's hand.

"I'm sorry," Sarraphin said gently. "He went up onto the platform in the cavern with Vagan and three others. After the explosion one of them tackled a Mage and they both fell. We couldn't wait because we'd promised we'd get out ourselves no matter what, so we could let everyone know what had happened in there. We're not sure that it was Jonnie, but given what he said to us when he volunteered to go up there, I think he was trying to make up for something and it's likely it was him. Vagan and the others are still there and will look for him, but I'm afraid that whoever it was could never survive a fall like that."

Kayla looked completely stricken.

"Kayla, Linden, before he left Jonnie asked me to tell you that he'd put things right for himself, and that he loved you both."

"So, it's like he knew something was going to happen?" Kayla said in a quiet voice, tears streaming down her face. "At least I got to see him again, and to remember how much we love each other."

"Kayla, please remember how much you've done for our land. All of you have had courage beyond anything that could be expected of you. Tom and Sarah, you have saved North Feasgar. Now begins the hard work of building something new, founded on good principles rather than evil." Galawand held out her left hand, palm up, and they knew she was inviting them to place their left hands on hers. With the four of them together, she placed her right hand over the top, saying quietly, "All is one."

***

As they walked away from the mountain, back to Karim's farm a little apart from the others, hand in hand, Tom and Sarah were quiet. They'd had so little time to themselves, so little time to talk, and it suddenly struck Tom that he had no idea what would happen for them now. Would she stay or would she go? He couldn't bear it, now that they'd fulfilled the job they'd been destined to do, if she disappeared back to England. He so wanted to be with her, but maybe that was totally selfish, because there was no way he wanted to leave this land to be with her. He loved being in North Feasgar, with Mary and Arthur, Hermione and Ryder. They were his family now, the good family that he'd never had before.

"What's up?" Sarah said to him, picking up on his distress.

"Sarah, are you going to go back?" he managed to say through his fear.

She squeezed his hand. "No way," she said simply. What more was there to say?

Epilogue

He woke to the feeling of rasping on the skin of his arm. It hurt! It felt like the rasp he'd used for metalwork at school, filing deep gouges into his skin, over and over. His whole body was hurting, like all his bones had been dismantled and put back together, but with all the muscles screaming, trying to hold broken bones in place, trying to tear out of his skin. Pain he'd never experienced the like of before. He moaned…

"Well, you've had more lives than a cat!" came a voice in his ear.

What? He opened an eye. All he could see was a pair of eyes glowing in the dark near him.

"Don't move. You're lying near the edge of the chasm. You'll have to do exactly what I say if you ever want to get out of here alive… Now, if you can move your hand, reach out your arm. On my back you'll find a container. Open it and take out the vial it contains. Put two drops on your tongue…"

A Jungian Perspective for the Older Reader

Once again, I'm using the medium of story to offer older readers a glimpse into the emotions, psychology and symbolism that often lie beneath the happenings of their external world. It may offer some understanding about what readers, or others you know, experience and find hard to understand and articulate.

In 'Through the Labyrinth' and 'Return to Greyvyn' readers were introduced to our two main characters, Tom and Sarah, as they undertook adventures in a different world that tested both who they were and the relationship growing between them. The coming together of the masculine and feminine parts of our psyches was illustrated through Sarah and Tom's growing friendship and trust, and the symbolism of the Anam Cara. As they came into contact with more characters in 'Return to Greyvyn', increasingly complex relationships were developed. In our lives we typically experience a need to discover what lies in our personal and collective shadow, to find parts of ourselves that we have 'lost', and which requires a descent into the dark. In this trilogy, this descent was represented by Sarah and Tom entering Greyvyn, the volcanic mountain located on the boundary of the North and the South, which may be seen to represent the boundary between our conscious and unconscious selves.

In this third, and final story in the Anam Cara Trilogy, 'The Rising of the South', our characters turn to face the shadow land of the south directly. This is a confrontation that threatens the whole of the land of Feasgar, and readers get the opportunity to find out more about what resides in the south, both good and evil. The dynamics present in 'Return to Greyvyn' are deepened, as they learn that they can no longer maintain the split from the south (the shadow) – it has to be faced, explored and made conscious. The repair that is needed is painful. They need to find their courage and trust themselves enough to stand up for what they value, letting themselves be seen and heard, much as we need to do ourselves if we undertake a path of inner exploration and face the challenges of individuation.

The story begins with Sarah in a state of mourning and despair. Her beloved grandfather has died and she's feeling abandoned by her parents. More than that, her grandmother has broken the river mill plate, her only means of returning to North Feasgar. She feels helpless and depleted. On an inner level, if, for example we dream of a death, it may indicate that an old attitude has been out-lived and needs to change to give way to something new. Such a dream is symbolic of the life-death-life cycle of renewal. In Sarah's despair, she happens upon another tarot card, The Star, which helps her to find a sense of meaning and a possible future growing out of the unhappiness she has experienced.[1] The Star gives her a sense of hope and strength, guiding her towards the inner resources that allow her to find her way back to North Feasgar.

The Mythic Tarot offers a psychological approach to the cards that helps us tap into archetypal patterns, and to 'read' the cards in a symbolic, rather than a literal way. Juliet Sharman-Burke and Liz Greene write that: "Mythic images are really spontaneous pictures, sprung from the human imagination, which describe in poetic language essential human patterns of development. Psychology now uses the term 'archetypal' to describe these patterns."[1] [p.11] An archetypal approach to using tarot cards looks at the shared meanings of archetypal events, such as birth and death, as inner experiences unfolding and at work within us.

The second tarot card that Sarah encounters later in the story is The Tower. This card is often interpreted as a 'negative' card; however, the Mythic Tarot emphasises that it represents the breaking down, the collapse, of old forms. Such a 'breaking down' experience requires us to look inwardly in an honest way at the edifices and self-stories we have built up – these represent our past values.[1] The degree to which it is painful to let go of these old views depends on our attitude; whether we are questioning and willing to confront what is represented by the Tower, or whether we try to hold onto it tooth and nail. As Sharman-Burke and Greene write, the Tower is going to fall anyway, whether we are prepared for it or not, because something has changed and we can no longer live within the confines that the out-dated value represents.

For North and South Feasgar, the falling of the tower is about the destruction of Darthmore, the centre of dark magical power in the city of Scathach. Scáthach is a Gaelic word meaning shadow, and was the name of a female guardian in Celtic mythology. The fall of Darthmore releases the destructive hold of the Mages on the south, which is necessary before the north and south can become, once again, a united land. Psychologically, with the shadow (our inner darkness) becoming integrated into consciousness, we find the opportunity for wholeness.

In the notes section at the end of both 'Through the Labyrinth' and 'Return to Greyvyn', I talked about the shadow, our unconscious psychological traits that lie hidden beneath our ego, which is our conscious sense of who we are. It is normal to feel afraid when confronting and trying to make meaning of our shadow. If we want to become whole and reach our potential, this is important work – we need to own the dark things inside ourselves, otherwise we will continue to see them only in other people. In other words, we project the things we don't like about ourselves 'out there'. According to Murray Stein,[2] shadow often emerges as the ego's hidden capacity to be selfish, willful, unfeeling and controlling; to operate from personal desire for power or pleasure. People try to hide these shadow traits from other people (and themselves), hence the tendency instead to only see those traits in others, for whom we will likely feel a strong dislike. Another well-known analytical psychologist, Marie Louise von Franz says that, "When an individual makes an attempt to see his [sic] shadow, he becomes aware of (and often ashamed of) those qualities and impulses he denies in himself but can plainly see in other people... in short, all the little sins about which he might previously have told himself: 'That doesn't matter; nobody will notice it, and in any case other people do it too'."[3] p.174

From clinical experience, a common example of projected shadow is when people are triggered by others who they label as braggarts, show-offs or skites, those who 'think too much of themselves'. Even if there is an element of truth in this perception, sometimes they may just be confident people who know themselves and aren't afraid of owning their successes and expertise. The 'tall poppy syndrome' is pervasive in many Western countries and around the world, and those who are envious and haven't assimilated their own shadow may try to chop these confident people off at their knees! Meanwhile the triggered person has trouble claiming praise for what they can do, secretly resentful that no one appears to notice their own successes.

Marie Louise von Franz[3] reminds us that if we feel rage when someone reproaches or confronts us about something, or when others who are 'no better' criticise us, we can be sure that there is something present that is unconscious and that we need to recognise and own. When such a need for shadow work arises, we may find ourselves in something of a crisis, feeling we need to find something, or experience something, but not knowing quite what that is; an 'un-ease', a feeling that something is missing. There may also be a sense of something dark approaching, perhaps appearing in disturbing dreams or fantasies.

We can also see shadow dynamics on a collective level: between countries, ethnicities, genders and religions. Groups of people, like individuals, may project their hatred onto the unknown 'other', or that which is different to their status quo. Marie Louise von Franz,[3] for example, draws our attention to the white supremacy and racial intolerance of the Ku Klux Klan in America, a 'secret society' that has often incited mob violence. The society dresses in white and projects 'blackness', both literally and metaphorically onto those they cannot tolerate. There are many other contemporary examples of ways that extremism in all its forms is playing out in the world today. Von Franz maintains that the 'problem of the shadow' plays a great role in political conflicts, splitting off people, political parties and agendas from each other into good and bad, in and out; right and wrong, and in the process spoiling the possibility of genuine human relationship and communication. Anything outside the dominant perspective becomes 'wrong' and is to be ridiculed, put down or destroyed. This can be seen contemporaneously being played out on the world stage.

South Feasgar reminds us too that there are 'good' characters residing there, representing those positive aspects of ourselves that have been unrecognised or not valued, split off and pushed into the unconscious. Maybe we were labelled as 'too sensitive' or 'too imaginative' by our parents and only received love and acceptance if we became more like them; maybe we were 'too clever by half' and had to learn to bury our natural curiosity and questioning way of being. If parts of ourselves are repressed and pushed down into our unconscious, we may have wonderful qualities that are left languishing in the dark, only getting aired through projected 'hatred' onto people who have those qualities that we secretly envy. It is easier sometimes to think of shadow as being 'all bad', forgetting that it contains really valuable parts of ourselves as well, potentials that have never been given a chance to take shape.

Shadow work is vital if we want to find meaning in our lives and try to reach our fullest potential. Carl Jung said: "How can I be substantial if I fail to cast a shadow? I must have a dark side also if I am to be whole." [4, p.35] It may be painful, but doing this work, finding the things we have repressed or forgotten, gives substance to who we are.

Through the Anam Cara trilogy, I have attempted to portray some complex psychological ideas using symbolism. There are too many to speak to them all, but they are present in the choices of names, such as Feasgar; materials, like obsidian; experiences, such as falling into a void or being muted; and people. As in a myth, there are wise people, like Galawand; and people who represent the dark side, such as Argin, or Willard in his less evil but bumblingly 'out for himself' way of being.

You may notice that some of the characters have been

paired: Tom and Sarah; Mary and Arthur; Jonnie and Kayla. While there is no intention of implying that gender needs to be paired in this way to form relationships, they illustrate the pairings of opposites in a symbolic way. In examining the way symbols form, Jung writes that they are often preceded by a pair of opposites: "From the activity of the unconscious there now emerges a new content, constellated by a thesis and anti-thesis in equal measure and standing in a *compensatory* relation to both. It thus forms the middle ground on which the opposites can be united."[5, p.479] The union of these two opposites represents a synthesis, which Jung calls the 'transcendent function'. It may involve the bringing together of two opposing principles, two conflicting viewpoints or positions, and results in a synthesis that breathes new life into a stuck position, or a way forward, with the opportunity for new possibilities. For example, one common point of tension is about individual versus collective/societal values. I've sometimes been asked "Do you think it's selfish to be in analysis/to want to individuate?" To be able to find the balance between these two positions, it is essential first to find out who you truly are, shadow and all. In the words of one of my clients in analysis, "Individuation is about becoming present to ourselves so that we can be available to society, which is the opposite to selfish. It leads us to being able to empathise and understand others, rather than being locked into complexes."

From the union of the opposites and the transcendent function, a symbol emerges that expresses something new, which is intensively alive and 'soulful'.[5] In the Anam Cara Trilogy, it is the task of Sarah and Tom, coming together and supported by their friends, to find a soulful connection to each other and new way of being for a united Feasgar.

South Feasgar has been created to represent the unconscious

(and sometimes conscious) power dynamics we are exposed to in our external world and may then internalise to influence our inner drama. It is a hierarchical world where people are classified according to 'Orders'. Three Mages, called the Elders, hold the ultimate control, from the tower in Darthmore. They are cloistered away by choice, keeping their power close and 'unknown', which makes it all the more effective for scaring people into compliance. The structure of the Orders distributes power so that no one has enough to challenge them. While the Mage Order, enabled by the Guardians, is in control, even their magic is limited to prevent anyone seeking more power than they have been allocated. They also wield power through anonymity, achieved by wearing a headdress that prevents identification, and by deliberately falsifying information about others, dividing people and groups from each other. The lowest level of the hierarchical structure is occupied by the 'uninitiated.' These people carry out all the support tasks that keep South Feasgar running efficiently, yet they are denied education, which keeps them in a subordinated position. Women are 'allowed' within Orders, but are still confined to the lower ranks within the Mage and Guardian Orders, thus marginalising them and restricting their influence.

To free the south and enable a union with the north, these rigid power structures must be broken down. Note too, that although the north is portrayed as 'good' and avoids the power and control dynamics of the south, it is still a self-limited society, being closed off from outside influence. This illustrates the way we can't live a full life without taking the risk of becoming conscious of our shadow material – we remain two-dimensional and soulless, as this is a major task in becoming whole.

To become the person we have the potential to be, means

moving beyond the effects of our experiences, making meaning from them and increasing our consciousness. Wholeness may be defined as the: "fullest possible expression of all aspects of the personality, both in itself and in relation to other people and the environment." [6, p.160] It relates to both a potential and a capacity, reflecting completion rather than a drive for perfection. To find a sense of wholeness is about the development towards ever-greater consciousness, which can be facilitated and observed through the process of analysis. Jung terms the path of actively seeking wholeness 'individuation'.

***

The three novels of the Anam Cara Trilogy have led Sarah and Tom on a series of adventures through which they have matured, found the value of relationship with each other and their friends, and have achieved their pre-destined task of helping North and South Feasgar to reunite. One of the guiding principles of the books emerged in 'Return to Greyvyn', in Sarah's dream about meeting Galawand, returning again at the end of 'The Rising of the South' with the notion of 'all is one'. This term actually came up spontaneously in one of my own dreams from many years ago and to my knowledge I had never read this phrase before. My dream was accompanied by a really strong feeling tone, indicating an archetypal dimension that was much greater than me. It lifted me up at a difficult time and gave me a sense that everything would be all right.

Parmenides, an ancient Greek philosopher, born c.515 BCE, was supposedly the original scholar to coin the term 'all is one'. Parmenides maintains that the multiplicity of existing things, their changing forms and motions, are actually an appearance of a single eternal reality.[7] Everything in the world is connected, part of one unity, even if they are seemingly separate. Jung's notion of the '*unus mundus*', the Latin expression for 'one world' develops this understanding further in saying that psyche and matter exist in one and the same world, each partaking of the other. There is a paradoxical possibility of reaching a state of unity following periods of opposition.[8] He saw this as the last stage of individuation, symbolised by the mandala. So, looked at another way, the 'whole' includes both the many, and the one; "an individual and all that exists – local and world community, global environment, cosmos." [9, p.157] We are all connected.

Mandala

References

1. Sharman-Burke, J., & Greene, L. (1992). *The mythic tarot book. A new approach to the tarot cards.* East Roseville, Australia: Simon & Schuster.

2. Stein, M. (1998). *Jung's map of the soul: An introduction.* Chicago: Open Court.

3. Von Franz, M. (1964). The process of individuation. In Jung, C. *Man and his symbols.* Dell Publishing.

4. Jung, C. (1933). *Modern man in search of a soul.* London: Routledge.

5. Jung, C. (1971). *Psychological types.* (2nd Ed.). Collected Works of C.G. Jung, Volume 6. New York: Princeton University Press.

6. Samuels, A., Shorter, B., & Plaut, F. (1986). *A critical dictionary of Jungian analysis.* New York: Routledge & Kegan Paul Ltd.

7. Britannica, The Editors of Encyclopaedia. (2017). "Parmenides". *Encyclopedia Britannica.* Accessed from https://www.britannica.com/biography/Parmenides-Greek-philosopher, 11 December, 2022.

8. Le Mouël, C. (2012). Experiencing the Unus Mundus. *Psychological Perspectives, 64*: 4, 437-442, DOI: 10.1080/00332925.2021.2043109.

9. Stein, M. (2022). *The mystery of transformation.* Asheville: Chiron Publications.